COMING HOME TO PUDDLEDUCK FARM

DELLA GALTON

Boldwood

First published in Great Britain in 2022 by Boldwood Books Ltd.

Copyright © Della Galton, 2022

Cover Design by Alice Moore Design

Cover Photography: Shutterstock

A CIP catalogue record for this book is available from the British Library.

Paperback ISBN 978-1-80280-896-4

Large Print ISBN 978-1-80280-895-7

Hardback ISBN 978-1-80280-894-0

Ebook ISBN 978-1-80280-897-1

Kindle ISBN 978-1-80280-898-8

Audio CD ISBN 978-1-80280-889-6

MP3 CD ISBN 978-1-80280-890-2

Digital audio download ISBN 978-1-80280-891-9

Boldwood Books Ltd
23 Bowerdean Street
London SW6 3TN
www.boldwoodbooks.com

For my dear friend, Gaynor Davies, who inspired and supported my first steps into novel writing, with my love.

1

Phoebe Dashwood was still angry as she took the Cadnam turn-off from the M27 and the road changed from motorway to countryside. The air coming through the partially open driver's window switched from diesel-scented to the fresh, clear, unmistakable winter smell of the New Forest. Usually, this would have been enough to soothe her – that blissful feeling of leaving the urban landscape behind and being in the countryside she loved. Beautiful Hampshire. But not today.

Although she had to admit, she wasn't quite as angry as she'd been when she'd left London at just after eight this morning.

She glanced at the dashboard clock. Barely two and a half hours ago. She'd made bloody good time. Hopefully, she hadn't gone through too many speed cameras. She hadn't been aware of any. All she'd been aware of in the mad dash out of the city that was thronged with commuters and people doing festive things was a desire to get away from Hugh. She'd stormed out of the Greenwich apartment they'd shared for six years with one hastily packed bag. It contained a couple of changes of clothes, her make-up, her shoes, her toothbrush, her phone charger, a small bag of Christmas presents and her credit cards. She was already beginning to regret that she'd brought so little. She was going to have to go back again.

Hugh would know that too. Which was probably why he hadn't tried to phone her. Typical Hugh. He never acted in haste. Rational was his middle name. It made him a very good vet. Phoebe wondered if he'd gone into work, carried on as usual with his Saturday, and the thought that he may have done exactly that made her feel cross all over again.

This was crazy. In her headlong dash from Greenwich, she'd only had one thought in her head. Get home. Fly back into the warmth of her family, her childhood home, sit by the wood burner in the lounge and sip hot chocolate, while Dad complained about the neighbours' battle to see who could put up the most Christmas lights. But now she was almost there, she was suddenly full of doubts.

Her parents would be pleased to see her. Of course they would. They wouldn't question that she was three days earlier than planned. But they would question the absence of Hugh. Her mother would take one look at her face and then hug her and Phoebe knew that all it would take was one hug and she'd crumple and start crying, and once she started she was afraid she would never stop.

She needed to think this through. Work out exactly what she was going to say. She couldn't just turn up and pour out the whole sorry story to her parents. For the first time, she wondered if she had overreacted. If maybe she should have stayed, talked to Hugh, found out the ins and outs of it all. She wished she was more like her mother, who was a primary school teacher – she taught Year 3. Louella Dashwood was always calm and measured and would never make any decision before she'd thought through every option. Louella Dashwood would not have stormed out of her home with just an overnight bag, no matter what the provocation.

Phoebe relaxed her hands fractionally on the steering wheel and sighed. She needed to decide exactly how much she was going to tell them about what had happened last night and she also needed to stretch her legs – and she was in the perfect location for both.

Making her second impulsive decision of the day, she turned left towards Lyndhurst, instead of right towards Godshill where her parents lived. She was close to one of her favourite places. The Blackwater Arboretum, home to a selection of trees from around the world and part of the Rhinefield Ornamental Drive, was one of the most beautiful areas of the New Forest. Walking through the ancient woodlands never failed to lift Phoebe's spirits.

Twenty minutes later, she indicated to pull into Blackwater, parked beside a wooden picnic table and got out of the car. She took in a lungful of fresh forest air, as she went to retrieve the walking boots and Barbour jacket she kept in the back of her car. It wasn't cold. It was typical Christmas weather. Grey skies and a top temperature of eight degrees. Average for the twenty-first of December, according to the weather notification on her phone, which also told her it was the shortest day.

Good, Phoebe thought, as she sat on the open hatchback of her car, lacing up her boots and tucking her long brown hair beneath her hood to stop it getting too wet. There was less time to be sad. If you were going to feel heartbroken, it was definitely better to do it on the shortest day of the year than the longest one.

There was a message from Hugh on her phone. She clicked on to WhatsApp.

I'm sorry. Please can we talk. Ring me when you get this.

Hugh rarely apologised. Phoebe felt her spirits lift fleetingly before they dipped sharply again. Apologising did not make up for the fact that she'd caught him kissing another woman.

Not just any woman either, but Melissa Green – who was the senior partner of City Vets where they both worked, and also their boss.

Melissa Green, who was known openly by her colleagues as Cruella De Vil because of her cut-glass accent, cool demeanour and fondness for scarlet lippy, was a hotshot vet. She was a trust-fund babe – her father, also a vet, had given her the prestigious practice six months after she'd qualified.

Melissa had never seemed to mind the nickname Cruella. Perhaps because it was better to be a glamorous baddie than to have Natalie Portman, girl-next door looks, Phoebe mused. But until last night Hugh had professed to love her hazel eyes and long brown hair. He'd always said he adored what he called her under-stated beauty. Had that really been true?

During the six years that Phoebe and Hugh had worked for her, Melissa had made Hugh a junior partner. Phoebe hadn't minded that her boyfriend had got the promotion and not her. It had been Hugh who'd got them both a job there in the first place, thanks to his father's contacts. Everything was about contacts in London.

Until last night, Melissa had always been utterly professional with them both. She wasn't the type of boss who did heart-to-hearts, but she ran the practice with brisk efficiency and she was fair, if a little ruthless. City Vets was the kind of practice where the well-heeled of Greenwich brought their pampered pusses and pooches and were happy to pay a fortune for the privilege. Never-theless, Melissa didn't charge the astronomical prices that some of the other practices in the area did. She'd always been fair to her customers and her staff alike.

Or at least that's what Phoebe had always thought. She hadn't much liked Melissa, but she had respected her. But all that had changed yesterday.

Tugging her coat tighter around her against the damply drizzled afternoon, Phoebe glanced back at her five-year-old red Lexus, a present to herself last year, and set off along the gravel path of The Tall Trees Trail.

The familiar soundtrack of birdsong and the stirring of a slight breeze through the trees and the sound of her boots on the path slowly soothed her. The air smelled of damp earth and old trees and rain, although it wasn't actually raining, more like a very fine mist, which Phoebe was glad of, because it meant she had the place virtually to herself.

As she walked, she felt the tightness in her shoulders lessen and the headache, which she'd only been half aware was there, slowly fade. It felt so good to be back in her forest. Her forest. Despite the circumstances, the fact that she still saw it as *her* forest made her smile.

Most of The New Forest, once the province of kings and queens who had hunted deer and wild boar there, still belonged to the Crown. It had been proclaimed 'a royal forest' by William the Conqueror and had featured in the Domesday Book, although now it was free to anyone who wanted to walk in an untouched, beautiful ancient woodland. These days, you were more likely to see ponies or donkeys grazing on the patches of heathland than other animals – the rights of common pasture still being recognised.

Her parents had been thrilled when Godshill had become part of the New Forest National Park. Her father was particularly pleased because it had put up the value of their house, which was now, according to the local estate agents, in a 'very desirable hamlet'.

Phoebe felt herself relax a little more as she walked. She had been brought up here. She and her younger brother, Frazier, had spent their childhood with the forest as their backyard. She hadn't realised how much she'd missed it. There were plenty of parks in London. There was a lot more green space in the capital than she'd ever imagined, but it wasn't like this. London was much tamer and more civilised and there were always people. You were never more than six feet away from a rat in London, or so the saying went. But Phoebe had been much more aware of the fact that you were rarely more than six feet away from a person in London. In fact, six inches was probably nearer the mark.

And, of course, there were the rats of the human variety – hmmm. Her thoughts turned back to Hugh, and with it came the conundrum of what she was going to tell her parents.

She wasn't an impetuous teenager any more. She was thirty-four. This wasn't a bust-up with a boyfriend she'd just met. She and Hugh had been living together for six years. Happily sharing an eye-wateringly priced flat in Blackheath next to Greenwich Park – owned by his father – although they did pay him a nominal rent. Mum had even started dropping hints about buying a hat on their last couple of visits. Not that marriage had been on their agenda. Neither she nor Hugh had seen the need. Perhaps that should have told her something. But they'd both been focused on the work they loved. Getting themselves established, dreaming that one day they might set up their own practice.

Suddenly, Phoebe felt very relieved that they hadn't been married. What would she have done if they were? Would she still have been running away?

She ran through an imaginary conversation with her mother, who she was sure would be just as upset and outraged as Phoebe had been at first. But then would come the questions.

'*So what kind of kiss exactly was it? Did you say it was at the Christmas party?*'

'*I did. Yes. It was under the mistletoe, and I know that makes it sound* as though it was inconsequential, a moment of madness, but it wasn't just a peck-on-the-lips kind of kiss, Mum. That's the point.'

'I see. And had Hugh been drinking, darling?'

'He had. Yes. We'd both had a couple. We were getting the tube home.'

'I see.'

In the cool light of day, it didn't sound so bad. But it had been bad.

Phoebe knew that if she hadn't been over the limit last night, she might well have left the flat then instead of this morning. She wouldn't have stayed up, pacing the kitchen with its squeaky new floor, waiting for Hugh to realise she'd left the party. For him to put two and two together because he hadn't known she'd been watching when he'd kissed Melissa.

In a weird kind of way, it wasn't even the kiss that had clinched things either. Clinch being a very appropriate word, Phoebe thought now. It had been the moments just before it.

Her mind flicked back to the previous night – had it really been less than twenty-four hours ago? The image she'd had of Hugh and Melissa freeze-framed in her head once more. They'd been silhouetted in the doorway, close to the six-foot Christmas tree that was festooned in silver and gold baubles. Its lights flashing green, red and blue on their faces. Melissa had pointed up at the mistletoe over the doorway and Phoebe had seen an expression on Hugh's face, a tenderness as he'd drawn the older woman into his arms and held her there for a few moments. Then he'd cupped her face in his hands, held it gently between his palms and he'd kissed her. A lingering kiss, lips touching lips, not just once, but back and forth. Not the kiss of strangers, half-drunk on Christmas punch, but the kiss of lovers.

And Phoebe, standing in the shadows of the hallway on her way back from the restroom, had felt her heart freeze as a tumult of emotions flooded through her. Shock, disbelief, nausea, pain and then finally anger, and she'd turned right back around and left the building. And not once had Hugh or Melissa even looked in her direction.

Jolted back to the present by the ping of an alert on her phone, Phoebe was back on the forest path, and she realised that she was walking towards a trio of giant fir trees. Their dark green winter foliage, triangular-shaped, stretching into points high above her head, was silhouetted against the winter whiteness of the sky. They looked like three enormous Christmas trees. Some joker had hung a blood-red bauble from one of the lower branches and, as she got closer, it twirled on its string, mocking her, gaudy and brash and out of place in the natural evergreen woodland.

In the winter light, it looked scarlet – the exact same colour as Cruella's blood-red lipstick. Oh the irony. Phoebe felt another sliver of ice spike her heart.

It was getting colder, despite the fact she'd been walking at a good pace. A couple of strands of her long hair had come loose from her hood and were now clinging damply to her face. She shivered. This was not helping.

She spun round and headed back towards the car park, longing only for the warmth of her childhood home. Much as it hurt, maybe she should just tell her parents the truth.

2

Phoebe took the scenic route back through the forest and it was getting towards lunchtime when she drew into Old Oak Way, the unmade road where her parents lived. There were only four houses in the road, all with big gardens and gates and enough space between them so that if you had a constantly barking dog no one would have heard it.

She could see that the usual Christmas lights competition amongst the residents was in full swing. The first house in the road had a Father Christmas sleigh on its roof drawn by eight reindeer and the one next to it had a Nativity scene complete with donkeys on its front lawn. By the time dusk came, they would all be ablaze with lights. So much for saving the planet.

Her own home looked a lot less flamboyant. As Phoebe drew through the double gates onto the gravel turning circle, she saw there was a string of lights draped around the front porch and icicle lights dripping from the white Tudor façade. They would be on a timer that switched on at eight. Dad wasn't mean, and he was a solicitor so they weren't broke, but he hated wasting money.

Her mother's Yaris hybrid and Dad's electric Nissan Leaf were in the drive. She parked behind them, glad both her parents were in. At least she'd only have to explain herself once. Then she walked slowly up to the front door, which opened about five seconds before she reached it.

Her mother was wearing a soft pink woollen jumper and trousers and her hair was coiled up in a loose bun. There was a blob of what looked like flour on her cheek. The smell of baking drifted out into the porch.

'Darling, how lovely to see you. I wasn't expecting you. We didn't say today, did we?' She glanced over Phoebe's shoulder. 'Is Hugh with you?'

'No. No, he's not.' Phoebe avoided her mother's eyes. 'I'm not interrupting anything, am I? Shall we go in?'

'Of course. Come on in. It's horrible out there, isn't it? Dank. And no – you're not interrupting anything. I was just baking. Mince pies.'

'Typical Christmas weather,' Phoebe said. 'Not a snowflake in sight and mud everywhere. It's not even that cold. No chance of a white Christmas. It's eight degrees.' She paused just inside the front door to take off her boots which she was still wearing. 'Mince pies. Yummy. I've come at the right time then.' She knew she was babbling on about weather and mince pies so she didn't have to explain about Hugh. 'Where's Dad?'

'He's out the back sorting out some logs for the wood burner. He'll be in in a minute, I expect. I'll get the kettle on.'

They went through the short hall and into the kitchen, which had always been the heart of the house and was where all visitors sat. It was a big square room with a conservatory off to one side that led out onto the back garden and a snug on the other side where the wood burner and sofas and television were. But not many guests got past the kitchen, simply because it was so warm and welcoming. It was full of reflected light from the ivory Shaker-style cupboards and a modern yellow range oven, which her mother said was the best present she had ever bought either herself or the kitchen. It was a room full of sunshine no matter what the weather.

Squarely in the centre was an oak breakfast island with high-backed stools placed around it. Phoebe perched on one. Today, the island was strewn with English Heritage magazines, a cake tin and two wire trays of mince pies with another waiting. The oven was clearly still on and it was hot.

Louella liked baking – she said it was a great antidote to Year 3 children – and she liked to feed her guests. There was usually a cake in the tin or some tea loaf – her speciality. Today, the room smelled deliciously of shortcrust pastry and sugar and spice, and on the wooden French dresser beside the door that led through to the snug, there was an uncut iced Christmas cake on a glass display stand. Phoebe's mouth watered. She loved Christmas cake. She hadn't had breakfast this morning and she'd usually have had lunch by now too. She wasn't one for missing meals, although she hadn't felt hungry until now.

Her mother put the kettle on and made them both coffee, checked on the progress of the latest batch of mince pies, transferred a couple from one of the cooling racks to a plate and pushed them towards Phoebe. Then she sat on a stool on the other side of the breakfast bar.

'Do you want to talk or would you rather I minded my own business?' she asked, her gaze level. 'Either is good with me.'

'Thanks.' Phoebe felt her throat tighten with emotion and gratitude. That was so typical of her mother. She was never pushy, never overbearing, she had a quiet perceptiveness about her that made her a great schoolteacher as well as a great mum. Even so, Phoebe knew she couldn't just turn up three days early for Christmas, without her boyfriend, and offer no explanation at all. 'We had a disagreement. I will tell you about it, but I'm still trying to get my head around it.' She took a mince pie and bit into it. 'Oh my God, these are delicious, how do you get the pastry so "melt in your mouth"?'

'Too much butter, I suspect,' Louella said ruefully. 'Terribly bad for you. Not that you ever put on an ounce, do you? You don't take after me.' She patted her tummy. 'I've put on loads lately.'

'You wouldn't notice,' Phoebe said loyally, although maybe her mother did look a little plumper. She'd always struggled with her weight. 'How are you? Apart from busy baking?'

Before her mother could answer this, the kitchen door burst open and her father appeared, filling the doorway – still in his big outdoor coat and with wood shavings down his front. His cheeks were rosy and his grey hair a bit windswept.

'Phee, love, I thought I heard a car. Good timing. I could do with a lift. Where's that lovely man of yours? Can I borrow him?' He broke off – clearly taking in his wife's 'shut up' expression but blundering on anyway. 'Don't tell me you haven't brought him. What's up with him? Snowed under with work, I bet. Lots of sick animals at this time of year and him too daft to turn them away. What?' he said, looking between his wife and daughter. 'You haven't had a bust-up, have you?'

Dad was as loud and unsubtle as her mother was intuitive and calm, Phoebe thought, lowering her eyes and biting her lip. They said opposites attracted and it was certainly true in her parents' case.

'James,' her mother said. 'Shut up.'

'I'm shutting up.' He mimed a zipping motion across his lips. 'There, I've shut up. Come and give your old man a hug, angel.'

Phoebe got off her stool and did as he said, and it felt so good to be swept into one of her dad's bear hugs. None of her family were small. Both Phoebe and her mother were five ten and her brother topped six foot, but her dad was big as well as being tall and his hug took her breath away.

'You're looking a bit skinny, angel,' Dad said when they drew apart. 'And peaky. You've been working too hard, haven't you? Wait until I see that Hugh. He should be taking better care of you.'

Out of the corner of her eye, Phoebe saw her mother roll her eyes. But, to be fair, it was hard to shut Dad up. He wore his heart on his sleeve, he always had, and he wasn't very good at editing what came out of his mouth.

He was better at work. He was a family solicitor – a very successful one. According to her mother, his clients loved the fact that he was so completely authentic and honest and never tried to pull the wool over anyone's eyes.

'We had a tiff,' Phoebe told him, 'and I was cross, so I left early. That's basically the situation.'

Her father's warm brown eyes met hers. 'Oh dear, oh dear.' His brow furrowed and he put his hands up in front of him, a little gesture of surrender. 'Your mother's right though. I talk too much. I'm going to let you two ladies catch up for a bit. I've got some, er, logs to sort out.' He pinched a mince pie, much to her mother's chagrin, and backed out of the room.

Phoebe looked at her mother, who was shaking her head.

'God love him,' the older woman said before getting up and going to the oven to liberate the last batch of mince pies, which she transferred to a cooling rack before sitting down again without speaking.

For a moment, the only sounds were the ticking of the kitchen clock and the hum of the fridge and the occasional bang from the room next door as James sorted out his logs.

Phoebe crossed and uncrossed her legs and then finally she said, 'It was a bit more than a tiff. Hugh kissed our boss at the Christmas party.'

She relayed the whole story and Louella didn't say anything until Phoebe got to the part where Hugh had come home an hour after she had, very drunk and not very apologetic, and then her mum reached a hand across the breakfast bar in reassurance and said, 'In your shoes, I'd have walked out on him too.'

'Would you, Mum?' Phoebe felt relieved for the first time and a little bit vindicated.

'Yes, darling. That's bad behaviour, even if he was drunk, and I'm surprised at him.' She leaned forward. 'But it's what's happened since that's important. What has happened since?'

'Nothing much. We had a blazing row when he got in. He said I was overreacting. He'd just had one too many beers, which always makes him more touchy-feely. I'm not even sure if he realised I'd seen them. I made him sleep in the spare room last night. Not that I got much sleep, as you can imagine. And this morning I left before he got up. I was still fuming, Mum. Not least because none of it seemed to have affected Hugh's sleep. He was snoring his head off.'

There was a little pause.

'I'm not surprised you're angry. But you are going to have to talk to him sooner or later.'

'Yes, I know.'

'Has he phoned you?' her mum asked.

'He sent me a message saying we needed to talk and that he was sorry.'

'But you haven't responded?'

'No, not yet. I wanted to clear my head. I stopped for a walk in the forest on the way.' Remembering the scarlet Christmas bauble, she swallowed an ache in her throat. 'The only conclusion I've come to so far is that I probably shouldn't have left before we talked properly, but I did. And I'm certainly not driving all the way back there again.'

'I can understand that, darling. But maybe it isn't such a bad plan to get some perspective. A couple of days apart will probably help.'

'My timing's not great though, is it? What with it being so close to Christmas.' Phoebe felt a tear roll down her cheek. 'I should still be at work. I phoned in sick this morning.'

'Neither was his, love. Don't beat yourself up.' And there was such kindness in her mother's voice and such compassion that Phoebe felt more tears gathering. She should have known her family would be in her corner, no matter what. 'There's nothing that can't be sorted with a bit of time and perspective,' her mother added. 'And coffee and some decent food. Now, have you eaten anything? Aside from mince pies, I mean. I can do you a sandwich. We've got some nice ham.'

'I can do my own sandwich,' Phoebe said, standing up. 'Thanks, Mum. I'll get my bag from the car. Then I'll come back and do a ham sandwich, then I'll think about phoning Hugh.'

'That sounds like a plan,' Louella said.

3

It wasn't much of a plan, Phoebe thought as she went outside to her car. But it was better than nothing.

She looked up at the white-walled, double-gabled house with its two chimneys and dark-tiled roof. Directly above her head in the left-hand gable was what had once been her bedroom window and she felt the same rush of pleasure she always felt when she looked at her family home. She was so incredibly lucky to have been brought up in such an idyllic place. And she loved the fact that her parents still lived here and hadn't downsized, which was what so many of her friends' parents had done. Which meant she could still come back here – a time out of time, an oasis of love and calm.

Not that she hadn't been happy in London. Although, it hadn't always been that way. She'd been homesick when she'd first moved away. She'd gone straight from sixth form where she'd done her A levels to the London Vet School, which had been a complete and utter culture shock. Although, her homesickness had been offset by the excitement of getting a place in such an esteemed school.

The London Vet School was one of the best places in the country to train. She'd needed A grades in Biology, Chemistry and

Maths even to be considered, plus A grades at GCSE level, not to mention a shedload of relevant experience, which she'd got by doing placements at various vets and farms around the New Forest, thanks in part to her grandparents and their connections.

Her maternal grandparents, Maggie and Pete Crowther, known to everyone as Maggie and Farmer Pete, had been dairy farmers for most of their lives at Puddleduck Farm, which was half an hour from Godshill and had been in the family for four generations.

Puddleduck Farm had got its unusual name, apparently, because Phoebe's maternal great-grandmother, Charlotte, had been a fan of Beatrix Potter and had been given a pair of ducks as a wedding present from her maid of honour. Rumour had it that a tradition had grown up around the gift. As long as there were puddle ducks at the farm and one of them was called Jemima, the business would always prosper.

The farm's name had been changed at around the same time. It had previously been called Forest Farm. Charlotte had clearly been as strong and as feisty as her only daughter, Maggie, to have instigated this name change to her husband's farm. All Phoebe knew was that her grandparents had certainly taken the tradition seriously. There were still ducks at the farm – one of them was probably still called Jemima.

Phoebe smiled, her head full of fond memories. She and Frazier had spent summer holidays and weekends there as soon as they were old enough to 'be sensible around the animals and not get under my feet'. These were her grandmother's words.

Maggie Crowther wasn't your average grandmother. For a start, she preferred to be called Maggie by everyone – even her grandchildren, *especially* her grandchildren. Being called Nanna or Gran or, heaven forbid, Grannie, would have made her feel old, she had proclaimed with a shudder. Maggie Crowther was a force of nature. Fair-haired and diminutive, she was the only one of her family who'd missed out on the height gene – she was five foot four – but what she lacked in height, she made up for in strength and attitude.

'I can fling hay bales onto a lorry faster than any man,' she was fond of telling anyone who'd listen and, back in the day, there hadn't been a man on the farm who'd dare argue with her. Phoebe doubted many people would argue with her grandmother these days either. They'd have got short shrift and possibly would have been chased with a pitchfork. Phoebe might have been scared of her too, if she hadn't loved her so much.

Farmer Pete had been less averse to the idea of the kids, especially Phoebe, calling him Grandpops when Maggie wasn't listening. He had died suddenly twelve years ago from a stroke a few months after he'd retired. Phoebe had been just twenty-two and she still missed him badly.

Maggie had dealt with the grief of losing her husband and soulmate by looking after animals. Or at least that's what Louella had always said and Phoebe was inclined to agree with her. Puddleduck wasn't a dairy farm any more – there had been no one left in the family who wanted to farm – but it was still home to a selection of stray animals that her grandmother had taken in across the years.

The first donkey or Neddie, as Maggie called them, had turned up just after Farmer Pete had died. He'd been skinny and malnourished with a sore on his flank and Maggie had nursed him back to health and had never found his owner – not that, Phoebe suspected, she'd tried very hard. He'd been joined by Roxy, made homeless when her owner had died, and because of that, Maggie's impromptu animal rescue shelter had become known affectionately by the locals as New Forest Neddies. A handful of dogs and cats had joined the 'neddies', who went up and down in number, but the name had stuck.

Phoebe felt a sudden urge to go and see if her grandmother was all right. She would be busy with the animals – she always was.

Despite the fact that she was seventy-two, she never sat down. New Forest Neddies was a full-time job; she didn't have much time for sitting down. But Phoebe knew she'd neglected her grandmother lately, too caught up in her own life to check up on her. She felt guilty that she'd been so neglectful. Maggie wouldn't be around for ever.

Maybe she should go now before she took everything into the house. She glanced at her vet bag and wondered whether to take that inside first. The car was usually its permanent home. Always on hand and packed in case of an emergency. They were bigger than most people assumed. They had to be to get everything in them: bandages, local anaesthetic, needles, saline flushes, suturing kit, stethoscope, and all manner of other paraphernalia.

For as long as she could remember, Phoebe had wanted to be a vet. While other children had played with dolls, Phoebe had collected miniature plastic and china animals – horses and donkeys, dogs, cats, rabbits, she'd even had a little racoon with a furry tail that had been part of a fridge magnet brought back by one of her friends from a holiday in America.

She'd performed pretend operations, converting a shoebox to an operating theatre and wheeling the animals in and out on a toy ambulance stolen from her brother. All of her operations, whether she had been delivering an imaginary litter of kittens or treating a fractured leg on a horse, had been successful. She'd looked after the toy animals as carefully as if they were real animals.

There had been real animals, too, who'd received the same loving care. They'd never been able to have a dog or cat at home because Dad was allergic, but she'd had guinea pigs and rabbits in the garden. Dad had made the hutches and an interconnected playground of runs for them that could be moved around the lawn to make up for the fact that she couldn't have the dog she'd dreamed of. Her mother had praised her for being the only child she'd ever met who'd promised to clean them out every day and who had actually kept her promise.

The memory was bittersweet. It felt weird being back here at her family home. Especially without Hugh. Phoebe knew she would never have stayed away from the forest so long if it hadn't been for him. When she'd qualified just over ten years ago, her first job had been at a practice in Camberley, which wasn't quite commutable for the hours she worked, but had meant she could visit home at weekends.

Hugh had worked there from time to time as a locum, but it had been a long while before she'd got to know him properly. The tall, handsome young man, who was as passionate about animals as she was, had been shy around women, but he'd eventually asked her out and they had fallen in love. A slow-burn kind of love based on mutual respect and friendship, Phoebe had thought when she looked back. The best kind of love.

When Hugh had said he'd got a permanent job at the prestigious City Vets in Greenwich and that he could get her one too, she'd hesitated to move even further away from the New Forest and into the city. But, somehow, London and her love of Hugh had become intertwined and so it hadn't been such a wrench to move there permanently.

'Working at a top London practice will look great on our CVs whatever we do in the future,' Hugh had said, his eyes shining with enthusiasm. 'I know you love the countryside, but we can visit.'

And that's how it had been for the past six years. London had become familiar, her second home, and living in his father's amazing flat together had been the icing on the cake.

Luckily, her family had loved him too. Even Maggie had liked him. And she was renowned for getting on better with animals than she did with people – they were far less trouble because they were reliable and didn't bore you senseless with their chatter, was something else she was fond of saying.

A flicker of indecision tugged at Phoebe's heart. She needed to phone Hugh, but maybe she should drive over and see Maggie first. She wavered. Or should she leave that until tomorrow? She was suddenly torn. The practice closed early on a Saturday, but that didn't mean Hugh would have gone straight home. He may have taken her 'sickie' at face value. He may not even know yet that she'd left London.

She was still wavering when her thoughts were interrupted by the sound of the front door opening and she saw her father silhouetted in the oblong of light that spilled out onto the porch.

'Are you OK out here, angel? Is there anything I can help you with?'

'I'm fine, Dad, it's all good.' Phoebe made a decision. She would get settled in first and spend some time with her parents before she dashed off to see Maggie.

She leaned into the back of her car and grabbed the overnight bag and the carrier of presents.

'Although you could take these in if you like, Dad? Thanks.' She handed him the bag. 'They need putting under the tree.'

He looked pleased to have something useful to do as he crunched across the drive to help and took the bag from her outstretched hand.

Phoebe followed him back into the house. It probably had been the wrong thing to do, making the mad dash down here. She should have stayed and talked things through with Hugh. They might have sorted things out and her parents would never have needed to know. Instead, she had just complicated everything by running away. But, she decided, Mum was right. A few days' time and perspective was what she needed.

* * *

'Phoebe, there's a sandwich here for you,' her mother called through to the snug once she and her father had added her presents to the growing pile under the tree by the fireplace. 'And I've switched the radiator back on in your room. I hadn't quite got as far as making the bed up, but there's fresh linen in the airing cupboard. Use the blue set.'

'Thanks, Mum. I'll do that now.' Phoebe paused in the kitchen doorway. 'I'm just going to try Hugh.' The sandwich was on the side, but she didn't feel hungry any more. The prospect of speaking to Hugh had stolen her appetite. She picked up the plate, not wanting to disappoint her mother. 'I'll take it with me.' She hesitated. 'Before I go, is Maggie OK?'

'Maggie's fine, love.' Her mother paused from putting mince pies into tins and glanced at her. 'I spoke to her yesterday. Why do you ask?'

'I haven't kept in touch as much lately as I used to. I feel a bit guilty.'

'You're busy with your own life, love. It's natural. You've grown up and moved on. That's how it should be.' She frowned. 'It doesn't help that she doesn't really do technology, does it? I've been trying to persuade her to at least carry a smartphone, but she's adamant she doesn't need one. You know what she's like.'

'*New-fangled nonsense*,' Phoebe parroted her grandmother's voice. 'Yes, I know. Hugh and I bought her a smartphone for her birthday and we set it up for her. I bet it went straight back in its box as soon as we'd left the farm.'

'I wouldn't take it personally. Frazier and Alexa bought her an Amazon Fire Stick so she could turn her TV into a smart telly and watch those old reruns of *Fawlty Towers* and *Keeping Up Appearances* that she loves.'

Alexa had been Frazier's childhood sweetheart and now, to the whole family's delight, because she really was a sweetheart, she was his wife. They'd been married eighteen months.

'They thought it would be a huge hit,' Louella continued, 'but I think she put that in the bin.' She lidded the tins of the mince pies and stacked them on the dresser alongside the Christmas cake. 'I must admit, I do worry about her over on that farm now she's older. It was better when Eddie was living in the van.'

Eddie had been a former farmhand who'd kept his fully fitted-out trailer on a patch of land at Puddleduck Farm, permanently plugged into the electrics and water, rent-free, in return for doing odd jobs around the place.

'What happened to Eddie? I thought he was still there.' Phoebe felt a pang of sadness. The old man had looked about ninety the last time she'd seen him. 'He didn't die, did he?'

'No, he went to live with his son in Southampton.'

'Oh good.' Phoebe felt a surge of relief.

'Maggie still sees him occasionally. He comes on the coach to Ringwood. He's deaf as a post these days and he's not so steady on his feet, but he still has all his marbles and he's always had a soft spot for your grandmother.'

'I know he has.' It was amazing, Phoebe reflected, quite how many people did have a soft spot for Maggie, considering the fact that she regularly said the planet would be a much better place if it had less humans on it and more animals. 'I'm looking forward to seeing her,' Phoebe said. 'But first I'll go and phone Hugh.'

She couldn't put this off any longer but she was not looking forward to it one bit.

4

Upstairs, Phoebe collected the bed linen from the airing cupboard and went into her old room. Her parents weren't the sort of people who kept the kids' bedrooms as they'd always been in case of visits – they were used for other things these days. Frazier's, which was the biggest, had been turned into a home gym when her father had decided it would be cheaper to work out at home than go to an expensive venue and he'd bought an exercise bike and a treadmill and some weights from eBay a couple of years ago. Phoebe bet they were all gathering dust. Her father was far too much of a socialite to want to work out on his own, no matter how much money he saved by cancelling his gym membership.

Her bedroom, she saw, as she pushed open the door, had become even more of a dumping ground for things which had no other home since the last time she'd seen it. There was a laptop case and a box of paperwork on the floor that looked as though it was teaching paraphernalia and a pile of books and other clutter on the little desk that now took up the space where her dressing table had once stood.

The wardrobe with its full-length mirror was still in situ,

though, and the pretty floral wallpaper was the same. The small double bed with its white iron bedstead was free of clutter. Phoebe made it up with the blue linen, then sat on it and hooked out her phone. She couldn't put it off any longer.

Taking a deep breath, she speed-dialled Hugh.

The phone rang several times and she imagined him in their flat, picking it up, finding his earbuds, putting them in place, settling himself down. Then, finally, he answered it.

'Hi. Thanks for ringing. Where are you?' Straight to the point as usual.

'I'm at my parents.'

'Ah.' There was a world of meaning in that 'Ah'. 'I thought you might have gone to Lettie's.'

He hoped she had, Phoebe thought, because that would have been less terminal. Lettie and Graham were friends of theirs. Well, they were more friends of Hugh's, and they lived just outside the city. It was probably the only other place she might go where she'd have needed to take her car. He clearly hadn't checked though. Or he'd have known she wasn't there.

'Did you go in to work?' she asked him.

'I did, yes.'

Phoebe felt a stab of pain and jealousy at the thought that he'd been working with Melissa all day. Presumably, they'd have talked about the night before. She wondered how that had gone.

She imagined that Melissa would have been concerned – as well as irritated that they were a vet down – and that Hugh would have been consoling her. '*Don't worry, she'll calm down. She just overreacted. A Christmas kiss. These things happen.*'

Phoebe's stomach twisted in pain.

'I saw you and Melissa under the mistletoe. In the hall,' she added, so there could be no doubt what she was talking about. 'I know what you said last night. But it didn't look like a drunken kiss from where I was standing.'

'Ah,' he said again.

There was a long pause and she closed her eyes. Why wasn't he jumping in to explain?

Then he said, 'I really didn't want to have this conversation on the phone, Phoebe.'

'Well, unless you're going to drive here, we don't have a lot of choice, do we?'

'No, I guess we don't.' She could hear him breathing. 'I'm not driving there.' His voice was cold.

She felt a little stab of shock. 'I see. I'm not worth a couple of hours of your time.'

'It's not that.'

Now she could hear movement in the background. He sounded as though he was pacing their kitchen. She could hear the squeak of the new flooring. He must be agitated. He only ever paced if he was really stressed. Good. He deserved to be stressed.

'As I said, Phoebe, I really didn't want to have this conversation on the phone, but here we are. I'm sorry. I'm really sorry you had to find out like that, but I've been seeing Melissa for a while.'

His words, so calmly and quietly spoken, sent a shard of ice straight to her heart and she was sure for a few seconds that she hadn't heard him right. Or that she hadn't understood him right. The whole room seemed to freeze-frame in her head. An old picture on the wall of her cuddling a Red Setter, carefree and happy, at Puddleduck Farm blurred and the desk clutter wobbled as she blinked. Her heart was thundering so loudly in her ears that she couldn't breathe, but then, when she did speak, all she could hear was her own ragged breathing.

'You what? What do you mean you've been seeing her?'

'We didn't plan it. I promise you that. It just—'

'Don't say it just happened,' she broke across him. 'These things don't just happen. They're choices that we make. We don't just suddenly fall into bed with people. Oh my God, have you been to bed with her?'

'No. No, I haven't. Nothing like that. We've just dated.'

'What do you mean you've dated? You live with me. How can you have dated someone else?' She could hear her own voice rising in horror. What on earth was he talking about?

Hugh sighed.

'Dated is the wrong word. We've connected. And we've been out a few times for dinner and suchlike.'

'But when? How?' She was completely thrown. This was so not what she'd been expecting. She'd been expecting him to apologise yes, but not for something like this. She'd been expecting him to say that at worst he'd just got too drunk, he didn't drink much usually, that he'd let his hair down – everyone had been working really hard and their job could be so stressful. She'd been expecting a scenario that had run along the lines of her imagined conversation with her mother. A storm in a teacup that could be resolved. A situation in which she might have been prepared to admit that she may have overreacted by flying back home. She might even have apologised for being so impulsive – after he'd grovelled enough, that was. But she had never in her worst nightmares anticipated this.

'I didn't go to see the new James Bond film with Graham,' Hugh continued quietly.

She had thought that was odd at the time when he'd said it, that either of them had liked James Bond, but she hadn't questioned him. No wonder he'd asked if she'd gone to Lettie and Graham's – Graham must have been covering for him.

'You took Melissa to see James Bond?' Phoebe hadn't had her

down as a Bond fan. An art-house film fan maybe – the type that she didn't much care for.

'No. No, I lied about James Bond. I'm sorry. We just went for a meal.'

'And Graham covered for you?'

'No. No, Graham didn't know – I just took a flyer that you wouldn't ask him.'

Bloody hell. That was so out of character. She couldn't believe she was hearing this. She had never known Hugh to do anything that wasn't carefully thought out, planned and then meticulously executed.

'I see.'

She didn't see. OK, Hugh hated confrontation, and he wasn't one for showing his emotions, but this was cold, even for Hugh. None of this made any sense.

'I'm so sorry, Phoebe.' He was still pacing. She could hear his footsteps again, the squeak of their flooring. A familiar sound in a world that had suddenly become so very unfamiliar. 'We were going to tell you, but we didn't want to wreck your Christmas.'

'Well, how very bloody considerate of you both. So what did you plan to do? Come down here and play happy families with my parents and act like everything was fine and then spring it on me at New Year?'

'No. God, I don't know. I haven't thought it through. Like I said, we didn't plan it to happen – oh shit, what a mess.'

The squeaking had stopped, but then Phoebe heard another sound in the background – as if someone, it sounded like a woman, had just cleared their throat. An awful thought struck her. What if Hugh wasn't the one doing the pacing? What if it was Melissa who was there, walking up and down in their kitchen?

She hadn't thought she could feel any worse than she did, but she'd been wrong.

'Is she there with you? Is Melissa there now?'

'Um...'

'She is, isn't she? She's there listening to our private conversation. Jeez, Hugh. You are unbelievable.'

She disconnected the call. Her fingers were shaking so much that it was hard to hit the red button on her smartphone.

For a few seconds, Phoebe sat still on the bed, the shaking that had started in her fingers had spread to her insides, but the overwhelming emotion that she felt was no longer shock. It was anger. How dare he invite Melissa into their home the moment she wasn't there. How dare he think he could sit there, refusing even to drive here and discuss this face to face, like any other decent human being would have done. Like the man who'd always professed to love her would have done.

She snatched up the phone again and pressed redial. This time, he answered it almost immediately. He probably thought she'd disconnected by accident. She'd never hung up on him in her life.

'You can tell Melissa Green she can stick her job where the sun doesn't shine,' she yelled at him. 'And she needn't expect me to work out my notice either.'

She disconnected again before he had time to answer.

For a few seconds, Phoebe was aware only of the anger and of the adrenaline that was coursing around her body. Her heart pounded with it and her head throbbed to the same beat in a relentless accompaniment. Every part of her was shaking. She felt as though every atom of her being was shaking.

Feeling hot and sick and somehow cold and shivery at the same time, she sat where she was, trying to control the trembling. Trying to process what had just happened. For maybe half a minute, she stared into space. The rage was dissipating as swiftly as it had arrived. Phoebe rarely got angry and when she did, it was more fleeting storm than lingering resentment.

She glanced at the sandwich that was still on its plate beside her on the bed. Thick white bread cut diagonally. A glisten of pink ham. She felt sick. No way could she eat it now.

Oh my God. Had the last ten minutes really just happened?

She stared at her phone. Barely even ten minutes, more like six. Was that all it took to tip your life upside down?

She put her head in her hands and pressed her fingers against her temples to ease the headache that was fast replacing the adrenaline throb. It was hard to believe that less than ten minutes ago she'd had a boyfriend, a home and a great job that she loved. Now, in one fell swoop, she had lost them all. It might have happened at supersonic speed, but it was going to take a great deal longer than ten minutes to get her head around it all.

5

Phoebe wasn't sure how long she sat on her bed, trying to make sense of it all, but she was roused from her thoughts by the jangle of the doorbell. It was one of those old-fashioned ones that reverberated, so it didn't matter where you were in the house, you couldn't miss it.

Her parents had visitors. Mum hadn't mentioned anyone coming round. It was probably a neighbour being Christmassy. That was all she needed. Hopefully, they wouldn't stay too long.

She got up slowly and went across to the wardrobe mirror and studied her face. She didn't look like a woman who'd just seen her entire life go down the pan and then had the chain unceremoniously flushed. She was maybe slightly paler and her hazel eyes looked darker than usual, but that was it.

If this had been a TV soap there would have been mascara streaks and evidence of tears. She'd been too shocked and angry to cry, she realised. Besides, she hadn't bothered with make-up this morning. She'd been blessed with lovely skin and she rarely used much more than lippy. This morning, she'd been in too much of a hurry to leave the flat to bother even with that.

Her wavy brown hair was fairly mussed up after the walk in the forest. It had grown a fair bit lately and was well past her shoulders. Hugh liked it long and she didn't have any strong feelings either way, so she'd let it grow. At least long hair was versatile. She put it up for work, a neat plait that kept it out of her face. You couldn't have hair dangling everywhere when you were examining patients. She hadn't bothered doing that this morning.

It struck Phoebe suddenly that it might be Maggie who'd called round. Maybe Mum or Dad had called her and she'd decided on an impromptu visit. If there was one person in the world who she'd have loved to see, it was her grandmother.

She opened her bedroom door and went cautiously to the top of the stairs. She could hear voices – whoever it was had been taken into the kitchen – and was that her father's laughter?

Then she heard her mother's voice. 'I'll have a look if you like. I'm sure she'd love to see you.'

The kitchen door opened and her mother came into the hall and glanced upwards.

'Oh hello, darling. I was just coming to find you. Sam's here. I've just made coffee. Are you coming down?'

Phoebe stiffened. Sam Hendrie was the son of her mother's best friend, Jan. Jan had owned Hendrie's Village Store and Post Office in Bridgeford, which was the nearest big town to Godshill, since the year dot. Sam worked for her there. He was the same age as Phoebe and she couldn't remember a time when she hadn't known him. Or a time when they hadn't been friends. Although, they'd drifted apart since she'd been in London. Phoebe knew there had also been a time when the two mothers had hoped their offspring might become romantically linked, but they had never felt like that. They had known each other far too long.

Not that she couldn't see he was attractive. Most people who met him thought he looked like a young Robson Green. He had the same startlingly blue eyes and rugged, almost craggy hand-someness.

Phoebe did not have any great urge to see him now, though. Sam was very good at seeing through the smiley-face façade she put on when she didn't want to show her feelings.

However, it would have seemed churlish to say, no, she was staying in her room, while she tried to work out how she was going to piece back the shattered fragments of her life.

She swallowed.

'I'll come and say hello,' she told her mother. 'How lovely.' Taking a deep breath she did her best to regain some composure before she went downstairs.

When she went into the kitchen, Phoebe saw that Sam was sitting on a stool at the breakfast island beside her father. It was the same stool she'd sat on earlier and both men had a coffee and a mince pie in front of them. Sam was wearing a wax jacket and jodh-purs and he stood up as she came into the room. Sam was like that – old-fashioned, with good manners and a wicked sense of humour. His dark hair was slightly shorter than usual and his blue eyes were sparkling with bonhomie.

'Hello, gorgeous. Happy Christmas.'

'Happy Christmas to you too, Sam.'

Phoebe went across and kissed his cheek. He smelled of outdoors with a hint of horse. Sam's passion was horses and when he wasn't working in the Post Office, he taught at the local riding school where he kept his own horse.

'Have you been teaching today?' she asked him.

'I have. Do I pong of horse? Sorry.' Before she could get away, he gave her a bear hug. Then he stood back to look at her properly. 'It's been ages. You're looking as stunning as ever.'

'Thank you.' It was gratifying to think that someone still thought so – even if it was just Sam.

Then he spoilt it by adding, 'If a bit pale?'

'I've been working too hard. It's that time of year.'

'Yeah. Tell me about it. Whoever said the Post Office is dead needs to swing by ours at Christmas. We've had queues down the street today. I had to work for a couple of hours this morning, despite the fact Ma's got extra help in.'

For the next few minutes, Sam, her parents and Phoebe exchanged pleasantries. She asked after his family and he updated them on his mother, who was thriving – she loved being busy – and his father who was a kitchen fitter and was also rushed off his feet – what with everyone wanting their kitchens finished before Christmas.

'It's crazy,' Sam said. 'It's just one day and everyone makes so much fuss. Pa's always complaining that if you try to order anything in early December people just whistle through their teeth and say, "Not sure we can promise getting it this side of Christmas."'

They talked about Brook Riding School and the fact that they'd just branched into riding for well-being, which was a course aimed at promoting people's self-esteem through connection with horses, and that Sam was one of their instructors.

He would be good at that, Phoebe thought. He was kind and he had infinite patience, both with people and animals, particularly the more vulnerable ones.

Not once did anyone mention the elephant in the room. Hugh. Or the fact that he was missing. Phoebe wondered if Sam had been primed not to say anything but decided her mother was more diplomatic than that.

Sam stayed at the Dashwoods for just over twenty minutes before draining his second mug of coffee and standing up.

'I'd better get off. I've still got a pile of Christmas card deliveries to make,' he told them, putting a fan of white envelopes on the breakfast bar addressed to Louella Dashwood and family and

Phoebe and Hugh. 'By day, I sort out other people's post and by night I become the postie for the cards Ma's too mean to stick stamps on,' he told them, grinning. 'These are from us.'

'I've got one for you and your mum somewhere,' Phoebe said. 'I'm not sure where it is.' They also had Hugh's name on them, she thought uneasily, so she was a bit reluctant to give them to him anyway.

'No worries.' Sam held out his hands, palms facing her. 'Drop them round when you find them. I take it you're here for a few days?'

She nodded. 'I'll do that.'

* * *

Sam dropped his gaze. There was something going on with Phoebe, that was for certain. He hadn't bought Louella's hasty explanation that Hugh was busy with work and was coming down separately. Not for one second. Surely Phoebe would have waited for him, not left him to it.

Then, as soon as he'd seen Phoebe's pale face, he'd known for sure it wasn't true. There was a lot more going on than anyone was saying. Phoebe was doing her best cover-up job, but she wasn't quite pulling it off. He hoped that whatever was troubling her and Hugh wasn't permanent. Christmas wasn't a good time to be falling out with people.

He said his goodbyes and escaped before he outstayed his welcome. He didn't want to pry and it was clear that Phoebe needed some space.

Outside, he got thoughtfully back into his old Subaru, which also smelled of horse and had a couple of bits of straw clinging to the driver's seat. Idly, he picked them off. Good job he wasn't giving anyone important a lift any time soon.

It would be a relief when Christmas was over. Sam liked the festive season as much as the next man, but he did find the whole thing a bit too hectic. He liked normality and routine and a peaceful life and Christmas was the opposite of all of these things. Nah, the whole thing had got way too commercial in his opinion. It caused unnecessary rows. It threw people together who didn't get on and would much rather be elsewhere, and it was disruptive.

Sam liked his own company and he was happiest when he was out in the forest, riding his horse, Ninja, along quiet woodland tracks with just the sounds of nature and birdsong for company. He just needed to get through the next few days and then life would return to normal.

He finished delivering the rest of his cards and was back home again within the hour. Five years ago, he'd bought a two-bedroom maisonette in Bridgeford, which had only just squeezed into the top of his price range because it was run-down and had been totally neglected by the previous owners.

It was impossible to find anything affordable in the New Forest, unless you were looking for either a park home or a retirement flat. The prices were crazily high. In 2019, the New Forest National Park had topped the table for being the most expensive national park in both England and Wales. He couldn't afford to buy in the New Forest but Bridgeford was the next best thing.

The maisonette's saving grace, as well as being just about afford-able, was its 100-foot-long garden. The previous owners may have neglected the inside – the kitchen had needed replacing and so had most of the flooring – but they'd clearly loved their garden. It was beautiful and had a greenhouse, several established flower beds, as well as a workshop and parking space.

It had come also with the freehold, so although Sam had to put up with whoever was in the flat below – it was currently rented out to a nice family, by the guy who owned it – the maisonette was a savvy investment. The prices in Bridgeford were only going in one direction – upwards – his parents had told him. He would never lose out.

Sam's father had helped him refurbish the place and Sam had learned more than he ever wanted to know about being a chippy in the process.

He'd had a lodger at the beginning, a lad who'd worked locally, but Matt had moved out in the summer. It had been useful having the extra money, but Sam hadn't got round to replacing him yet. He preferred living alone.

The maisonette was also very handy for work. Hendrie's Post Office and Village Shop was ten minutes away. He could have walked there. Not that he did very often. His days always began early – he was over to sort out Ninja at six every morning. His sixteen two bay thoroughbred cross Welsh cob was at part livery at Brook Riding School. This meant they did some of the work of looking after Ninja, which included feeds and part stabling when Sam couldn't get there. He couldn't have afforded their livery prices, but they gave him a big discount, in return for giving riding lessons to kids at weekends. He didn't have a flash, high pressure job like some of the other livery owners. He'd never wanted one.

Sam had never been on the same academic levels as Phoebe, their lives had gone in different directions after school, but he wasn't daft. Street smart and savvy was a description that fitted him well. He was good at maths and he was good with people. Both of these things came in handy for working in the Post Office and he was as popular as his mother and well liked by the locals.

It was the life Sam had chosen and the life he loved, he thought now, as he let himself into the front entrance of the flats and sprang up the two flights of stairs to his own front door. The only thing missing was romance. He'd had the odd girlfriend, but there hadn't been anyone serious since Judy. It was actually quite tricky to find a woman who was as besotted with horses as he was.

Judy had been that woman. She had loved horses and had two of her own. She'd kept them in a posh livery yard on the other side of the forest and she did one-day events all through the season. On the surface, Judy had been his ideal woman.

They had met while out riding in the forest. Judy was the daughter of two London stockbrokers, her father was as rich as Croesus and her mother was the most upmarket woman Sam had ever met. She had a plummy voice and a silky blonde bob and when she visited Judy's livery yard, she wore an Ariat hacking jacket and riding boots – Ariat was one of the pricier equestrian brands – despite the fact that Judy told him she had never so much as sat on a horse herself. But Sam had known the second that Judy had taken him to meet her parents – this was after they'd been dating eight months – that they hadn't liked him. Or, more to the point, that they hadn't thought he was anywhere near good enough for their daughter. No way would their future son-in-law be the son of a postmistress and a chippy. Oh, they were pleasant enough, but they were also dismissive.

'They'll grow to like you,' Judy had told him. Because Judy, despite her privileged upbringing and lifestyle, had no such qualms about class and money.

But Sam had known that they wouldn't. They would never actively come out and say he wasn't good enough – they were far too smart for that – but it was there in every glance, every conversation, and in an occasional barbed comment to Sam when Judy wasn't around. He had felt the strain, even if she hadn't, and he had loved her too much to ever want to put her in the position where she'd have to choose between him or her parents. In the end, they had drifted apart and had eventually decided to go their separate ways. The last time he'd seen her had been back at the beginning of

August at a show. Sam still missed her sometimes. But there was no point dwelling on the past.

Inside his own home, Sam put the coffee percolator on to boil and bent to stroke Snowball, his fluffy black cat, who came to greet him, tail as erect as a flagpole, purring madly.

Seeing Phoebe had jolted Sam. He wasn't sure why. Their friendship had drifted a bit since she'd been in London. Maybe it was just the fact that she'd looked so sad beneath her mask of brightness.

'Women, eh,' he said to Snowball, who blinked amber eyes and twined himself around his legs. 'Life's much simpler when it's just us boys, isn't it, mate?'

6

Phoebe had finally told her parents what had happened in the conversation with Hugh, although she'd toned it down a little bit. She hadn't mentioned the fact she'd told Cruella to stick her job for one thing. This had turned out to be a good call because her father's immediate reaction had been to want to drive straight to London to punch Hugh's lights out. And while this might have been gratifying, it wouldn't have helped anything.

It was two days since that shocking conversation with Hugh and there had been no further communication between them. He hadn't even sent her a WhatsApp message, which she'd thought he may have done, out of guilt.

OK, so if he had phoned her, she would have hung up on him again, but that was hardly the point. Phoebe couldn't even explain that logic to herself.

It was now lunchtime on the day before Christmas Eve and Phoebe was driving through the forest on her way to see Maggie. She'd tried phoning ahead to tell her grandmother she was coming, but her mother had been right. Maggie hadn't answered the phone.

Neither had she been able to leave a voicemail because the landline's inbox was full.

'It drives me mad,' Louella had said with a hint of irritation in her voice. 'I have no idea what she's doing – or if she's all right. Days go past sometimes and I don't hear from her.'

'That is worrying,' Phoebe had agreed. 'What if she got ill or fell over, heaven forbid.'

'You are preaching to the converted,' Louella had said, shaking her head. 'You wouldn't believe how many times I've driven over there after a seven-day silence to find Maggie happily pottering around with her animals, completely oblivious to the fact that she's totally out of contact with the outside world. I've tried to persuade her to carry one of those things you wear round your neck. But she won't have it. Too expensive, she says.'

Phoebe had sympathised. Maggie had always been a bit like that. But for some reason, she'd assumed her grandmother might change as she grew older and more vulnerable. It was worrying. Puddleduck was a huge place for a lone woman to manage. Maggie was still fit as a fiddle, but not many seventy-two-year-olds would still be running a smallholding of several acres, even if much of the land had been sold off now.

Puddleduck had been a thriving dairy farm when Phoebe was small. One of her earliest memories was of herself in oversized wellington boots, tramping through the mud and dark-brown puddles across the yard, holding tightly to one of her grandfather's big hands.

His gravelly voice came echoing down the years, 'Now, mind their feet and mind their gurt backsides. They're gentle creatures and they wouldn't harm you on purpose, but they might not notice you're there, and we don't want any mishaps. I don't want to be telling your mother you've been trampled by one of my girls. She'll have my guts for garters.'

'I'll be really careful,' Phoebe had promised earnestly. 'What are garters?'

'They're for holding things up. Stockings and suchlike.' Her grandfather had reddened and started blinking. 'Never mind what they are, we don't want to upset your mother, do we? Or she'll be shouting at us.'

'We don't want any shouting,' Phoebe had agreed and they'd both giggled because everyone knew that Louella never did much shouting. She wasn't a shouting type of mother.

Not that Phoebe had ever been allowed to get too close to the huge soft-eyed Friesians. Not when she was tiny. But one of her favourite things had been when her grandfather had lifted her up onto the old five-bar gate that enclosed the yard where the dairy herd were kept just before milking. There was a big scratching post in there built especially for the cows. It looked like a giant bottle brush on a pole, with brown prickly bristles like those on the yard broomsticks, and she loved to watch the cows scratch their backs on it, moving back and forth with blissful expressions on their faces.

'They can't do it like we can,' her grandfather had explained, 'because their legs don't work that way. You've never seen a cow scratch her back with a hoof, have you?'

He would mess around at this point, trying to reach his back with his arm and pretending he couldn't and nearly falling over in the process, before finally giving up and using the back of a door or a chair to scratch his back with instead. During these antics, he would be making cow sound effects. A moo here and a moo there. Her grandfather was an excellent mimic. Phoebe had always ended up choking with laughter at his hilarious impersonations.

'If you or I couldn't reach a bit of our back that needed scratching, then we'd ask another person to help,' he explained. 'Your mum might ask your dad or you might ask your brother, but a cow can't do that, see. So that's why they've got their special scratching post.'

It was amazing what memories flicked into your head, Phoebe thought as she drove through the entrance of Puddleduck Farm, parked the Lexus on the gravel frontage and got out. She glanced up at the farmhouse, which looked very much the same as it always had. A long L-shaped building with a red roof – the L was an extension to the original building – much of it covered in ivy.

She walked towards the wooden blue painted front door. She hadn't thought about that conversation with her grandfather for years. Oh, what Phoebe would have given to hear him impersonating a cow now. She felt a pang of sadness. An ache for days long gone. She knew this was partly due to her mood. She was still trying to process what had happened with Hugh. She wondered if he was with Melissa. Other than at work, that was. Had he moved Melissa into their bed already? Had he really moved on that effortlessly or was he missing her?

Phoebe wished suddenly that she hadn't left so hurriedly. Because her imagination painted scenarios that were much crueller than what the reality probably was. Or maybe not!

She knew she would have to go back sooner or later and face him. But she was still too raw to want to talk to him, even to arrange that.

She found the front door unlocked as usual and stepped inside onto the flagstone floor. The house felt colder inside than it had out, despite the chill of the December day.

'Maggie,' she shouted, but she could tell immediately that the house was empty. Although, there were dogs barking somewhere outside.

Tutting, she bolted the front door behind her and then, just in case she was mistaken, she checked out the downstairs rooms. There were four. The back room with its great inglenook fireplace was empty, although the room smelled as though a fire had been recently lit there. On the wide wooden mantelpiece above the fireplace, a single card with a reindeer galloping across its front was the only concession to Christmas. That was odd, Maggie usually got loads of cards.

The smaller back room, which mostly got used as a dumping ground for things that didn't live anywhere else, was also empty of people, although not junk. Phoebe had trouble opening the door, which turned out to have a pile of blankets and a dog basket just behind it. A guitar that had been propped up against the wall fell over with a loud twangy jangling noise. Surely Maggie hadn't taken up playing the guitar.

From somewhere outside, a dog was still barking. But no dogs appeared.

Phoebe continued her search.

The office, which was where her grandfather had once done all the paperwork and admin for the farm and which Maggie still used, was surprisingly tidy. There were boxes of paperwork around the walls, but at least they were neatly filed and labelled. They had dates on them in her grandmother's neat handwriting.

The kitchen was empty too. Trails of breadcrumbs scattered the worktops and there was a half-cut loaf on a chopping board, a carving knife alongside, and a butter dish with the lid left off.

On impulse, Phoebe checked the fridge. There was milk, cheese and a few mouldering tomatoes. There were also several lidded plastic tubs that looked as though they might be meat. A quick sniff revealed they contained raw tripe.

Yuck. That had been a mistake. Almost gagging, Phoebe screwed up her nose. Hopefully, they were for the dogs and her grandmother hadn't resorted to a diet of bread and tripe.

She was about to withdraw from the fridge when a flurry of movement behind her made her jump out of her skin.

'Hold it right there. Don't move. I'm armed.'

Phoebe spun round to find herself face to face with her grandmother, who was holding what looked like a baseball bat high in the air.

Instinctively, she raised her hands. 'Maggie, it's me. It's OK. It's Phoebe.'

Her grandmother's face crinkled up into laughter. 'I know it's you, you walnut. Well, I did, about two seconds before you turned round. What are you doing in my fridge? What are you doing here at all? You should have rung and told me you were coming. You gave me a right old shock.' She dropped the baseball bat and put her hand across her heart. 'You do know it's dangerous to sneak up on defenceless old people. You could have given me a heart attack.'

'From where I'm standing, it's you who was doing the sneaking around. You don't look in the slightest bit defenceless either.' Phoebe glanced at the baseball bat. 'And, for your information, I did phone. Your voicemail is full.'

'Is it? Useless, flaming thing. It's always full.'

'You're supposed to delete the messages,' Phoebe scolded and then, unable to contain herself for a second longer, she rushed across the room to hug her grandmother. 'Oh, it's so good to see you. I've missed you.'

The old lady hugged her back and, as they drew apart, Phoebe saw that her eyes were dancing with laughter. 'You know how I am with technology. I do try. Did I give you a scare?' She prodded the baseball bat with one booted foot. 'I've been practising on a bale in the hay barn. Very therapeutic it is, knocking ten bells out of a bale of hay. I've got a few of these bats kicking about. Woe betide anyone who breaks in here.'

'They don't need to break in. The front door isn't locked,' Phoebe chided. 'And you should be careful keeping weapons in your house – these days, you can get sued by the burglar. Especially if they can prove you had malicious intent and weren't just grabbing the nearest thing to hand in self-defence.'

'Who's to say I haven't taken up baseball? I've got a few balls lying around too. I'm not stupid, you know.' She smiled. 'Oh, Phoebe. It's good to see you. Let me get a proper look at you.' Maggie stepped back a pace so they were at arm's-length once more and they studied each other.

Phoebe saw, to her great relief, that her grandmother looked very much as she always did. Her still thick blonde hair was cut short, as it always had been, with maybe a few extra grey strands mingled in with the blonde around her ears. Her upturned nose was stuck up in the air – if you didn't know her, you might have thought her snobby, but it was just the way she carried herself – and her chin jutted determinedly. She didn't look frail or any more vulnerable than she'd ever looked despite the fact that she would be seventy-three next year.

Louella's worries seemed suddenly misplaced.

'You're getting skinny,' Maggie said without preamble. 'What's going on? Are you too busy to eat properly in London?' She narrowed her eyes. 'And you don't look very happy for a girl who's living the dream. Has London lost its sparkle? Or is it that Hugh? If he's been messing you about, he'll have me to answer to.'

She never missed a trick, Phoebe thought. She'd always been like that – straight for the jugular – and somehow when Maggie was asking, she didn't mind. It didn't feel intrusive or nosy. Perhaps because she had always had the feeling that Maggie loved her so completely and unconditionally. Not that her mother didn't, but Maggie was different. Maggie had always been in her corner one hundred and ten per cent. Phoebe had the feeling that if she'd turned up one day and said she'd decided to try out a spot of mass murder for a hobby, Maggie's first response would have been to say, 'Well, I'm sure you've got your reasons.'

'I'll tell you about Hugh in a bit, but, yes, you're right. We've split up.'

'I see.' Maggie quirked an eyebrow and shot her a curious look. 'Shall I make us some lunch?'

'Not if it's tripe on toast.'

'That's for the dogs, as you very well know. I can offer you a full range of soup – well, I can offer you vegetable or pea and mint?'

'Canned soup?' Phoebe asked curiously. Her grandmother had always looked down on food that came in cans.

She tutted. 'No, darling. Home-made soup. It's in the freezer. I batch-cook it to save time. Are you familiar with the concept of batch cooking?'

Phoebe laughed again. She'd forgotten how much she enjoyed this banter. 'Where are the dogs anyway?' she asked. 'I assume Buster's still around, is he?'

Buster was an elderly black Labrador. Her grandmother didn't know how old he was, but he was arthritic, and back in the summer when Phoebe had last seen him, she'd thought that he couldn't have much longer in the world.

'I locked Buster outside when I came in to do burglar bashing,' Maggie said in a no-nonsense voice. 'I didn't want him getting hurt.'

'What about you getting hurt?'

'I left the top half of the back door open. I knew I could whistle for backup if I needed it.'

There was no arguing with that logic. Phoebe rolled her eyes.

'Pea soup sounds amazing,' she said. 'Can I do anything?'

'You can clear a space on the table so we've got somewhere to eat it,' Maggie said.

Phoebe did as she was told, heading across to the long farmhouse table that had been in place for as long as she could remember, against the far wall of the kitchen. It was solid wood and probably too heavy to move. She shifted several free newspapers and a pile of what looked like unopened Christmas cards. So that was why there was only one on the mantelpiece.

'Why haven't you opened your cards?' she asked, when they were sitting next to each other with fragrant steaming soup heated in the microwave and chunks of bread and butter.

'I've been busy. I'll get round to it.' Maggie gave a little frown and tore off a chunk of break. Then she held Phoebe's gaze with slightly worried hazel eyes. 'To be honest, I didn't send many cards this year, so I'm feeling guilty. If I open that lot, I'm going to feel even more flaming guilty because I won't have sent half of them a card, will I?'

'It's not too late. I could help you do some.'

'It is too late. There's not much sadder than a late Christmas card, I've always thought. Besides, they'll know they were an afterthought then, won't they? They'll know I'm only sending them one because they sent me one.'

'True.' That was a change. Maggie had never been in the slightest bit bothered about what other people thought of her. Maybe her mother was right and she was feeling more vulnerable than she let on. Maybe that explained the baseball bat too.

Before Phoebe could comment any further, they were interrupted by the sound of a bang and an ear-splitting, raucous noise that was somewhere between a chainsaw and a lawnmower with rusty bearings.

Phoebe jumped out of her skin. 'What the hell was that?'

'Don't worry, that's just Diablo.' Maggie put her spoon down. 'He's one of the reasons I'm so busy. He must have escaped again. He follows me around. I'd better shut the top half of the door or he'll be in here scrounging bread. He loves it...' She leapt to her feet and headed for the back door. Phoebe followed her curiously.

The farmhouse kitchen narrowed into a utility room at one end and this had a stable-style back door that led outside. As they approached, Phoebe saw that while the bottom half was indeed closed, the top half was currently filled by the head of a shaggy brown donkey with cheeky dark eyes and a white nose, who was clearly eager to get through it. When he saw them, he nudged the wood with his nose and kicked the lower half of the door with an impatient hoof.

'Get out of it,' Maggie shouted at him. 'Yer great daft beggar.'

The donkey took no notice at all, just bent his head and blew on her hands, and Phoebe didn't miss the way her grandmother rubbed his long brown ears and the tenderness on her face before she turned towards her granddaughter with an exasperated look.

'Can you give me a hand to shift him, love?'

There was nothing quite like being back at Puddleduck Farm!

7

Shifting a small, but very stubborn brown donkey, who had no intention of going anywhere except into the kitchen was harder than Phoebe had imagined. It took about fifteen minutes to bribe him back into the field he shared with the two other donkeys, which was the nearest field to the house on the northern side of the farm, abutting the road.

Puddleduck Farm was made up of a collection of fields and a scattering of outbuildings, which included the dairy block, a haybarn and feed store. From the air, if you had drawn a line around the boundaries of the farm and its original grazing land, it would have made the shape of a boot. Like Italy, the toe of the boot pointed left and the heel was to the right. Puddleduck Farm itself was nestled in the heel and accessed by a permanently open gate that separated it from the road which bent around the boundary.

Their nearest neighbours, Beechbrook House, were alongside the toe of the boot, or at least the entrance to Beechbrook House was alongside the toe. The house itself – an impressive mansion at the top of a slope – was accessed via an imposing entrance between a high stone archway, with a life-size sculpture of a stag standing on top of the arch. The drive that led up to the house looked from the road to be about a quarter of a mile long. Not that Phoebe had ever been there.

Beechbrook House was owned by Lord Alfred Earnest Holt, the local landowner, who tenanted out many of the surrounding properties. Maggie and Pete Crowther had owned their land – it had been won fair and square in a poker match back in 1905 by Maggie's grandfather, Henry, who had farmed it for a brief while before passing it on to his son, Edwin – he'd been married to Charlotte, who'd changed the name – and they'd passed it, in turn, to their only daughter, Maggie.

The road that bordered both Puddleduck Farm and Beechbrook House ran along the back of the boot, down the heel towards the toe and from there alongside a good deal more of the Holts' land, most of which was enclosed by a twelve-foot-high red-brick wall. There was also a natural border of woodland across the fields that separated Puddleduck Farm from Beechbrook House.

As Phoebe walked back from the donkey field with Maggie, she noticed that the farm buildings looked much more dilapidated than they had the last time she'd been here. The haybarn, with its corrugated roof, which had always looked rickety, now had bits of roof missing altogether. Some of the fencing didn't look in a very good state of repair and the timber-built kennel block, which had been new eleven and a half years ago, looked in need of some TLC. All of its occupants who were in their outside runs barked crazily as they went past, and as they passed the old milking shed, which now housed cats and any animals that might need quarantining for any reason, a dozen or so geese came hissing towards them, their white wings flapping.

'Don't mind them,' Maggie said, as Phoebe glanced at them warily. 'They're all bark and no bite.' She shooed them away with an authoritative hand and most of them did back off obediently, although one big fellow was determined to peck the back of Phoebe's leg and kept darting in for another go. 'Apart from Bruce Goose,' Maggie added. 'He's a bit more persistent than the rest.'

'I don't remember you having geese before,' Phoebe said, ducking out of range of Bruce Goose's stabbing yellow beak.

'Someone in the village was moving and he couldn't take them.'

Sensible chap, thought Phoebe.

'And you have more ducks, don't you?'

'I may have a couple of extra ducks. People assume I take ducks when they see the name of the farm,' Maggie said cheerfully.

'And how about the wolfhound?' Phoebe said. 'I've not seen him before.'

'Tiny?' Maggie smirked. Tiny was a total misnomer for an enormous Irish wolfhound. He was only about two inches shorter than Diablo and he had appeared alongside Buster, the ageing black Labrador, as soon as they'd gone outside. He clearly adored Maggie and he and Buster had escorted both women and Diablo back to his field. Phoebe didn't think she'd ever seen such an enormous dog, but there was such a daft look in his brown eyes when he'd come to greet them that she warmed to him instantly.

'Tiny's owners had to downsize and they didn't have the space to take him,' Maggie told her when they finally got back to the farmhouse kitchen.

This time, Maggie didn't bother shutting the stable door, so both dogs had sneaked in too and they established their positions at Maggie's feet as soon as she sat back down at the kitchen table, lying as close as they could get.

'Tiny's no trouble anyway,' Maggie added and the wolfhound opened one eye at the sound of his name and his great grey tail thumped once on the flagstones. 'People are so irresponsible. They dash out and buy a puppy without a thought to the future. Anyway,

I had space for another dog. I've rehomed a couple of the kennel dogs lately.'

The kennel dogs were the ones Maggie thought had a good chance of getting another home. They were the young ones, the pretty ones, the small ones. Maggie actually had quite a good turnover of those.

She probably did have space, Phoebe thought, but Tiny was as big as several dogs and he wasn't in the kennel, so clearly wasn't going to be rehomed anyway. She had also noticed several cats slinking around in the barn. Maggie had told her they earned their place at the farm by keeping the mice down. Phoebe had no doubt they did, but they still needed looking after and must add to her grandmother's workload, not to mention the upkeep and vet's bills. No wonder she didn't have time to open her Christmas cards.

'But Puddleduck Farm is still a rehoming centre and not a forever home animal shelter?' she asked, as she reheated their soup in the microwave and carried it back to the kitchen table.

'Of course it is.' Maggie's voice was over-bright. As if she was trying to convince herself as much as Phoebe. 'I can't afford to keep all these waifs and strays permanently.'

'Do you still get help with fundraising from the locals?'

'Yes, I do.'

'And how about help to look after the animals?'

'I've got Natasha – she comes in every weekend and any other time she can.' There was an edge to her grandmother's voice and a warning flash in her eyes. 'Now will you stop asking pointless questions and eat your soup.'

Phoebe bit her tongue and did as she was told. She knew her grandmother could be a bit sensitive when it came to the animals that she adored. The animals that had filled the hole her grandfather had left.

She sometimes wondered what would have happened if both

her grandparents had still been alive. Farmer Pete and Maggie had had such great plans. They had worked hard for their retirement – that was an understatement – and they planned to enjoy every second. Their plan had been to sell on the dairy herd, buy a big motorhome and tour Europe, starting with France.

Farmer Pete had never really known his dad who had died in the D-Day Landings when he was just two years old and had been buried in a commonwealth cemetery. So that's where they had planned to start. He wanted to go and visit the grave, touch his father's name on the monument. He wanted to do these things for his mother, who had never been there, as much as he did for himself. 'I just want to see it, even if it's only the once,' he was fond of telling anyone who would listen.

They had got as far as selling the herd and buying the motorhome when Farmer Pete had died. It had been a stupid accident involving a tractor. Even now, Phoebe didn't know the full details because twelve years ago, when it had happened, Maggie had been too devastated to talk about it. All Phoebe knew was that it had been something to do with a brake failure. The tractor hadn't even been that old.

According to Louella, if it hadn't been for Neddie, and later Roxy, Maggie would have given up right there and then. The donkeys had saved Maggie's life. They had got her through the grief and given her something to focus on. Something to care for and love. The donkeys had been the beginning of the rehoming centre. Not that either of them had ever been rehomed.

Maggie had said they were mascots, as important as Jemima Puddleduck had once been to her mother, so therefore couldn't be rehomed, and besides, she liked them, so Neddie and Roxy had stayed. They were still here, living the life of Riley and looking a lot fatter than when they'd arrived.

'Am I allowed to ask another question now I've finished my soup?' Phoebe ventured, shooting her grandmother a glance.

'One more and then it's my turn.'

'Where did Diablo come from?'

Maggie wiped breadcrumbs from her mouth with a green paper napkin and shrugged. 'He was found injured on the road. Not badly, but he'd cut his neck. A motorist drew my attention to him – although, he was practically here already. He was getting acquainted with Roxy and Neddie over the fence. I've been trying to find out who owns him ever since.'

Phoebe suspected she hadn't tried all that hard. 'He doesn't belong to a commoner then?'

'I don't think so. All the roamers have to be marked for identification purposes and he doesn't have a mark.'

'I see. Is he all right now? I mean, the injury healed OK? You don't need me to take a look?'

'He's fine, love, thanks. No after-effects – in fact, from what I've learned about his escapee tendencies, he probably just jumped out of someone's field. He's very adept at escaping. He's a little devil.'

'Hence the name Diablo?'

'Precisely. Right, that's enough questions. It's my turn. And you're getting off lightly because I've only got one question.'

Phoebe braced herself.

'What's happened with Hugh?'

Phoebe didn't tone down anything for Maggie. She told her the full story, no holds barred, ending with the devastation she'd felt when she'd realised that this was so much more than a fleeting lovers' tiff.

'I must say it sounds like you're well rid of the man,' Maggie said, having listened without interrupting verbally, although there had been several outraged looks and shakes of her head. 'I'm disappointed, though. I'd had him down as being better than that.'

'But you weren't entirely surprised, were you?' Phoebe said, remembering her grandmother's perceptive comments earlier.

'I've always known he was the ambitious type and I had wondered, if it ever came to it, what he would put first – you or the job?' She gave Phoebe a searching look. 'And now we know.'

'You think he wants to be with Melissa to forward his career?' Phoebe had to admit that this hadn't occurred to her.

'I think it's possible. It never ceases to amaze me the lengths some people will go to in pursuit of personal ambition. Or who they'll trample on along the way.'

Maggie sounded so sure about this that Phoebe was tempted to ask her if she'd had any personal experience. But she held back. She wanted her grandmother's opinion and she wouldn't get it if she was sidetracked. Maggie might be brusque and feisty and the most stubbornly independent woman she'd ever met, but she was also wise and kind and very astute, with a heart bigger than the sun.

'It's also possible he just had his head turned by a powerful woman. How much older is she? Isn't she your siren type?'

'She's thirty-seven. Three years older than him. I'm not sure about a siren, but she's certainly the temptress type.' Phoebe felt her heart dip. 'Her nickname's Cruella. Although she does like animals. Being a vet.'

'Not all vets like animals,' Maggie said lightly. 'Some of them are in it purely for the money. I wouldn't have thought that applies to Hugh – he has enough money coming his way – but he's definitely power-hungry. He's still trying to impress his father, isn't he?'

'Yes, I suppose he is. I hadn't thought of that.' Phoebe remembered how Hugh changed to being subservient and ever so slightly fawning when he was in his father's presence.

'Boys either try to impress their fathers or they rebel outright against them. Your Hugh is the type who wants to impress. I'm guessing he isn't too fond of living in his daddy's property either, but he doesn't earn enough to rent a place like that in London, even on a junior partner's salary.'

'Are you saying what he did isn't that bad?' Phoebe felt slightly put out.

'No, darling. Definitely not. I'm simply trying to work out what his motives are. If you know someone's motives, then you can understand why they behave as they do and that can be helpful.' Her hazel eyes, so like Phoebe's own, were kind. 'The only thing that really matters here is how you feel. Do you still love him? Would you take him back if he realised he'd made a mistake and came begging? Or is it too early to tell?'

Phoebe paused to consider this and, for a moment, the only sounds in the old farmhouse kitchen were the ticking of a clock somewhere and Buster's breathing and Tiny's gentle rhythmic snores.

'I honestly don't know,' she said eventually. 'I was pretty shocked when he told me that he and Melissa had been "dating", as he put it.' She mimed the inverted commas in the air. 'I hadn't been expecting that.' She remembered the kiss and the fact that it hadn't been casual. 'Although, some part of me knew when I saw them kissing. Knowing that I've lost my job as well is just muddying the waters. I made it far too easy for them, didn't I?'

'I wouldn't beat yourself up about that one just yet. I'm sure Cruella will know perfectly well that you could sue her for constructive dismissal, even if you do hand in your notice formally. She'll be amenable to compromise, I'm sure.'

'I can't work there again though. Not knowing that the two of them...' She broke off, aware that her grandmother was shaking her head.

'You don't have to. All I am saying is that it's unlikely you'll walk away empty-handed if you decide to quit. It would be in her interests to give you a pay-off and a good reference. You won't lose out professionally.'

Phoebe closed her eyes and she heard her grandmother's voice continue very softly in the room.

'The best thing to do when you're not entirely sure of the way forward is to wait until you are. Does that help?'

'Yes, it does,' Phoebe answered, opening her eyes. As always seeing Maggie was like balm in a crazy world. 'And thank you. Mum said you're coming over for the Christmas Eve supper tomorrow. You are coming over on Christmas Day for the main event too, aren't you? Shall I come and collect you?'

'Whatever for? I'm perfectly capable of driving half an hour there and back to see my family.'

'I thought you might enjoy travelling in style in my nice Lexus.'

'Pah. I prefer my trusty Land Rover, as you very well know.' Maggie's voice had taken on a haughty tone.

'Have it your own way.' Phoebe waved a careless hand. 'If you prefer that old boneshaker of a vehicle to heated-seat luxury.'

'I do.'

'Fine.'

They were back in banter territory.

Phoebe had felt like she'd never smile again when she'd arrived. But she was still grinning when she finally waved goodbye. Even if she was also still a little worried about how her grandmother was really coping. Puddleduck Farm was a lot for just one person, let alone a seventy-two-year-old woman and far from winding down it seemed, Maggie was taking on even more in her old age.

8

Sam's Christmas Eve tradition was to have evening fish and chips with his parents and any other relatives and friends who might be in town. This year, it was just him and his ma and pa. The fish and chips came from The Posh Plaice in Bridgeford. On this particular Christmas Eve, Sam had volunteered to both collect and pay for the meal and take it around to his folks, who lived above the shop and Post Office in a flat which his father called the Tardis, as it was much bigger inside than it looked from outside.

Fish and chips might not have sounded that special to most people, but it was to his mother, because she didn't have to cook it. His father was slightly old-fashioned and he liked a plain cooked meal every night. Meat and two veg on the table at six. Ma complained about this regularly but was perfectly happy to do it, as far as Sam could make out, because if ever his father offered to whisk them off for a meal out, she tended to refuse.

Sam wondered sometimes if his mother just loved her fixed routine or whether she was actually worried about going too far away from the flat. He'd learned from an aunt once that his mother had suffered with postnatal depression after Sam had been born, hence she'd never had any other children, and this had developed into agoraphobia. His mother herself had never spoken about it with him and Sam thought she was fine now. But he'd learned that agoraphobia wasn't, as some people assumed, a fear of open spaces but an anxiety disorder that made it difficult for sufferers to go to certain places that triggered fear for them.

Jan did go out and she didn't seem afraid – she went regularly to the bank, she came to the stables sometimes to see Ninja and she had been known to go on holiday, although only in the UK – she didn't like flying – she also had coffee and cake with Louella. But she wasn't keen on going anywhere she didn't know well.

Sam might have worried that she wasn't happy, but she clearly was happy. Or at least she was very content. Jan Hendrie's glass wasn't just half full, it was brimming over, no matter what the outside world dealt her.

Her customers adored her and came into the Post Office to chat as much as they did to buy essentials. As well as being a Post Office, the shop sold most things that a big supermarket did, albeit pricier versions, but it was always packed. Once, when there had been talk of the Post Office part closing down, the locals had started a petition and its future had been secured very quickly. His mother certainly didn't need to go out to visit friends. They all came to her.

Sam was driving back to his parents with the fish and chips when a silver Mercedes with blacked-out front windows cut across him. Sam slammed on his brakes, more irritated than he'd usually have been because he knew who the driver was.

'Idiot,' he shouted, gesticulating out of the window. Not that there was any sign he'd been seen. The Mercedes just accelerated away. Forty in a thirty. Typical. Sam swore under his breath. 'Think you own the bloody road,' he muttered, enraged, because while Rufus Holt, who was undoubtedly driving the car, didn't own the road, he did own a hell of a lot of the land around Bridgeford and the New Forest. Or, more to the point, his father, Lord Alfred Holt owned it, which meant it would one day pass along with the title of lord to his eldest son – Rufus. Sam knew, as all the locals knew, that Alfred Holt had inherited the title of lord and had sat in the House of Lords, as well as being a lord of the manor. And from what Sam had seen of him Rufus already acted as if he was Lord of Bridgeford.

A couple of weeks ago, Sam had had a much more serious run-in with Rufus Holt. He'd been riding Ninja along a quiet country road, close to the stables, when the silver Mercedes had passed too quickly. It had slowed down a little, but not enough, and his bay horse, who was nervy at the best of times, had shied at something in the hedge and had sidestepped into the path of the car, which had been forced to slam on its brakes and squeal to a halt. This had unnerved Ninja further and he'd ended up foaming and sweating and jigging in the middle of the road so it was all Sam could do to stop him from bolting.

The driver's window had slid down and Rufus, who'd looked utterly furious, had leaned out. 'You idiot. You nearly got us both killed. Can't you keep your horse under control.'

'I nearly got us killed?' Sam had retorted. 'You were going way too fast. Haven't you seen the speed limit through the forest?'

'Horses shouldn't be on a road. They should be in a field. People like you are a total menace.'

Sam had caught a flash of a stony-faced gaze before the window slid up again. Thanks to Ninja's antics, he had his hands too full to retaliate. But he'd been left fuming. It was that line, 'People like you', that had enraged him the most. What was that supposed to be mean? Plebs, peasants, inferiors? It certainly hadn't been complimentary.

For the next few hours, the incident had replayed itself over and over in his head and Sam thought of all the things he'd wished he'd said in retaliation. In another life, he'd have hauled Rufus Holt out of the car and smacked him one. That would have been very satisfying. Not that Sam was in the habit of smacking anyone. Physical violence was abhorrent to him, but the man had been so totally obnoxious, it was the only thing he could think of that would have made him feel better.

Sam disliked the whole 'lord of the manor' thing at the best of times and Rufus Holt didn't help. The injustice of a society where some people worked their socks off their entire life and were forever poor but still managed to be civil and decent to those around them, not to mention have integrity and good manners, and some people just didn't – well, it stank.

Seeing Rufus again so soon had taken the shine off what had otherwise been a very pleasant day. Sam gave himself a little shake and a good talking-to. 'Oh, get over yourself, Sam. He's just an arrogant nob. Forget him.'

But he still felt unnerved when he arrived back at his parents' with the fish and chips, and let himself in through the side door, which had a holly wreath pinned to it, and went on up to their flat. Rufus Holt threatened to spoil Sam's Christmas Eve entirely.

* * *

Phoebe's family tradition was to have a Christmas Eve buffet, which Phoebe had helped to get ready. Not that there had been a lot of preparation needed. Louella focused most of her efforts on the traditional meal on Christmas Day, which they had at lunchtime – although, lunchtime was usually closer to two than one. The buffet was about chilling out with the family, but Louella wanted to chill out too, so it was mostly comprised of party food bought in – although, she did always make the mince pies and the sausage rolls. There was a selection of quiche and nibbles, like olives, mozzarella-stuffed tomatoes, nuts and dips, and some rather lovely mini choco-late rolls covered in glitter that Phoebe had her eye on. Mum had got the same ones last year and they were delicious.

It was now seven and Phoebe had just seen her brother's car pull up on the drive. She ran to the front door to let in him and his wife, Alexa. She was really looking forward to seeing Frazier – her brother was one of her favourite people, and Alexa was lovely, inside and out – but she was also anxious about seeing them, because the last thing she wanted to do was to have to go through the whole sad story again. Better to nip it in the bud now.

She swung open the door and before they had a chance to get through it, laden down with overnight bags – they were staying until Boxing Day – and carriers of presents and bottles, she said, 'Happy Christmas, guys. I have news. I'm telling you now to get it out of the way. Hugh and I have had a disagreement – that's most probably terminal – so he won't be joining us for Christmas.' Her words all spilled out in a rush and she was aware of Frazier's surprise and Alexa's sympathy but also of another look that flashed between them. Something a little shifty and embarrassed. No doubt she would find out what that was about later.

'I'm really sorry to hear that,' Alexa said, sounding it. Her pretty face was screwed up in consternation, her dark eyes concerned. Alexa had a girl-next-door prettiness that was as natural and genuine as she was.

'Yes. Same, sis.' Frazier's voice was gruff. He wasn't good with emotional stuff. He was definitely the strong and silent type, but he did add a little awkwardly, 'Need a hug?'

'I never say no to a hug.' She hugged them both, smelling Alexa's Loulou perfume and Frazier's Peaky Blinders shampoo in the close proximity of the hall – Frazier was a huge fan of *Peaky Blinders*. The familiarity of them both – or was it their warm hugs? – made her want to cry a bit. God, she was emotional at the moment.

But at least she had told them about Hugh, so it wouldn't be an unspoken conversation, hanging over the celebrations. The elephant in the room. Or, at least, not so much of one as it would have been if she'd said nothing.

Two minutes later, they were all in the kitchen and there were more hugs and sorting out of where to put presents and bags.

'Alexa, I've just made fresh coffee,' Louella said.

A disembodied voice from the direction of the sideboard announced, '*Freshly ground coffee is made from beans grown in South and Central America, Africa and South East Asia.*'

'Oh, I'm so sorry. I'll switch it off.' Louella leapt to her feet. 'So we don't have a computer piping up every five minutes thinking we're speaking to her.'

Everyone laughed, as they always did when anyone mentioned Amazon's virtual assistant, which had caused much hilarity in the past, much to Alexa the human's embarrassment. She must have heard every Alexa joke going a thousand times over, but she was very good-natured about it.

'If anyone wants to know a Christmas fact, they'll have to ask Frazier,' she said, smiling at her husband. 'He's on top form tonight.'

Everyone looked at Frazier. He'd been blessed with a photo-graphic memory for quirky facts and his party piece was to reel them off.

'Come on then, son,' said their father. He was obviously getting in the spirit of things. He was wearing a jumper that said, 'I only get my baubles out once a year.'

'Yes, go on. Impress us,' Phoebe prompted. 'It's not a proper Christmas without a few festive facts.'

Frazier scrunched up his face as if struggling to remember something. Then he held up a hand and tilted his head as though listening. 'Did you know that "Jingle Bells" was once broadcast from space?'

'No way,' Phoebe said, amazed.

'Yes way. In December 1965, two astronauts aboard the USA spaceship Gemini 6 played a prank. They told Mission Control they'd seen an unidentified object about to enter earth's orbit and then just as things were getting a bit tense, they played "Jingle Bells" over the airwaves.'

'Is that true?' Louella asked, shaking her head in amusement.

'It's gospel. I swear,' Frazier said. 'It's in the *Guinness Book of Records*. The first song ever played from space. You can check if you don't believe me.'

Phoebe clapped her hands and everyone else laughed.

'Also,' Frazier continued with an authoritative tone in his voice, 'Santa has to visit 822 homes a second in order to deliver all the presents on Christmas Eve, which means he has to drive at 650 miles a second.'

'Definitely speeding then,' their father remarked. 'Although I don't suppose there's any flying traffic police fast enough to catch up with him.'

Phoebe felt some of the tension she hadn't even been fully aware of dissipating beneath the cheery atmosphere. It was so lovely to be back with them all, despite the circumstances.

'Rudolf very nearly wasn't called Rudolf.' Frazier was in full flow now. 'They were originally going to call him Reginald, but it didn't have quite the same ring to it.'

'Reginald the red-nosed reindeer. Hmmm,' Alexa said. 'See what you mean. Wasn't the song based on a story that was originally some marketing ploy?'

'The story was certainly a marketing ploy,' Louella chipped in. 'It was a children's story, published by an American department store, I seem to remember.'

'And one more fact before we start talking about sensible things,' Frazier said. 'Did you know that mistletoe is an aphrodisiac. It's an ancient symbol of fertility and virility, so watch out if anyone asks you for a quick kiss under the mistletoe. Who knows where it might lead?'

Phoebe felt a spike of pain at the mention of mistletoe, and she was aware of her mother's swift glance in her direction, as the others, oblivious, began making mistletoe jokes.

'Right then,' Louella's clear voice rose above the hilarity. 'Is anyone hungry? Gosh, look at the time. It's gone seven thirty. Did Maggie say when she was planning on joining us, Phoebe?'

Phoebe glanced at her mother, grateful for her swift, if clumsy, change of subject. 'No, but I told her seven, sharp. She is quite late, isn't she? If she's not here soon, I could drive over?' she offered. 'I haven't had anything to drink yet. I did ask her if she wanted a lift, but she said no.'

Fortunately, at that moment, the doorbell jangled out its strident summons and Phoebe escaped to let her grandmother in.

But as soon as she saw her face, she knew there was a problem. Maggie's usually ruddy complexion was pale.

'There's been an accident with Jemima. I was going to phone you, but I thought it would be quicker to just bring her with me. She's in the Land Rover.'

'Who's Jemima?' Phoebe asked, even though she had a feeling she could probably guess.

'She's my favourite duck,' Maggie confirmed her suspicions. 'She's been bitten. By a dog, I think. Or it could be a fox. There's an open wound. We can't let her die, Phoebe. Not on Christmas Eve.' Her voice wobbled. 'That would be too awful.'

9

The very last thing that Phoebe had anticipated doing on Christmas Eve was to be kneeling in the back of a Land Rover with her veterinary kit laid out beside her and an injured duck on a blanket in front of her.

Fortunately, Jemima was very tame and she submitted peacefully to Phoebe's examination as she carefully parted the white feathers to examine the wound on Jemima's side. It wasn't as bad as it looked – injuries always looked worse on her white patients. There was no muscle or bone showing. This didn't mean it wasn't serious. Birds usually died from shock or infection after a bite and, in Phoebe's experience, quite a high percentage did die, no matter what you did. Not that Phoebe would be telling Maggie this.

She cleaned the wound and thanked her lucky stars that stitching it was not essential – stitching in these circumstances was liable to trap bacteria and most open wounds tended to heal better. Then she smothered the wound in antibiotics for ducks, that Maggie had had the presence of mind to bring with her from her own first-aid cabinet.

'The best thing we can do is take her back to yours and keep her quiet,' Phoebe told her grandmother. 'She'll need to be isolated from the others. Is that possible?'

'Yes, that's fine. I've got an isolation pen.' Maggie blinked several times. 'I know it sounds crazy to be this worked up over a duck. But she's one of my favourites. She's such a sweet little thing.'

Her voice was husky and Phoebe knew she was close to tears. Her feisty, strong-willed grandmother who was perfectly happy to live alone in the middle of nowhere and would think nothing of sneaking up on a burglar with a baseball bat turned to mush when one of her beloved charges was hurt.

'It doesn't sound crazy.' Phoebe shot her grandmother an empathetic glance. This was why they had always been so close, she thought. It was their love of animals. It bonded them. This passion, this strong protectiveness that extended to the whole of the animal kingdom. She only ever saw Maggie this vulnerable when she was around an animal that needed help.

'Your father would probably say we should cut our losses and have her for lunch on Boxing Day,' Maggie added, clearly trying to regain some of her usual bluster.

'And he'd be totally wrong,' Phoebe said, even though they both knew that she wasn't a vegetarian herself.

Maggie hadn't been a vegetarian either while Farmer Pete was alive. But she was now – she'd made the life choice on ethical grounds a couple of years after he'd died. Phoebe knew that some people might have called her a hypocrite – having been a dairy farmer for most of her life, but Maggie wasn't a hypocrite. She'd simply found that she was less and less able to stomach what she called the exploitation of animals as she'd grown older. Setting up Puddleduck Shelter had been part of her attempt to redress the balance. And she'd worked tirelessly at it ever since.

* * *

Sam's Christmas Eve had been far less eventful than Phoebe's. He'd waved goodbye to his parents with a promise to be back the following day for the big Christmas meal. As usual, they would have turkey with all the trimmings in the evening.

He was in bed by ten. Sam was a lark, not a night owl, which was just as well, as he was usually up by five thirty. Bizarrely, though, he couldn't sleep tonight. He doubted whether it was the excitement of Christmas, but there were all sorts of things whirling around his mind. The altercation with Rufus Holt, which had flicked back into his mind after he'd seen him again today. The fact that Phoebe was back without Hugh. He hoped she was all right. The fact that Ma had been looking a lot more tired than usual when he'd seen her tonight. Not that he was entirely surprised about that. At least she could have a few days off now. The shop was closed through to the New Year.

In the end, he got up and padded over to the bedroom window, his feet almost soundless on the stripped-back boards and big rug, and drew back the curtain and looked out at the night sky. The clouds had cleared and it was colder than it had been for a few days. Above the trees in his garden, he could see a bright silver moon and a sprinkling of stars. There was the sound of distant traffic and, two gardens along, a neighbour's Christmas lights shone out a Happy Christmas greeting.

This time last year, Sam had been with Judy. He'd still thought they had a future. They'd been looking forward to going for a meal with his parents the following day. His parents had loved Judy. And this time last year, he'd only met her parents the once – he'd still had high hopes that she was the one.

He wondered what she was doing now. Whether she was seeing anybody. He could have found out via social media, but Sam wasn't a fan of social media – the intrusive, trivial nature of it, where a careless, throwaway line could hurt without the writer of it ever even knowing, much less caring.

He had a sudden urge to send Judy a text to wish her happy Christmas. He glanced at the LED display of the radio alarm he still used and saw it was just before one. He couldn't send her a text so late. She would think he was drunk – or worse, lying in bed alone, thinking about her. Neither option was very palatable.

With a small sigh, he headed back to bed. He should try to get some sleep. His alarm was set for just after six. A lie-in but not much of one. Ninja didn't know what day of the year it was. Sam planned to be at the stables just after seven, as always. Christmas Day was forecast to be bright and clear. He was hoping to head off for a forest ride before he got togged up and went over to Ma and Pa's for the Queen's Speech and the big evening meal. He put Judy out of his mind.

* * *

On Christmas Day morning, Phoebe drove over to Puddleduck Farm to check up on her patient and was relieved to find Jemima looking bright-eyed and a lot less subdued than she had been the previous day. Her beak was a healthy yellow and her eyes were bright. That was a good start.

Maggie had put the bird in a penned-off covered area within the hay barn, with a baby bath of water also in the pen for her to splash around in. Ducks needed to be near water that was deep enough for them to at least get their heads into, which Jemima had been doing when Phoebe arrived.

The outbuilding was used mainly for storing hay and its sweet scent filled the air. Phoebe finished her examination and gave Maggie the 'thumbs up'. 'She's doing great,' she told her. 'No signs of infection. Keep your fingers crossed.'

Maggie was looking a lot happier too, Phoebe thought, as they both sat on hay bales in the barn and chatted. Maggie was wearing some mud-spattered trousers, boots and a thick coat and Phoebe was dressed in the jeans, fleece and the Barbour coat she'd left home in. Her running-away outfit, she thought a little ruefully.

'Have you thought any more about what you're going to do?' Maggie asked, tuning in to her thoughts. 'Have you heard from the man?'

'No and no,' Phoebe replied, noting Maggie had dispensed with his name now, and sipping coffee from a flask they had brought out with them. 'But I am wishing I'd brought more clothes. I literally have these jeans and some slightly smarter ones, which I'm going to have to wear for Christmas lunch. I didn't think that through, did I? I'll be the scruff at dinner.'

'I wouldn't worry about that. I can definitely out-scruff you,' Maggie said, with an ironic lift of her eyebrows. 'I could wear this if you like. Better still, I can come in my old milking outfit. It's a boiler suit with unmentionable stains all over it and I have some ancient boots with the toe coming away from the sole that go with it nicely. I could stick a bit of hay in my hair as a finishing touch.' She demonstrated how the hay might look, twirling it this way and that, and they both giggled.

'Why do you keep boots that are falling to bits?' Phoebe asked, glancing at the ones she had on, which also looked pretty worn out.

'It's the comfort factor. They fit my bunions perfectly. You'll understand when you're as old as me.'

'Something else to look forward to,' Phoebe said, lifting her eyebrows. She glanced back at Jemima. 'On a more serious note, one thing I know for absolutely certain is that I can't give up being a vet. I love it.' Giving up her job had been playing on her mind ever since she had treated Jemima.

'What about giving up being a vet in London?' Maggie asked.

'Could you do that? Would you consider moving back here and looking for a position?'

Phoebe's mind flicked back to City Vets, the big reception, Jen and Laura, the two cheerful receptionists, the upmarket treatment rooms, the clients. You got to know your clients well when you worked in practice. And you got to really care about them too – or, more specifically, you got to really care about their animals.

Most of her Greenwich Park patients were dogs and cats. There was the occasional house bunny and hamster and one or two birds. She knew she would miss them – especially the odd one, like Bella, the three-legged Jack Russell, who she'd seen often because the little dog was always getting into trouble. She'd lost her back leg after a disagreement with a car – that had been before Phoebe's time – but having only three legs hadn't slowed her down one bit. Phoebe had stitched her up twice after she'd got into altercations with other – much bigger dogs. She'd also sorted out an injured front paw, all within the space of a couple of years. Bella was feisty and fearless and surprisingly waggy. A real character. Phoebe knew she would definitely miss Bella. She would miss most of the patients she'd got to know since she'd worked there and she knew she would miss several of their owners.

She also knew she couldn't go back. Not to City Vets, with Hugh and Melissa parading around like lovesick peacocks. And was there really any point in moving back to London when the only reason she'd been there in the first place was because of Hugh? Not to mention his parents' flat, and the job that had come up so handily.

City Vets was a short hop on the overground train from where they had lived. The area was beautiful. Blackheath had a village vibe. There was a greengrocer, a butcher and several nice restaurants. Even the charity shops were fancy. But she could never have afforded to live in Blackheath independently.

She gave a deep sigh, forgetting fleetingly that she wasn't alone, until Maggie cleared her throat.

'Penny for them.'

'I was just thinking that I can't afford to live in London on my own anyway. But, then again, I'm not sure if I'd have settled there in the first place if it wasn't for Hugh.' She felt a sudden spike of anger, not just at Hugh for so effectively tipping her life upside down, but at herself for having put all her eggs in one basket in the first place. 'Mind you, I'm not sure I can afford to live in the New Forest either.' She glanced at Maggie. 'House prices are just as astronomical round here. I'm guessing the rents are still sky-high too.'

'You don't have to go dashing off to find your own place. You can stay with your parents. Or, if that feels like too much of a backward step, what about your friend, Tori? Has she got a spare room?'

Phoebe noticed Maggie hadn't mentioned that she could stay in one of her own spare rooms, but she let this pass without comment. Maybe Maggie was assuming she wouldn't want to stay in a draughty, damp farmhouse that was in serious need of modernisation and had a haphazard mobile signal, not to mention being off the beaten track.

'I've hardly spoken to Tori lately,' she admitted, feeling guilty, because they'd been close for most of their lives. They'd sat next to each other on the first day of primary school and had pretty much been best friends ever since.

She had sent Tori a Christmas card, though, and a small gift. That was something they'd never stopped doing, despite the fact they had lived a hundred miles apart and rarely saw each other.

She hadn't received one in return, but that was probably because Tori was late with posting things. She was incredibly busy and always working to a deadline. She was the owner and editor of *New Forest Views*, the local free magazine. Besides, Tori would have sent it to London, not to her parents.

Phoebe hadn't told Tori about Hugh yet. Partly because she

knew she had never been that enamoured with him. Phoebe was in no rush to hear her friend trying to sound sympathetic about the split when in reality she'd probably think it was for the best.

'I'll go and see her tomorrow,' she said. 'Assuming she's here and hasn't gone away anywhere for Christmas.'

Maggie nodded approvingly. 'What I'm trying to say, my darling, is that you don't have to make any decisions in a hurry, do you? You have options. You can think about things, regroup.'

'Yes, I know. I can take some time out and have a proper think.' Phoebe felt brighter at the thought of options. Suddenly the future didn't look quite as bleak.

A quiet quack interrupted their conversation and Maggie glanced at Jemima, who was standing at the wire boundary of her pen, looking at them, hopefully.

'She's bored, bless her.' Maggie unzipped the bumbag at her waist and grabbed a handful of something orange. 'Grated carrot,' she explained. 'She loves it.' She got up, a little stiffly, making Phoebe wonder if her arthritis was playing up, and went towards the expectant Jemima, who wagged her tail in appreciation of the carrot. 'How long will she have to be cooped up for?' Maggie asked, glancing back at Phoebe.

'It really depends on how quickly she heals. Are the others safe? From whatever it was that bit her?'

'I think so. I found a gap in the fence. I've sorted it. Usually, foxes don't come that close – there are too many dog smells, but you get the occasional opportunist, and Jemima tends to roam further than the others. She likes to come in the kitchen.'

'What with dogs, donkeys and ducks in there, I'm surprised there's any room for humans.'

'I didn't say I let her come in the kitchen any time she likes,' Maggie replied in her haughtiest tone. 'I'm not completely oblivious to hygiene rules and regulations, young lady.'

'I'm glad to hear it.' Phoebe shot her a grin. 'I'm not judging you. What goes on in Puddleduck Farm kitchen is your business, not mine.'

Maggie softened then and dropped her defensive look. 'I know. You're not your mother's daughter, are you? She seems to think I share my kitchen table with a menagerie.'

'Whereas the reality is that you might just have the odd dog taking up half the floor.' Phoebe thought about Tiny and Buster.

'And the occasional determined cat.' Maggie snorted with laughter. 'For a farmer's daughter, your mother is way too fussy.'

'It's because of Dad's allergies,' Phoebe said loyally. 'She has to be careful.'

'She's been like it since she was small,' Maggie countered. 'I can't think how she gets on, spending her days with snotty-nosed kids.' She broke off. 'Hark at me. Your mother's got a heart of gold and endless patience. We both know that. Right then. I suppose we'd better get ready for this Christmas meal malarkey. Shall I go and find my milking overalls?'

'I dare you,' Phoebe challenged.

They left the barn together and Phoebe felt warmth stealing through her. There was no doubt that she was on the same wavelength as her grandmother. That was part of it, but Maggie had a gift that Phoebe doubted she was even aware of. She had the ability to lift you when you were feeling down. It was more apparent when she took charge of an injured creature. But she could do it with humans too. She had the ability to turn tears into laughter quicker than anyone Phoebe had ever known. No matter how down Phoebe felt, after twenty minutes in her grandmother's company she would be laughing again. For all of her bluster and stroppiness, Maggie had an abundance of compassion too, mixed in with a great sense of humour. What a priceless gift that was.

10

Phoebe was quite relieved when Maggie didn't carry out her threat of wearing her old milking overalls to her mother's posh Christmas Day lunch.

The long dining-room table in the conservatory was rarely used. It was mostly a handy dumping ground for her dad's briefcase and an increasing pile of free magazines that no one ever had time to read, but at Christmas it came into its own. It had been laid with sparkling silver cutlery, the best lead crystal glasses were out, a gorgeous red and gold floral display of winter flowers was the centrepiece and there were alternating red and green crackers on every plate.

Red candles in two candelabras at either end of the table flickered softly over the remains of a meal that had been both ginormous and fabulous and everyone was now sitting around the table with that gorged, slightly dazed look that people had after a big meal. Her mother was also looking relieved that she could finally relax now nothing had been burnt or forgotten, and her father was looking content and full of bonhomie.

Phoebe had felt slightly guilty that she hadn't helped with many of the preparations, despite the fact that her mother had shooed her out earlier in the day with the words, 'Go and sort out your grandmother and that duck of hers. Or she won't come to dinner. Alexa has offered to help out here.'

'I'll go wash the pots,' Phoebe said now, deciding to make up for earlier. She stood up decisively.

'You don't need to do that,' Louella said. 'Have some coffee first. And I have some lovely cheese and port if anyone has a gap...?'

There was a collective groan from around the table.

Even Frazier looked defeated and her brother had an appetite the size of a horse's. 'Can we save it for Boxing Day lunch?' he begged.

'But I've got a whole ham for Boxing Day,' Louella said, then relented. 'Don't worry, I'm kidding about the cheese. Why don't we retire to the snug? Leave the washing-up, love, honestly.'

Phoebe hesitated, still on her feet.

'Before we leave the table,' Frazier began, with an unusual hint of seriousness in his voice, 'Alexa and I have got some news.'

From the other room came the disembodied voice of the ever-helpful robotic Alexa. '*The current news is that visitors to shops are down twenty per cent this December and the Queen sends good wishes to the nation and hopes this will be a better year.*'

'Oh, I'm sorry, I switched her back on for the movie listings?' Louella said. 'Please ignore her.'

Phoebe noticed her brother looked unusually thoughtful. Hopefully, the news wasn't something bad – no, surely, he wouldn't have saved that for Christmas Day.

Both of their parents were looking at Frazier expectantly and he cleared his throat, a little shyly, 'We've been desperate to tell you, but we wanted to wait until we were all in one place.' He glanced at his wife with a look of such tenderness that Phoebe knew in the instant before he told them, just what the news was. 'We're expecting a baby. We were going to wait until New Year to tell you, but we can't. We're too excited, aren't we, love.'

Alexa's face was flushed. 'I hope we're not tempting fate,' she said. 'But, no, we couldn't wait and this seemed the perfect time of year to tell you all.' She glanced at Phoebe, 'Although I was a bit worried when you told us you'd split up with Hugh. It felt wrong to be feeling so happy when you were sad.'

So that explained the slightly embarrassed look she'd seen her brother and Alexa exchange when she'd told them her news.

Phoebe blinked, feeling incredibly touched by her thoughtfulness. That was so typical of her sister-in-law. 'Oh, please don't be worried on my account. A baby is wonderfully exciting news. I'm going to be an aunt! Wow!'

'And I'm going to be a grandmother.' Louella's voice was full of wonder. 'Oh my goodness. That's the best news ever. Congratulations, you two.' She jumped up and raced around to hug them both. 'Oh, Alexa, is that why you brought that low-alcohol wine?'

'*Low-alcohol wine must be 1.2 per cent alcohol by volume and its ABV should be indicated on the label.*'

'You've not been drinking much either, have you, love?' Louella looked at Frazier. 'Is that because you're supporting Alexa? Have you made a pledge?'

'*A pledge is a solemn promise never to reveal a secret.*'

'Can someone please go and turn that blasted thing off,' their father, James, said in exasperation, 'before I throw the flaming thing in the bin.' He leaned across the table and called through to the other room, 'Alexa, can you shut the hell up.'

'*I don't know that one*,' Alexa countered.

Phoebe escaped into the kitchen to do as he suggested. It was wonderful news about the new baby. She couldn't have been more thrilled for her brother and sister-in-law. At thirty-two, Frazier was just two years younger than her, but he'd always seemed about ten years older in maturity. He'd followed Dad into the family solicitor firm and was doing great and he'd always said he wanted his family young too. She wondered how long they'd been trying.

It had been enormously sweet of them to be so concerned about her and Hugh too, she thought, switching off Alexa and then putting her in a drawer for good measure. She hooked out her mobile phone.

A couple of hours earlier, Hugh had sent her a message. It had been just two words: Happy Christmas. Was he serious? After everything that had happened, did he really think that was all there was to say? Did he expect her to respond with a reciprocal greeting? She had felt herself beginning to get angry again just thinking about it.

She hadn't replied and she hadn't told anyone in her family either. She didn't want to bring up the subject of Hugh when everyone was so happy. She didn't want to dampen the festive mood. The one thing she had made a decision about was that she needed to go up to the flat and collect her things, sooner, rather than later.

She would do it in the break between Christmas and New Year. Get it over with and work out how she was going to move on. Because she knew for sure that any last vestige of hope of Hugh getting in touch to say he'd made a huge mistake and please would she come home had been smashed. Those two words that would have seemed so innocuous in almost any other circumstances had told her that this was final. Hugh had moved on, without, it would seem, the slightest trace of regret.

The door opened and she glanced up to see Maggie standing there, her face solemn. 'I don't know what you're looking so glum about,' the old lady said. 'I've just found out I'm going to be a great-grandmother. Good grief, I thought being a granny was bad enough.' She screwed up her face as if it pained her to say the word granny.

'I'm sure we can continue the tradition of calling you Maggie,' Phoebe said with a little smile because she could see the sparkle in the old lady's eyes. She might be protesting loudly, but it was clear she was much more enamoured with the idea of having a new baby in the family than she was letting on.

* * *

The biggest surprise in Sam's Christmas had been when his mother had served up sprouts with chestnuts and pancetta instead of the usual plain, rather soggy ones that accompanied their turkey.

'It's a Nigella recipe,' she told him and his father. 'Do you approve?'

'Very nice, love,' his father had said, prodding a chestnut with his fork and looking slightly mystified.

Sam had suppressed a smile. His dad liked plain food. He was as traditional as they came and regularly told anyone who'd listen that he didn't see the point of fancy food. 'The fancier it is, the more it's been messed with. Waste of time.'

Not that Dad would have been thoughtless enough to say this to his wife when she'd been slaving over a hot stove for hours.

Sam had helped with the pots, then given his parents their present, which was a voucher for the carvery so they could have a Sunday lunch out, plus a bottle of Mum's favourite scent and a pair of socks for his father.

They'd given him a trio of ManCave shampoos and a bottle opener and a £50 note in his card.

'I never know what to give you,' his mother had told him, her eyes warm. 'I thought you could maybe get something horse-related.'

'Cheers, Mum.' He had kissed both his parents, they'd watched Christmas TV, then he'd played a couple of games of ten-card rummy, which was his father's favourite, and as the evening had drawn towards nine, he'd made going-home noises.

It had been a relief that another Christmas was over and done with.

Sometimes he wished he came from a bigger family. He had no siblings and his two aunts, on his mother's side, had moved to North Wales, where they shared a smallholding which was difficult to leave because of the animals, although they did occasionally get cover and make a flying visit. Even his grandparents had emigrated to Spain when they'd retired. They didn't fly back for Christmas any more – it was too expensive – so they usually came for their annual visit in the summer when they caught up on doctor's appointments and checked to make sure their bungalow, which was rented out, was still in one piece.

At other times, Sam was glad of the peace of being part of a small family. There were rarely any disagreements, which he knew was not the case with many people. Some of the post-Christmas stories he heard from both their customers coming into the Post Office and his friends at Brook Stables were enough to make your hair stand on end. Christmas, it seemed, was the prime time for depression divorces, and all manner of bust-ups. This was not the case in his family.

Sam had made it home and was tucked up peacefully in bed by ten, which suited him just fine.

* * *

It was now Boxing Day and as Sam trotted Ninja along a forest track, not far from Brook Stables, his thoughts turned towards Phoebe. He wondered how she was getting on. He hadn't heard anything from her since he'd dropped off the cards. Hopefully, that meant that she and Hugh had sorted things out.

Christmas might be a prime time for break-ups, but it must also be an incredibly sad time for break-ups when the fairy tale of everyone else's Christmas was being rammed down your throat every time you switched on the TV or radio. Unless of course you were watching a soap when tragedies and murders abounded during the festive season.

This was his fairy tale of Christmas, he thought, taking a lungful of clean air. The soundtrack of birdsong and the skittering of a squirrel along the branch of an overhead tree. The steady rhythm of Ninja's hooves on the damp ground and the rustle of the occasional breeze through leaves. The forest was both peaceful and fully alive. There was nowhere else like it. Sam felt more at home when he was riding along this network of paths that he knew better than his own house than he did anywhere else on earth.

The view of his horse's long bay neck outstretched in front of him, his own gloved hands on the leather reins, the feeling of being almost a part of another living creature, Sam loved it all. The beauty of his surroundings never got old. Even in December when the paths were pitted with puddles and littered with old leaves, the New Forest was beautiful.

It had got colder these last few days. There hadn't been ice on the water trough this morning and there was none yet on the puddles, but there had been a crispness in the grass, a slight silvering of leaves. And, in places on the forest floor where the sun hadn't yet reached, a sparkling of frost still glittered.

It was now just after ten thirty. Sam was just considering turning for home – they'd been out an hour – when he heard the sound of a distant horn and then the faint but discernible noise of baying hounds. The Boxing Day Hunt.

Ninja heard it too. The horse stiffened. His bay ears pricked and he was suddenly on high alert.

Accustomed to his horse's rhythm and pace, Sam gathered the reins a little as Ninja began to dance on the spot. It was odd how horses knew and responded to the mournful sound of the horn. As far as Sam knew, Ninja had never hunted to hounds. He'd been bred by a woman who disapproved of hunting and Sam didn't hunt himself, but Ninja knew there was something afoot. As if by some telepathy, he picked up on the excitement of the chase, the primal call of the wild.

There was a dog at the stables that belonged to one of the livery owners that did the same thing. Little Ella, who'd once been a Greek stray and who looked like a mix of Staffie and collie with a sprinkling of spots on her black and white nose, always pricked up her ears when she heard the hounds. Then, she would scent the air, throw back her head and howl along with them. Quivering and trembling yet sitting stock-still in the yard. It was hard to tell whether she was excited or scared, but she was definitely answering some ancient call to hunt with the pack and Sam knew she'd have tried to run off to join them if her owner hadn't tied her up, wary of the danger.

Ninja was acting the same way now. His nostrils flared as he snatched at the reins and danced. He was fired up enough when they were some distance away, he'd be a nightmare to control if they came by in full flight.

Sam did some quick calculations. It was impossible to gauge exactly which way the hunt would go, but, with luck, he'd avoid them if he doubled back and took a shortcut, down a farm track he knew.

Ninja was happy to speed up. When Sam asked him to canter, he didn't need telling twice, and for the next ten minutes, Sam focused on putting as much distance as possible between them and the hunt. It was hard to work out whether it was further away or closer – for a while, he thought it was the latter and then he came out at the top of the farm track which overlooked fields and he saw the hunt in full flow across a field in the distance. They were travelling away from him. He couldn't see a fox, but the hounds were obviously onto some scent. The red and black jacketed riders were now streaming across a field which Sam knew was owned by a local farmer.

Sam reined in an overexcited Ninja, who was now foaming with sweat, despite the chill of the day, and paused to watch as the hunt got further away. Sam sent up a silent prayer for the fox if there was one. Maybe there wasn't. Only drag hunts were legally allowed in the forest, but there were loopholes and exclusions, which meant that plenty of hunts managed to chase foxes, while still appearing to stick to the letter of the law. Some people thought they were above the law.

An image of Rufus Holt flicked into his mind and he felt a needle of anger rising up in him. That entitled nob was probably out there in his red jacket, racing hell for leather across that field, heedless of the danger of potholes to his horse, ignoring the law. Although, Sam was more concerned about potholes and his horse's delicate legs than he was about the law.

Holy crap, what was wrong with him? If he wasn't careful, the man would become an obsession. 'Have a word with yourself, mate,' he said out loud and Ninja's long ears pricked at the sound of his voice.

Sam talked to him softly, feeling some of his horse's tension ebbing away as he responded to the reassurance of his rider, and feeling his own tension easing back too. By the time he finally set his horse in the direction of home, Sam had managed to put Rufus Holt and the hunt firmly back out of his head.

11

When Phoebe finally plucked up the courage to phone Tori on Boxing Day evening, her friend sounded delighted to hear from her.

'I'm really sorry things haven't worked out with Hugh, but I'm thrilled that you're back and it might be for good,' she said. 'When are you coming over for a catch-up?'

'When can I?' Phoebe asked, feeling bad that she'd thought Tori might be judgemental. She should have given her more credit, and she suddenly desperately wanted to see her.

'The sooner the better, as far as I'm concerned. But let me know because I'm not at home. I'm at Woodcutter's. Did I tell you I'm doing it up?'

Woodcutter's Cottage was the house that Tori's grandparents had left her eighteen months earlier. They'd gone on a world cruise for their retirement and before they'd gone, they'd bequeathed their three cottages, all dotted about in the New Forest, which they'd rented out until that point via Airbnb. They'd left two of them to Tori's parents and the smallest one, Woodcutter's, to Tori.

Phoebe did have a vague memory of her saying she was doing it up. 'What are you doing to it? I thought it was in quite good condition.'

'Come and see,' Tori said. 'But bring your oldest clothes and wrap up warm. I could do with a hand. I promise you, it's the perfect antidote to Christmas. That's if you were needing an antidote,' she added softly. 'I know I did. It can all get a bit much, can't it?'

'I might need to borrow some old clothes,' Phoebe said, wondering where the lump in her throat had suddenly sprung from. 'I stupidly didn't bring much with me. But if that's OK, I'll gladly help out with whatever you're doing.'

'You might live to regret that,' Tori said cheerfully. 'But it will be superb to see you.'

* * *

Phoebe drove over the day after Boxing Day, having spent the last of the festive family days playing charades with everyone, which pleased her father, and doing as much clearing up as she could so that her mother could talk babies with Frazier and Alexa.

She'd also made sure Jemima the duck was OK, which meant Maggie was happy, and she'd arranged with Hugh that she'd pick up as much of her stuff as she could fit in the car. That would be tomorrow. She'd made the arrangements by WhatsApp. He'd tried to phone her back, but she hadn't picked up his call, so in the end he'd just responded by text too.

The exchange had made her feel better – as though she still had an element of control over the situation. Small victories.

Woodcutter's Cottage was a tiny, two-up, two-down, seventeenth-century cob cottage with a thatched roof, tucked away up an unmade road beside a woodland near Linwood, which was a stone's throw from Puddleduck Farm. Its history was lost in the mists of time, but presumably it had once belonged to a woodcutter. It was the kind of place that Phoebe would have loved to live in if she'd ever had the money. So many of the cottages in the New Forest were second homes to rich outsiders or holiday lets, which had meant that the ones that were left were highly prized and even more expensive.

She parked in the second allocated parking space, beside Tori's Range Rover, and looked up at the whitewashed cottage with its green front door, four front-facing windows and untidy thatched fringe. It was like a child's picture. It even had a smoking chimney.

When Phoebe got out of the car, she could smell woodsmoke and freshness. It was cold today. Her breath puffed out into the chill morning air.

Tori had said she was in the back garden, so Phoebe walked through the side gate and round to the back of the house. She found her friend up on the raised decking with a paintbrush in one gloved hand and a big tub of wood stain beside her. The fence that surrounded the decking looked as though it was half done.

Phoebe called out a greeting as she approached. 'Wood staining in December. You must be crazy. Not to mention frozen.'

'I am crazy,' Tori called cheerfully. 'But you know that already. I am also frozen. You're right. But once your fingers and toes go numb, it's not so bad.' She was wearing a big coat over a boiler suit and a black fur-lined trapper hat that covered her auburn hair, although the odd reddish-brown tendril had escaped. She also had a blob of red wood stain on her nose – at least Phoebe presumed it was wood stain; it was the same colour as what was on the fence.

Phoebe climbed up onto the raised deck.

Tori put down the paintbrush and came the few steps to meet her and the two women hugged. 'It's so brilliant to see you,' Tori said. 'You look great by the way for a woman who's been through the mill.' Her eyes darkened. 'Hugh wasn't my favourite person, but I really am sorry that it didn't work out. I know you loved him.'

'Thanks. I'm OK. Or at least I'm getting there. You look great too.'

'I've put on weight,' Tori said, not sounding too worried about it. 'I've joined a dinner dating club. I'll tell you about that in a bit. Do you really want to freeze your socks off out here with me?'

'Of course I do. Did you say something about old clothes?'

* * *

A few minutes later, with Phoebe changed into the set of old clothes that Tori had brought for her, and clutching mugs of hot coffee, they were back out on the decking. While they'd made coffee, Tori had explained that she'd decided to let Woodcutter's Cottage out via a holiday cottage company.

'Grandma Alice had it on Airbnb, and I carried on with that for a while, but it's much too hands-on for my liking and I've already got a full-time job. So I decided to go with the holiday company. They do a managed package – they arrange the letting, the cleaning, the upkeep and everything. Well, they do once they've signed you up. You wouldn't believe how picky they are. Everything has to be totally together, inside and out. I've been dealing with this woman called Pippa – Pernickety Pippa, I call her. The things she wants doing, you wouldn't believe.'

'Hence the wood staining.'

'Exactly. The sooner I can get it photographed and on their books, the better. And as it's been dry lately – if not exactly warm – I'm taking full advantage.'

'We can chat while we paint,' Phoebe said, picking up a brush.

'That sounds perfect.'

For the next hour, they caught up on each other's lives. Phoebe told Tori all about the Hugh and Melissa situation and Tori was as outraged as Maggie had been and used a lot more expletives.

'You're well rid of him,' she said eventually. 'Seriously, Phoebe, it's much better to find out now than later. At least you didn't buy a house with him. You were planning to, weren't you? Does that mean you've got lots of money saved?'

'I've got enough to tide me over for about six months. As long as I don't rent anywhere too expensive.'

'You can have my spare room,' Tori said instantly. 'No rent required. It would be brilliant to spend some quality time with you.'

'Thank you.' Phoebe felt incredibly touched. 'Are you really sure?' She hadn't thought much about living arrangements beyond getting away from Hugh. She'd expected to be staying at her parents for a while.

'Of course I'm sure.' Tori narrowed her green eyes. 'One of the reasons I'm really busy at the moment, aside from work deadlines and Pernickety Pippa, is New Forest Diners.'

'That's the dinner dating club you mentioned?'

'It is. It's brilliant, Phoebe, honestly. It's a supper club event. They happen fortnightly at various places in the forest and there are a couple of seriously hot guys that go. You could come along and see. I don't mean now,' she added hastily, as Phoebe opened her mouth to protest. 'I mean when you're in the mood to go casual dating again. We could have a ball.' She paused. 'Although I have heard it said that the best way to heal a broken heart is to get straight back on the horse again.'

'That's a mixed metaphor if ever I heard one,' Phoebe replied. Dating anyone – casual or otherwise – was definitely not on her agenda. 'I think I'd be better off focusing on getting another job first. And picking up the rest of my stuff from London.'

'I can give you a hand with that too if you like?' Tori offered. 'Did you say you were going tomorrow?'

'Well, yes, but you've got all this to do.' She waved a hand to encompass the fence and decking. 'I thought you were in a hurry.'

'I'm getting twice as much done with you helping. Anyway, there's rain forecast tomorrow. I'll have to stop. We could take my Range Rover if you like. We could get more in that too.'

'OK, but I'm paying for the fuel and the low-emission zone.'

'You've got yourself a deal.'

* * *

Phoebe had to admit that she was glad of Tori's company the next day. Especially when they arrived at the flat and she saw that Hugh hadn't done as he said and gone out, he was in the kitchen doing something on his laptop.

He stood up awkwardly when they appeared and when Tori withdrew diplomatically back into the hall, Hugh put his hands in his pockets and came across to Phoebe.

'I'm very sorry about the way things have turned out,' he said. 'Are you OK?'

'I am OK,' Phoebe said quietly, meeting his eyes, which were hard to read. It felt so weird to be standing here facing the man who until a few days ago she'd have said she loved very much. She'd expected him to look different. To have grown horns or something. But he looked exactly the same as he always did. Smartly dressed, even in his leisure time.

He broke the gaze first. He stared at the floor and then at somewhere to the left of her face. So, he was feeling guilty. He couldn't even properly meet her eyes.

'Have you made up your mind not to come back to the practice?' he asked eventually.

'I think that's between myself and Melissa, don't you?'

'Yes, that's true, but we... she doesn't feel it's fair that you should be pushed out because...' He shifted uncomfortably from one foot to the other. 'I believe she's drawing up some sort of relocation package.'

'Relocation package. Really.' Phoebe shook her head in amazement at their audacity. 'Well, how very thoughtful of her.' She looked at his face. Hugh hated confrontations and his cheeks had gone a dull red. Anger or embarrassment – it was hard to tell. Perhaps it was a mixture of both. 'You can tell Melissa that I'll be in touch,' she said icily.

'I will. Um, there's some post for you by the bread bin.' His Adam's apple bobbed and he cleared his throat. But he didn't say anything else. He'd clearly exhausted his repertoire of ways to say sorry. She wondered if Melissa had asked him to be here to see her or whether he'd genuinely felt the need to face her directly.

To say that Hugh came from a family of stiff-upper-lipped Englishmen would have been akin to saying that the Pope was slightly religious. He'd once told her that as a child he had never heard his mother and father argue, which had sounded great, until he'd added that he'd never really seen them show any emotion towards each other at all. They didn't hold hands or hug or laugh uncontrollably. Showing emotion – any emotion – was frowned upon. It went far deeper than big boys don't cry. In Hugh's family, no one ever even parped in public. That was what bathrooms were for. If you were ill or upset about something, however big it was, you kept quiet about it and you didn't mix with others until you felt better.

He'd been sent away to boarding school at an early age with the instructions, 'Work hard. Make us proud. Achieve.' And Hugh had always tried very hard to do just that. He'd been incredibly academic, which had pleased his parents, both of whom had embraced his ambitions to be a vet, although he'd once told Phoebe that he thought his father would have preferred him to be a doctor. Both his parents were consultants and worked in private practice.

Phoebe had pieced most of this together from fragments that Hugh had let slip. Once, after an evening when they'd both been drinking, Hugh had told her that on his tenth birthday, his mother had cancelled his party an hour before it was due to take place because he'd made the mistake of telling her he had earache. He'd been confined to his room 'to rest' and was allowed no presents, and no 'over rich birthday food' until two days later.

Phoebe had listened in horror before she had said to him, 'How did you bear it, Hugh?'

And he had looked at her slightly askance and said, 'It was just how it was. It was normal.'

Phoebe had been sure, back in those idealistic, heady days when they'd first met, that she could make up for all the love Hugh had never had. She had thought she could fix him. But it was only now, as she faced him in the kitchen where they had shared a thousand little daily tasks that she realised that this had never been within her power.

Hugh hadn't been taught about love and warmth and compassion. Was it any wonder that he wasn't able to feel it? Why had she been surprised that he'd finished with her over the phone? Why had she even been surprised that he'd sent her a Happy Christmas text? He was so used to compartmentalising his world into little boxes, it probably hadn't even been that hard to do it with her. Remove girlfriend Phoebe. Replace with girlfriend Melissa. Even so, it felt weird to realise that she could never have really known him.

Phoebe was relieved when he went back to his laptop and got busy. He didn't interfere as Phoebe emptied the flat of everything she wanted. Not that there was all that much that was jointly owned, she thought, as she and Tori carried out boxes and bags to the Range Rover. The flat had been fully furnished when they'd moved in.

Along with the post that Hugh had mentioned, which was mostly Christmas cards, was a small brown parcel from Tori. Phoebe thanked her. 'Something to look forward to,' she murmured.

'Don't get too excited,' Tori said with a grin.

Less than forty-five minutes later, they both climbed back into the Range Rover for the final time. Hugh had barely looked up from his laptop when they'd left. That had stung.

'Do you need to say anything else to Hugh?' Tori asked her gently. 'Or are you all done?'

'I'm all done,' Phoebe said. 'As far as I'm concerned, I won't need to say anything to Hugh Lawson ever again. Although I might have a few words still to say to Cruella.' She told Tori about the 'relocation package' Hugh had mentioned.

'Unbelievable,' Tori said, shaking her head in disbelief as she started the engine.

'Yes,' Phoebe said, glancing at her knees. 'Thanks again for this. It's been much easier, having you here with me.'

'That's what friends are for,' Tori said softly, tucking a strand of auburn hair behind her ear as she pulled out to join the busy London traffic.

Phoebe didn't look back. She'd expected to feel sad, saying goodbye to the place where she'd lived and worked for the last six years. She'd thought that she had put down roots there. But all she felt, as they drove away, was a surprising lightness and a growing sense of freedom.

12

Phoebe moved into Tori's first-floor flat, which was in Bridgeford above an off-licence, which Tori told her was incredibly handy in the first week of January. She knew her parents were pleased, despite their protestations that 5 Old Oak Way was her home for as long as she wanted to stay. They were pleased because, as far as they could see, she had picked herself up, dusted herself down and was moving on – at least on the surface.

The first thing on the agenda was to try to find another job that wasn't too far out of the area. This was easier said than done. There weren't that many veterinary practices within a commutable distance. The New Forest wasn't like London. Not that Phoebe was in a huge hurry: finding the right position was much more important than finding just a job.

'I've got enough money to tide me over for a bit, like I said,' she told Tori one Saturday morning soon after she'd moved in. 'And, for your information, I will be paying rent.'

'Is that so?' Tori's eyes sparkled with merriment, and she put her hands on her hips in a mock-confrontational stance. 'I'm not sure if I approve of you spending your savings on rent when you don't need to. I'm happy for you to wait until you get the right job. I'm also happy for you to carry on paying me in kind – there's plenty more wood staining to do.'

Phoebe groaned. They'd done quite a bit of that over the limbo period between Christmas and New Year and in every other spare moment when Tori wasn't doing her day job. Neither of them had bothered staying up late to see in the actual New Year. Tori didn't do late nights, she was an early bird, and Phoebe had been happy to have an early night this year too. 'I dream about wood staining fences,' she said. 'Last night, I had a nightmare I'd painted myself into a corner on your decking and couldn't get out.'

'That sounds far too close to reality for my liking.' Tori shuddered.

'Anyway, I wouldn't be spending my savings on rent. I'd be spending my relocation package?' Phoebe had laughed at her friend's surprise. 'Or should we call it my guilt money?' She shook her head. 'I guess it doesn't matter what we call it. The point is that I've got it. A nice little severance package in return for my absolute discretion.'

'You're kidding me!' Tori's green eyes flashed with outrage. 'Is that what Cruella said?'

'Not in so many words. No. She didn't actually say, "Don't tell anyone I stole your boyfriend," but the inference was clear. She'd be grateful if I was "discreet when discussing the circumstances of our parting," and that she didn't need to give me any kind of package as it was me who'd chosen to leave but that she'd decided to do it as a "gesture of goodwill."'

Cruella had rung Phoebe to say all this and she'd had to bite her lip to avoid responding with a furious tirade. Tempting as it would have been to tell her to stick her offer, common sense had prevailed.

'So it's a gagging order. The cheeky mare. I think I might have thumped her if she'd tried that with me.'

'I don't think I've ever thumped anyone in my life,' Phoebe said, pausing to consider this. 'Although I've been tempted a couple of times. But, to be honest, I wasn't planning on telling anyone anything about the circumstances of our parting anyway. I mean, why would I want to do that? I just want to put the whole thing behind me.'

'I know,' Tori said with feeling. 'So when are you coming to one of my dinner parties?'

'Ask me in about six months.' Phoebe said brightly, but inside she was shuddering. She could think of nothing worse. The thought of dating anyone else was about as far off her radar as it could possibly be. It would be a long, long time before she trusted anyone again. Even as a dinner companion.

* * *

Frazier and Alexa were very pleased to hear Phoebe planned to stay in the New Forest. They asked her if she'd be their baby's godmother.

'I'd be honoured,' she told them. 'Godmother and aunt. Thank you. What a privilege.'

Sam was also pleased when she caught up with him in the Post Office one day. 'Let's catch up for a drink some time,' he said. 'If you need a friend, I am always available. And if you ever want a wing man, let me know.'

'I don't think I'll need a wing man for a while, but thanks, Sam,' she told him with affection. 'And, ditto, if you need a wing woman. I'm happy to oblige.'

But the person who was the most thrilled she was staying was Maggie.

'We'll get to talk more,' she said, when Phoebe turned up at

Puddleduck Farm to tell her what she'd decided to do, adding in a rare burst of sentimentalism. 'How lovely.'

'We could talk more on the phone,' Phoebe pointed out. 'If you ever deigned to pick it up.'

'Pah,' Maggie said. 'I don't like phones. Besides, I have far too much to do here to sit down and have cosy chats on phones. But don't you worry about me. If you're too busy with your own life to come over for the odd visit, then that's fine.'

Phoebe had put her hands up in laughing self-defence. 'Of course I'm not too busy to come and visit. I'm here now, aren't I? I was just saying that we could also talk on the phone sometimes – just as you could talk to Frazier and Alexa on the phone, and Mum and Dad. It would stop them worrying about you so much.'

'All right. Don't go on. I'll try.'

'You could try locking the front door too,' Phoebe added idly. 'It was open again today.'

'Was it? I must have forgotten to lock it.' She looked unrepentant and Phoebe didn't push her. Most of the locals knew that Puddleduck Farm was a rescue shelter and that several dogs would be wandering around loose at any one time. It would have taken a brave burglar to take on Tiny, even though he was a big softie and was unlikely to have given them more than a lick.

It was good to see more of her grandmother and Phoebe visited often, timing her visits deliberately so she could help with cleaning out kennels or feeding animals. Apart from Natasha, who had helped out at weekends ever since she was fifteen – she was now twenty – and the occasional person who'd adopted a dog or cat and wanted to help out occasionally, Maggie didn't seem to have any extra help.

Phoebe guessed she couldn't afford to pay anyone to come in, but it worried her that Maggie had so much work and expense. New Forest Neddies had grown from just a few donkeys to a much bigger outfit than she suspected Maggie had ever planned when she'd begun.

* * *

One day at the end of January, Phoebe was surprised to find a black SUV parked outside Puddleduck Farm with the words 'County Vets' on the side.

When she went inside, she discovered a grey-haired vet, who Maggie introduced as Duncan Petwell, sitting at the kitchen table. Surely that couldn't be his real name. But he certainly didn't contradict it when Maggie introduced them.

He turned out to be a nice guy who'd called by at Maggie's request to look at Neddie, who was off his food, which was unusual, as well as to drop off some arthritis medication for Buster.

'Maggie tells me you're on the hunt for a new position,' he said to Phoebe. 'A friend of mine is an equine vet in Marchwood, just this side of Southampton. He's looking for someone to join the team. I could put in a good word for you?'

'My experience is with a small animal practice,' Phoebe said cautiously. He was probably older than she had first thought. He had deep laughter lines around his eyes.

'Marchwood is a mixed practice, so don't worry about that.' He gave her his card. 'Do let me know if you'd like me to put in a word.'

'Thanks, I will.'

When he'd left, Phoebe turned to her grandmother. 'I could have sorted out Neddie for you. And Buster. You don't need to pay another vet.'

'I didn't want to take advantage,' Maggie said, blushing a little, which wasn't like her. 'You can't be doing me favours just because we're related. You need to earn a living.' She hesitated. 'It was different with Jemima. That was an emergency.' She shrugged.

'Besides, Duncan's partner used to look after the herd before this lot arrived. He gives me heavily discounted rates. He knows it's a "non-profit" organisation.' She mimed the inverted commas around non-profit in a voice loaded with irony.

Phoebe picked up the bill, which was still on the kitchen table. It wasn't that discounted. Duncan Petwell certainly wasn't just charging cost prices and he was also charging for his time. She frowned. 'It must cost a fortune looking after all of them. Do you get enough to cover it from fundraising?'

'Not really,' Maggie confessed. 'Not these days. It used to be better when I did the adoption packages, but I've let that slip a bit. Eddie was more hands-on with that kind of thing. He used to take the photos and print out the packs on the computer and suchlike.'

It was hard to imagine her grandmother's old farmhand being a whizz on the computer, although Phoebe supposed he wouldn't have needed to be that much of a whizz to print out a few pages of text and pictures. It was even harder to imagine Maggie doing anything on a computer, with her dislike of all things technology.

'So how do you fund it?' Phoebe asked softly.

'I've got bits and pieces put aside. I manage.' She lowered her eyes and Phoebe guessed what she hadn't directly said.

'You're funding this place with your savings?' Phoebe kept her voice as gentle as she could. 'That doesn't sound sustainable.'

'It'll see me out.'

Phoebe looked at her in alarm. She knew her grandmother wasn't young any more, but she was so active and fit. To Phoebe's eyes, she hadn't looked any different for years. She didn't even have much grey hair. 'Is there something you're not telling me?' she asked anxiously. 'You're not ill, are you?'

'Of course I'm not ill. But I'm not going to live for ever. And I probably won't be here when I'm eighty.'

Phoebe felt guilty suddenly. 'I could help you a lot more if I'm here.'

'I'm fine, love. Truly I am. All I'm saying is...' She leaned over and put a weather-beaten hand over Phoebe's, 'Well, I'm not going to be around for ever, so I don't need infinite money to run this place.'

The warmth of her grandmother's hand enclosed Phoebe's and she looked at the raised veins and short nails, and she wondered if Maggie ever wanted to be anywhere else. She'd always worked her socks off. Being a dairy farmer had been a very tough life and it hadn't got any easier when she'd retired. If things had worked out differently, Maggie and Farmer Pete would have been enjoying a peaceful, well-deserved retirement without the prospect of ever having to get up and face a dark and freezing winter dawn again. But running Puddleduck Farm as an animal rescue centre had put paid to all that and it seemed Maggie was working just as hard now as she ever had.

'OK, well, at least promise me you'll call me if you need any vet stuff doing – supplies, check-ups, minor injuries. Don't use Duncan Petwell so much.'

'All right then. If it will stop you going on.'

'And if I ask you a question, will you give me an honest answer?' Phoebe added softly.

'I'm always honest,' Maggie said, with a flash of ironic humour in her eyes because they both knew that wasn't true.

'If you could be anywhere in the world, doing anything you liked, money no object, what would you be doing?'

Maggie considered this for less than a second. 'I'd be right here talking to you,' she said. 'So stop your senseless worrying.'

It wasn't a very satisfactory answer, but Phoebe could see that it was all she was going to get for now.

13

Phoebe didn't tell her mother her concerns about Maggie funding Puddleduck Farm from her savings and having hardly any help. Louella had enough going on with the new term and her father was busy on some high-profile divorce case at work. But she did tell Sam about the conversation she'd had with her grandmother when they finally met one Friday evening for their long-overdue drink in the Brace of Pheasants, one of Godshill's best-kept secrets. The Brace was a lovely country pub that had a blazing log fire in an inglenook fireplace, did great home-cooked food – pies were its speciality – and served real ale.

* * *

Sam studied her thoughtfully across the aged wooden table on which he'd just put their drinks – half a real ale for him and a small white wine for her. 'How old is she now?'

'Seventy-two. But she never seems to age.'

'Yes, I know what you mean. But it must be really hard work keeping that place ticking over. Does she have any help?'

'Not much, from what I can gather. There are some volunteers who come in from the village. Some more than others. There's a girl, Natasha, who helps at weekends and on her days off. But Maggie does the cleaning and the feeding and the overseeing of all the animals, including rehoming the odd one from local adverts.'

'And the cards we put up in the Post Office,' Sam said. 'Wow. She must be tired out.'

'I know. I think there are more animals than there used to be and it's a huge commitment – she can't exactly take a day off or even leave the place for very long. I feel bad, Sam. I haven't been over to Maggie's enough. She's still paying a vet to come by and see to the animals. I could have been doing that. But she was too proud to ask. You know what she's like.'

Sam heard the worry in Phoebe's voice and hunted for the words to make her feel better.

'I know what she's like, but at least you're here now,' he said, 'which must be a huge comfort to her.'

'I'd like to help out more though. I guess I'll just need to keep turning up and doing whatever looks like it needs doing.' She sipped her wine.

'Maybe it's worth advertising for some volunteers,' Sam suggested, thinking on his feet. 'You'd be surprised how many people would love to help out at an animal sanctuary. Animal-mad teenagers, or retired folk with more time on their hands. I can put up a poster in the shop if you like? We've got a notice-board. Obviously we wouldn't charge, so she has nothing to lose. I'll ask some of our regular customers, too. And I can ask around at the stables.'

'Thank you. I'm sure she'd appreciate it.' Phoebe frowned. 'But maybe I won't mention it, just in case she objects. Honestly, Sam, she's ten times as stubborn as one of her donkeys. She's so damn feisty and independent.'

'It must run in the family,' he said, wanting to make her feel better and deciding to lighten the mood. He clicked his tongue. 'Genetics have a lot to answer for.'

He chuckled as Phoebe clocked he was talking about her and opened her mouth to protest.

'I'm paying you a compliment,' he added gently. 'Those can be very good qualities to have. They're probably why you became a successful city vet and I'm still working in my mother's Post Office.'

'Don't you dare put yourself down.' She looked even more outraged about that than she had about him accusing her of being stubborn. 'Besides, I'm not a successful city vet any more. I'm an out-of-work vet.'

'A temporarily out-of-work vet,' Sam corrected. He'd forgotten how much he enjoyed her company. And how pretty she was. Hell, where had that thought come from? The last thing Phoebe needed was a man making a move on her. He was here in a 'strictly friends' capacity.

The weird thing was that he'd never really seen her as girlfriend material. Even when they were kids, he'd thought she was out of his league. It had always been clear that Phoebe was going places. Sam had known she was academically brilliant, unlike him. He'd done OK at school, but he'd always been Mr Average, whereas Phoebe had excelled in all her chosen subjects. She was an A-star student who'd sailed effortlessly through her exams. She'd told him that this was because she worked hard and Sam had always congratulated her enthusiastically whilst knowing inside that it didn't matter how hard he worked, he would never shine in an academic background.

He hadn't been surprised when she'd ended up with high-flyer Hugh either. Sam had met him a few times when the pair of them had visited. The guy had been pleasant enough, but Sam had known they had little in common.

'Earth calling, Sam,' Phoebe said, waving a hand in front of his face, and Sam realised that she'd just asked him a question.

'Sorry, what was that?' He blinked a few times and came back to the present.

'I was wondering if you'd like another drink? It's my round.'

'OK, thanks. Just an orange juice. I'll go if you like.'

'Not necessary.' She snatched up their empty glasses before he could move. 'Feisty and independent, remember?'

She disappeared towards the bar, and Sam noticed that a couple of guys glanced appreciatively in her direction. He clearly wasn't the only one who thought her attractive, although she seemed oblivious to their stares. Her time in London had changed her a little bit, he observed. She had a poise about her that was new and her long wavy hair, which she was wearing loose about her shoulders tonight, looked different. A new cut maybe? Sam wasn't up on women's hairstyles, but she definitely looked different. Maybe it was the clothes she wore – although she was still dressed casually, the same as she always had. A crop top and faded denim jeans that showed off her pert behind.

He blinked as the image of 'beautiful woman' overlaid the image of 'old friend'. He shook his head to clear it. There was absolutely no reason Phoebe couldn't be both, of course. But it was slightly disconcerting that his view of her seemed to have shifted sideways without his permission.

She had just paid for the drinks and was coming back from the bar. Sam dropped his gaze in case she caught him staring.

She put their glasses on the table and sat down. 'I got an orange for me, too. Have you eaten? They're still doing food. The pie menu hasn't changed, has it?'

'I've had my tea, thanks. But what about you?'

'I've eaten too. You know me. I never miss a meal.'

At least she looked more relaxed than she had earlier. That was good.

There was a little pause as they both sipped their drinks and then they spoke at the same time. He indicated for her to go first.

'I was wondering if you were still seeing that lovely Judy. I thought you two were perfect for each other.'

'Sadly, her parents didn't agree,' he blurted before realising he should probably have edited that, but it was too late now, so he carried on with the unmodified version. 'We never really hit it off is what I'm saying – me and her parents. They made it crystal clear from the off that I wasn't son-in-law material.'

'Oh, Sam. That's horrid.' Her hazel eyes held his. 'How did Judy feel?'

'I never told her that her parents weren't keen on me. I didn't want her having to choose between us.' He took another slug of orange juice. 'We were drifting apart anyway.'

She nodded and he saw a flash of understanding in her eyes and compassion. But no sympathy. For which he was grateful. He'd have hated her to feel sorry for him.

'Your turn,' she said lightly. 'What did you want to ask me?'

'A similar question. I was going to ask what had happened with Hugh? If you don't mind talking about it, I mean? I thought you two were set for the duration.'

She told him about what she'd seen at the Christmas party and all that had happened since, and he listened quietly. She faltered in places, but he was relieved to see that while Hugh had obviously hurt her badly, she wasn't still crushed by his betrayal.

'The man's a muppet,' he said when she'd finished her story. 'You can do a lot better.'

'I know,' Phoebe said with determination in her voice. 'But that day is far in the future. I have a lot more important things to sort out first. Like me getting a job. I've just applied for a position at the practice in Bridgeford. That would be very handy. I could walk to work.'

'You could.' Sam felt warmed. 'You're planning to stick around then?'

'I am.' She sipped her drink. 'Partly because of Maggie. But also because since I've been back, I've realised how much I love it here. Don't get me wrong, I enjoyed London too. The sheer buzz of the place was unbelievable. I loved the diversity of it all. The theatres, the brilliant food. But, truthfully, my heart's here with my family, friends and the forest.'

Her eyes misted a little and he wondered if she was thinking about Hugh.

'I just need to work out how I can help Maggie more without treading too much on her prideful toes. So it would be great if you could put up a poster or cards or whatever you think would be most effective in the shop.'

'I think both would be good.'

'I'll knock up a poster then. Thanks, Sam.'

'My pleasure. I'll keep my fingers crossed that you get the job. Also, Phoebe, if ever you need any help with anything at Puddle-duck Farm – give me a shout. I'm sure I can spare a few hours.'

'Thank you,' she said, giving him a sweet smile.

14

February began with Phoebe getting an interview at the practice in Bridgeford, which she had high hopes for because it was so close to home, and she had all the right experience. She was really disappointed, not to mention a bit shocked, when she got a polite no, just two days later.

'Did they give you a reason?' Tori asked, screwing up her face in consternation.

'Nope. Just a standard line.' Phoebe read from the email on her phone. 'On this occasion, your application has not been successful.' She sighed. 'I guess my face didn't fit. They certainly made up their minds very quickly.'

'Sometimes that happens because they have someone in mind already,' Tori mused. 'But the law means they have to advertise the position externally, even though it's already been filled. Maybe it was that. Do you have any others lined up?'

It was a Friday evening and they were having a late supper in the open-plan kitchen-diner of Tori's flat, eating squares of Welsh rarebit which Phoebe had made. They took it in turns to make supper, which usually happened about seven thirty – Tori rarely finished working on the magazine before then.

She hired office space in Bridgeford, which was a ten-minute drive from home. She shared the space with an advertising company, which meant it was cheap – one of them also sold advertising for the magazine – and also she liked the buzz of an office.

Today she'd worked late because they were coming up to deadline. It was now just gone nine, hence Phoebe doing Welsh rarebit, which was quick, as well as her current favourite thing to eat, especially when it was spread with a thick layer of chutney which she'd bought from the local farm shop.

Phoebe had made light of the rejection email which had come that morning, but the truth was that it had knocked her confidence big time. She had spent ages on the application and had been thrilled to be invited for interview. She hadn't told Tori, but it was the first time she'd ever applied for a job. She'd got her first job at Camberley through a contact of her grandparents. And thanks to Hugh's father's connections, she hadn't had to do a formal application to work at City Vets either. Neither had Hugh. They'd both gone along for an informal chat and had been signing their contracts a week later. It had all been so easy.

'Didn't you say that Maggie's vet had mentioned a position and was going to put in a good word for you?' Tori asked, looking at the amount of chutney that Phoebe had just piled on her Welsh rarebit and grimacing. 'Can you actually taste the cheese underneath that lot?'

'Yes thanks. It's yummy, and yes he did, and yes I have applied for that too. But I haven't heard anything back yet.'

'I'm sure you will soon. I'd think most surgeries would be thrilled to have a vet of your calibre.'

'Thanks for the vote of confidence. But you don't know anything about my calibre.'

'Oh yes I do.' Tori helped herself to another slice of Welsh rarebit. 'This is delicious by the way. A – you've always been uber passionate about animals. And B – you're one smart cookie. Only the cream of the crop get into the London Vet School. You're the only person I've ever met who got straight As in every subject.'

Phoebe felt herself go pink – she'd never learned to take compliments. 'It takes one to know one,' she said, deflecting the attention from herself and indicating the framed graduation photo of Tori which was on the dining room wall. Tori had graduated with a First in Media Studies and had worked briefly as an intern at a publishing house in London before being offered a job there and then finally setting up on her own two years ago.

'There's nothing like a bit of mutual backslapping,' Tori said, 'but thank you. I appreciate it.'

Tori's phone, which was on silent, buzzed with a call and vibrated across the table between them.

Tori glanced at it. 'That's Laura, my assistant editor. She was finishing something off for me. I'd better get it. Just in case.'

She snatched up the phone and Phoebe heard her say, 'Yes, that's right. She is,' as Tori glanced in her direction. 'I don't know. I could ask her if you like? Can you give me some more info?'

She listened to the answer, which took some time, then pressed a button on her phone and gave Phoebe a quizzical look.

'Feel free to say no – I've put her on mute – but Laura has a vet emergency and she wondered if you could help. It's, um, a bit of an unusual pet.'

'Go on,' Phoebe said, curiously.

'It's a crayfish that belongs to her little girl. Apparently, Violet has a pair. Reggie and Ronnie Cray.' She gave a little smile. 'You couldn't make it up. But the thing is, Violet is very attached to these crayfish. Violet's on the autism spectrum so she's pretty sensitive and Laura has been dreading the day when something happened to one of them – and now it has.'

'What's happened?' Phoebe asked, feeling her heart dip. This didn't sound like a simple matter and what she knew about crayfish could be written on the back of an emery board in big letters.

'Laura's not sure, but she thinks one of them is dying. She says it was OK earlier, but now it's lying on the bottom of the tank. Unfortunately, Violet just came down because she was having a nightmare and she spotted it – and now she's inconsolable.'

'I see.' Phoebe's heart dipped a little more.

'Laura's tried phoning her own surgery, but it's out-of-hours emergencies only and the vet's out on call helping some show poodle that's having a litter of pups. Laura thinks it might be too late if she leaves it until he can get to them.'

'Are you saying she wants me to go over now?'

'It does kind of sound like it – she lives about ten minutes away.' Tori frowned. 'It's a big ask, I know. Shall I say no.'

Phoebe shook her head. 'I'm pretty sure I can't do anything. Officially, I probably shouldn't be practising anyway, seeing as I'm between jobs, but I'm happy to take a look. Tell her yes.'

'Are you really sure?'

'Yes, it's fine. I suppose at the very least I can explain to Violet that crayfish don't live very long and take it from there.'

'Yes, that would be brilliant. It might sound better coming from a vet than her mother. I'll drive you,' Tori said.

'Thanks. That's perfect.' And it meant she could google crayfish on the way.

* * *

In the ten minutes it took to get to Laura's house, a semi in Bridgeford not far from the practice where Phoebe had just been turned down for the job, Phoebe discovered two facts about crayfish. They tended to live between two and three years when kept in captivity and they could also be prone to infections.

'Water quality is really important, but I expect she's aware of that,' she told Tori as they walked up to Laura's front door, which opened before they reached it. Laura must have been watching out for them.

'Thanks so much for coming over.' Laura ushered them inside and along a narrow hallway. 'The tank's through here.'

Not that they needed to be directed, Phoebe thought, as she could hear a sobbing child before they got into the room itself.

'Violet, darling, the vet's here. Can you stop crying for a minute while she looks at dear Reggie.'

No pressure then, Phoebe thought, giving the sobbing Violet what she hoped was a reassuring look.

The tank was big, she was pleased to see, and she couldn't see any fish. So presumably the two crayfish had it to themselves.

'The first thing to ask you,' she said to Laura, who was looking incredibly pleased to see her and also worryingly hopeful, 'is have you made any changes to the tank at all? Have you added any items? Weed or a new food or anything like that? I see they have a nice shipwreck to play in.'

'It's Reggie's favourite place,' Violet interrupted her through several loud sniffs. 'He's always in there.'

'I don't think we've done anything different than usual.' Laura was shaking her head. 'Temperature's the same. The pH is the same. I just checked. I know they don't live all that long in captivity, but these two are quite young. Or at least that's what the man at the aquatic shop said when we got them.'

Phoebe nodded and took a step forward. 'OK, well, let's have a little look-see, shall we?'

Her heart was thudding madly as she peered into the well-lit tank.

'Do you have a net at all?'

Laura handed her a green gauze one and Phoebe carefully shifted the tank lid to gain access.

She could see immediately that the crayfish was on the gravel at the back of the shipwreck. Not all of him was visible. It was a shame that Violet had come down and spotted him. If Laura had spotted him first, she could probably have replaced him before her daughter had realised he'd died. Phoebe knew that wasn't the perfect answer. But that would have saved Violet having to be heartbroken quite so young. She couldn't have been more than six, bless her.

She had a brief vivid flashback to a time when her own mother had replaced one of a pair of goldfish that she and Frazier had owned. Louella had sworn blind to the eagle-eyed Phoebe that it had simply changed colour. Years later, she'd finally confessed that Goldie had in fact been Goldie the Fifth before she'd failed to get a perfect replacement.

As Phoebe reached into the tank to capture the very still and clearly deceased crayfish, the room around her stilled and all she could hear was Violet's ragged breathing and the humming of the aquarium's air pump. She was just about to tell the little girl that she was very sorry but dear Reggie had unfortunately passed on when something started niggling at the back of her mind.

A line from a long-ago textbook flicked through her head – *crayfish are vulnerable when they are shedding their exoskeleton and will take shelter.*

Phoebe's heart skipped a beat as she suddenly realised what had happened. Reggie wasn't dead. He had simply shed his outer shell and was hiding somewhere while his new one hardened up. That's what crayfish did. That's what all crustaceans did.

To test her theory, she very gently moved the edge of the ship-wreck and saw immediately that there were three long waving claws in evidence beneath it. Two that belonged to Ronnie and the other, she assumed, to the shyer, currently vulnerable, Reggie.

Ronnie came out into view, but Reggie slid back a centimetre.

Phoebe beckoned Violet over to the tank and said in hushed tones, 'Your Reggie is absolutely fine. You know when you get too big for your coat and your mummy buys you a new one?'

Violet stuck her thumb in her mouth.

'Well, that's what your Reggie has done. This bit that you thought was Reggie–' she indicated the discarded shell that was the perfect replica of a crayfish '–isn't him at all. It's his old shell. It got too tight for him, so he decided to take it off and now he's got a nice new one growing. Can you see him hiding in his favourite place?'

Violet's eyes had gone very round as she removed her thumb and leaned close to the glass. 'So that's not really Reggie?'

'No. Reggie's here. Look. You can see his claw.'

Violet stared and the look of pure joy that spread across her face when she realised Phoebe was telling the truth made every bit of their late-night mercy dash across town worthwhile.

Laura and Tori had leaned in for a closer look too. Now Laura was smiling and Tori was shaking her head in disbelief. The room felt a degree warmer than it had been a few moments before.

'Wow. Why didn't I think of that?' Laura said as they all straight-ened again. 'I knew they shed their shells, but I didn't realise they were quite such a complete replica. It's amazing. How much do I owe you?' She looked around for her bag and then spotted it on a chair. 'I really can't thank you enough.'

'Please don't,' Phoebe said. 'I really haven't done anything.'

'Oh, you have. You've made my little girl very happy and for that I'm eternally grateful. I must give you something.'

'No, really. That wouldn't feel right. I'm just so glad I was able to help.'

Laura was still trying to press money on her when Phoebe and Tori finally got away a few minutes later.

In the dark car as they clipped up their seat belts, Tori nudged Phoebe's arm. 'See. I was right about calibre, wasn't I? You're a genius. Not only can you heal sick animals – you can bring them back from the dead.'

Phoebe snorted. 'That is not what happened.'

'I know, but it would make a brilliant headline, wouldn't it? "Vet Brings Little Girl's Crayfish Back From Dead!"'

'Don't you dare!'

'I wouldn't dream of it. Don't worry.'

They both laughed. Phoebe knew hers was part relief that the evening had finished on a high. Thank goodness she'd remembered about crayfish shedding their shells in time.

If nothing else, this evening's escapade had helped to replenish some of her missing confidence. That was definitely a good thing.

15

Halfway through February, there was a violent storm. The forecasters had predicted that it would hit the east coast of England, but storms rarely affected the south as much as the rest of the country. This one was the exception.

Gales roared all night, howling down the chimney of Tori's flat and rain hammered on the windows. Phoebe woke up a couple of times, hoping that Maggie was OK over at Puddleduck Farm. It was the kind of storm that would rip tiles off roofs and it would definitely spook the animals.

She woke up early, feeling tired, and decided to ring her grandmother a bit later. Today was the day she was heading off to see Duncan Petwell's friend, the equine vet at Marchwood for an informal interview.

Tori had gone off early to cover an event in Southampton and she phoned Phoebe, obviously still in transit on her car phone. 'Just to let you know, the road's closed at Netley Marsh. We've just been diverted. I wasn't sure if you were going that way. There must be a tree down or something.'

'OK, thanks. I'll leave a bit of extra time,' Phoebe said, thanking her lucky stars that she was ready and had it covered.

She'd barely put the phone down when it rang again.

To her surprise, it was Maggie. 'Darling, I hate to bother you, but I've got a problem. Are you busy?'

'Um...' She caught herself before she said yes. Maggie wouldn't be phoning if she didn't really need her help. She hated phones. 'What's the problem?'

'Some of my fencing's down. It's the storm. There's a tree down too. But the main thing is the neddies. They've gone.' There was a thread of panic in her grandmother's voice. 'I need some help to find them.'

'I'm on my way,' Phoebe said, glancing at her watch.

She'd been about to leave for the interview and was wearing a smart suit, blouse, jacket and skirt – not really tramping-across-fields clothes. She hastily swapped the skirt for jeans, grabbed her Barbour coat – her boots were in the car – and left the flat.

On the way to Puddleduck Farm, she phoned the Marchwood Practice and explained that she'd had an emergency and could she possibly reschedule. A cool-voiced receptionist said she was sure that was fine and hung up before Phoebe could ask when.

She bit her lip. The interview was the least of her worries at the moment. If there were fences down at Puddleduck Farm, the donkeys could escape onto the road.

Just under fifteen minutes later, having put her foot down, Phoebe parked at Puddleduck Farm, pulled on her boots, and went to find Maggie, who was in the kitchen and clearly very relieved to see her.

'It's Five Acre field's fence that's down,' she explained as they went out to the back yard. 'It could be worse. It's the fence that backs onto the Holts' estate, not the road side, but they've all gone – Roxy, Neddie and Diablo. I can't even see them.'

Phoebe saw that her grandmother was carrying halters over her arm and a bucket. 'We'll find them, don't worry. We should probably go in different directions. Do you have any more halters?'

'In the barn on the hook. If you catch Roxy – she's the light-coloured one – the others will follow. Grab another bucket and some pony nuts. Roxy's a foodie. Well, they're all foodies, but Roxy's in charge.'

They were walking as they talked and Phoebe did as her grandmother said, grabbing halters and another bucket and filling it with a scoop of pony nuts. 'Any idea which direction they went in?'

Maggie shook her head. 'Maybe the woods?' She pointed towards a distant patch of woodland. 'I'll try to the right of the woods.'

'OK. I'll go to the left.' Phoebe resisted the temptation to point out that this was where a mobile phone would have come in very handy. They could have kept in touch. Maggie looked worried enough already.

At least the wind had dropped now. The storm had finally blown itself out, but there were twigs and bits of branch everywhere, alongside the damaged fence where the fallen tree still lay on the grass. A testament to the power of nature, Phoebe thought as they tramped across the wet fields.

The land they were now walking across sloped gently upwards towards the band of woodland that shielded Beechbrook House.

Puddleduck Farm, in its heyday, had consisted of 168 acres, but when her grandparents had retired and sold the herd, they had also sold much of the land to their neighbours, the Holts. Everyone in the locality was aware of the Holts. It was hard not to be as Lord Alfred Holt was one of the major landowners in the vicinity, but Phoebe wasn't sure whether she'd have recognised them if she'd actually met one.

Maggie had told her that she and Farmer Pete hadn't met the

Holts at any point during the sale of the land. It had all been done via solicitors and some dodgy-looking henchman (at least Maggie had described him as a dodgy-looking henchman) who was acting on their behalf.

As Phoebe and her grandmother, and presumably a stray trio of donkeys, were now trespassing on that land, she found herself hoping that the Holts and the dodgy-looking henchman were in good moods today.

Phoebe was puffing by the time she got to the outskirts of the woodland. She'd got really unfit lately and she'd put a little bit of weight on, what with all the home cooking. It wasn't even that much of a slope. When she'd lived in London, she'd done a lot of walking – everyone in London did a lot of walking – but she'd hardly done any exercise since she'd been home again. She could feel the difference.

The woodland was fenced, or semi-fenced, although the fields running up to it no longer were. The Holts must have dispensed with the boundary fence that had once been there when they'd bought the land. There was also a rusting old gate and a rickety sign by the path that led through the woods which said, 'Private Property. Trespassers will be shot.'

Presumably that was a joke. Just in case it wasn't, Phoebe hesitated for a few seconds, listening and letting her eyes adjust to the dimness of the woodland. It was dark beneath the trees, which weren't far apart, more man-made plantation than ancient woodland. Chances were, the donkeys hadn't come this way – although they could easily have breached the fence, which didn't look donkey-proof at all.

There was no sign of movement beneath the trees. All she could hear was the sound of birdsong. Deciding that the donkeys weren't in the vicinity and knowing her grandmother would be at the other end of the woodland anyway, Phoebe turned left, walked along the treeline for a few hundred metres and then finally found herself at the very outer edges of the land that had once belonged to her grandparents. There was a fence here and a five-bar gate, but it was open. Beyond the gate, she could see a private unmade road that she was pretty sure led up towards the back gardens of the house.

It was worth checking. The donkeys had to be somewhere. They couldn't have vanished into thin air. Even so, maybe it would be better to drive round to the front entrance and go via the gatehouse rather than sneaking around the back. Phoebe was just wondering whether this would be the most sensible plan when she caught the movement of something a hundred or so metres away. Was that a donkey?

She went through the five-bar gate, skirted the road and found herself on the outer edges of the garden. Whatever she'd seen had disappeared. She was beginning to think that it must have been a deer – deer were good at melting away into undergrowth.

Phoebe paused again. In front of her was an expanse of velvet green lawn the size of a small playing field. It led up to the main house, which was a long, pale grey three-storey building with a parapet roof and a colonnaded terrace. A set of wide grey steps, maybe marble, led up to the terrace and, oh my God, on the far side, there was definitely a donkey heading towards the first step.

Phoebe let out a small gasp. She had to divert the donkey. It wasn't Roxy, the alleged ringleader. This donkey was brown. It looked a bit like Diablo, the one who'd been determined to get into her grandmother's kitchen. Steps were obviously no more of a deterrent than doors as he placed one delicate hoof on the step and began to head determinedly up onto the terrace.

Phoebe darted out onto the lawn and banged the bucket she was carrying so the pony nuts rattled within it. 'Chook, chook, chook,' she called, which was actually the call her grandmother used for the ducks and geese, not her larger charges, but Phoebe had no idea what call the donkeys might respond to.

She thought she saw Diablo's long brown ears flick back at the sound of her voice. He didn't stop though. He was halfway up the steps now. Phoebe ran as fast as she could across the lawn. She banged the bucket again, but Diablo wasn't listening. He'd continued up the steps and was on the terrace itself, which she could now see was L-shaped – it must extend around the side of the house. Suddenly Phoebe realised where he was headed. Just out of her vision around the short part of the L, she could now see an outside table and chairs made of wrought iron and she could also see the other two donkeys. She could only see their rear. Their spindly tails were flicking, but they were focused on something that was even more interesting than a bucket of pony nuts.

It was a person, Phoebe saw, her heart sinking as she followed Diablo towards him. A small person, sitting in a chair. No, not a small person, a child, she realised as she got closer. He hadn't yet seen her. He was too busy chattering away to the donkeys and feeding them something from a bag that rustled.

Phoebe cleared her throat so as not to startle him, but he looked up anyway and she saw the brief flash of happiness on his face as he registered another donkey visitor, followed by his surprise when he saw her too.

'Hello,' Phoebe said.

'Hello.' He jumped to his feet, clearly astounded to see a human.

Phoebe saw instantly that although the donkeys must have been as much of a surprise to him as she was, they were obviously a much more welcome intrusion.

He had a mop of black hair and the most intense dark eyes she'd ever seen in a child, which narrowed suspiciously as he looked at her. 'Who are you?'

'I'm Phoebe Dashwood,' she said, wondering whether to offer him her hand, but she was too far away for him to shake it. They were separated by the length of a donkey and the three fat rumps were hindering her from getting much closer. She could see now that the bag contained bread and he'd been tearing off chunks for the delighted donkeys. On the table in front of him was a chessboard – and by the look of the pieces a game was in progress. But there was no sign of anyone else.

'I'm Archie Holt,' the child said, his face still solemn. 'I'm eight. Did you know that you're trespassing?'

'Um, yes. I'm very sorry. I was trying to catch my donkeys. Well, they're not exactly mine, they're my grandmother's. They escaped from their field when a tree fell on the fence.'

Archie nodded, taking this in.

Then, before either of them could say anything else, there was a flurry of movement behind him and a figure emerged from the house through a doorway Phoebe hadn't even noticed. She just had time to take in the sight of a tall, dark-haired man hurrying onto the terrace with swift angry strides before he was beside them. He looked furious and his clipped, icy voice cut across the February air.

'What the...?' He broke off, clearly editing whatever he'd been about to say when he saw the child. Instead, he stopped still, visibly struggling for self-control. The anger was coming off him in waves.

Phoebe took an involuntary step backwards. Even the donkeys looked a bit rattled.

Except for Diablo, who hadn't managed to get his nose into the bag yet and was completely unfazed. He took a step forward and nudged Archie's arm rudely.

'Get These Animals Off My Property Immediately.' Mr Angry gave each word extra emphasis as if there was a full stop between them. His words were directed at her.

'I was about to...'

'Now.' He didn't even let her finish the sentence. He grabbed the boy's arm and hauled him away from the donkeys. Then he shoved him none too gently towards the door he'd just emerged from. 'Get to your room.'

An unprotesting Archie didn't look back and Phoebe felt a surge of anger on the child's behalf. 'Was that really necessary?'

'Are you questioning me?' His eyes, that were as dark as the boys and ten times as suspicious, fixed on hers. 'Unbelievable.' Now the child was gone, he was, if anything, even angrier.

She held his gaze, disconcerted but also riled by his attitude, and opened her mouth to reply, but again he cut across her.

'First, you terrify my son out of his wits with these... creatures...' He spat out the word creatures, his hand sweeping the air over the donkeys' heads. 'And now you have the audacity to question me. On my own property. You do realise I could have you prosecuted.'

Phoebe had been ready to apologise, but his tone was winding her up. OK, so she was on his property, but he didn't need to be quite so arrogant and snooty about it. 'He was not terrified,' she said in a voice as icy as his. 'He was feeding them.'

As if to prove her point, Diablo grabbed the paper bag containing the bread from the table with his teeth and swung it eagerly so the contents dropped onto the terrace in a shower of crumbs and bits of crust. The other donkeys surged forward to snaffle the bread.

Diverted, Phoebe abandoned the bucket, moved forward and slipped a halter over Roxy's determined white nose. It was pointless trying to tug her away from the bread, but fortunately there wasn't much left.

Painfully aware that the wrath of the rude man might descend on her again at any moment, she waited for the donkeys to finish their impromptu meal without looking in his direction. Then she picked up the bucket once more and, praying fervently that the others would follow Roxy and the promise of pony nuts, she turned the donkey in a circle and led her off the terrace.

The other two followed. Thank you, God.

When Phoebe risked a look back, she saw that the man had gone. That was a huge relief too. That had been quite enough of a confrontation with their neighbour.

Phoebe and her charges had just reached the edge of the bowling-green lawn – she'd decided to leave the same way she'd come in – when she heard the unmistakeable sound of a loud donkey parp. When she looked back over her shoulder, she saw that Neddie, who was bringing up the rear of the little trio, was doing what donkeys do best, although he hadn't stopped walking. He was leaving a trail of poop across the lawn and with every step there were sound effects.

Phoebe closed her eyes, torn between laughter and tears. If their neighbour had been even remotely reasonable, she would probably have stopped and cleaned that up. She had a bucket, she could probably find a shovel somewhere if she had a look for one. In normal circumstances, she'd have gone back and asked for one. But she certainly wasn't doing that now. The whole exchange had left a sour taste in her mouth and all she wanted to do was to get away as fast as possible.

She quickened her pace. Besides, Maggie would probably laugh her socks off when she told her about this.

16

Maggie was amused, but she didn't laugh as much as Phoebe had thought she might.

They were now sitting in Maggie's kitchen, the donkeys having been temporarily relocated to the front field, which was smaller but had secure fencing, and discussing the incident.

'I think you must have met Rufus Holt,' Maggie said with a slight frown. 'That's a shame. He has a reputation for being a pain in the butt. Lord Holt, his father, is quite a sweetie, by all accounts.' She paused. 'Not that I've ever met either of them properly. They're pretty reclusive. But people talk, don't they.'

'Well, I wouldn't go running round to introduce yourself any time soon.' Phoebe gave a theatrical shudder. 'He's not a very nice man. He couldn't have been more unpleasant if he'd tried. He accused me of terrifying his son. Which wasn't true. His son was happily feeding them bits of bread when I got there. And the way he hauled him out of his chair was borderline cruel. The little boy had been perfectly fine up until that point. I told him what I thought about that too.'

'Oh dear.' Maggie's eyes darkened.

'What is it?' Phoebe asked carefully.

'Nothing.' Her grandmother stared at the table and then back into Phoebe's eyes. 'I don't suppose that went down very well.'

'No, it didn't. He threatened to prosecute me for trespassing. Which was just plain unreasonable in the circumstances. Not that he gave me the chance to actually explain the circumstances. He was too busy shouting.' Shouting wasn't the right word. He'd been too icy to shout. But he'd certainly got his disapproval across loud and clear. Phoebe could feel herself getting riled again at the memory of Rufus's hostility.

Maggie got up, went to the Aga and put the kettle back on the hotplate. 'You see, the thing is, I don't own the land that New Forest Neddies is on any more.'

'I know that. You sold the grazing to the Holts when you sold the dairy herd.'

'Yes, we did. We didn't think we'd need it. But we actually sold more than we should have done. In view of what's happened since – with the neddies and suchlike.'

Her grandmother brought two mugs of coffee back to the kitchen table and plonked them down with a thud on the old wood.

'I had to rent some back from Old Man Holt when I started taking in animals. That includes the top field and the smaller one. The bottom line is that the only bit I still own is the gardens, the yard and the land where the barns stand. But I don't own any grazing.'

'Which means you don't really want to upset them,' said Phoebe, catching on fast as the implications hit her.

'Precisely – there are conditions attached to me renting the grazing and one of them is that the animals are kept under control and don't cause a nuisance.'

'So you really didn't need me going up there and shouting the odds at our landlord.' Phoebe felt her heart sink. No wonder Maggie had sounded so worried this morning. It hadn't just been the prospect of the donkeys escaping onto the road. It had been the thought of them running riot over the Holts' land – and not only had they trampled all over his terrace, but they'd also pooped on his lawn.

'Shit,' she said to Maggie.

'A rather apt word in the circumstances,' Maggie replied, and now there was a spark of humour in her eyes.

For a moment, they both laughed, but it was Phoebe who sobered first. She'd had no idea that her grandmother no longer owned any land. That was a shock. She'd assumed that they'd just kept enough to house the donkeys. But why would they, when they didn't have any donkeys back then? They had come after her grandfather's death. There would have been no point in keeping any land which would have just needed maintaining. Not when they'd been planning to go off travelling. They had planned a total downsize.

Phoebe gulped down her coffee, emptying most of her mug, which was rapidly cooling. Then she stood up. 'It probably wouldn't hurt if I went and apologised to Rufus Holt then, would it? I would have apologised in the first place, had he given me the chance, but he didn't. Would it help to smooth things over if I did it now?'

It was the very last thing she felt like doing, and she'd been rather hoping that Maggie would say it wasn't necessary, but she didn't.

'If you can bring yourself to do it, then it might. But don't go grovelling. The Crowthers don't grovel.'

'There will be no grovelling,' Phoebe assured her. 'But I promise I won't make it any worse.'

* * *

Phoebe decided to go straight away before she changed her mind. She checked her appearance in the bathroom mirror. There was a grass stain on her face and her hair, which had been neatly plaited and pinned back this morning, ready for the interview, now looked dishevelled. She did a quick repair job. This was embarrassing enough already without her looking as though she'd been dragged through a hedge backwards – a Holt Hedge at that.

'I think I'd better go to the front entrance this time,' she told her grandmother when she emerged from the bathroom. 'I'll take my car.'

'Take some duck eggs with you too,' Maggie said. 'A peace offering.'

Ten minutes later, complete with a half-dozen eggs, Phoebe was driving along the road that bordered both Puddleduck farmhouse and the Beechbrook Estate. There was a twelve-foot-high wall that ran along the boundary of the estate for about a mile on the perimeter road, but Beechbrook House itself was on a slight hill, so it was possible at certain points in the road to see the long curving driveway that led up to the house itself.

The boundary wall was red-brick, but in places on the bends of the road, the bricks were darker than others and Phoebe guessed these were where cars had smashed into it and the wall had needed to be repaired.

Phoebe had never realised quite how long the wall was before, but then it had been part of her childhood for ever. She had never been inside the estate, although she had occasionally wondered as a child what lay beyond the imposing brickwork.

Her thoughts flicked back to the child who did live here. Archie Holt. She hoped he was OK after his encounter with the donkeys – or, more to the point, his father's fury.

She shook herself. *Don't go there, Phoebe.*

At the gatehouse itself were two great stone pillars about thirty-foot high with an archway joining them and on top of the arch was a stag. Full-size, by the look of it – its proud antlers were a spiky silhouette against the white February sky as it surveyed the surrounding countryside.

Phoebe indicated to turn into the drive. The gatehouse wasn't as small as it looked from the road. It was about the size of Woodcutter's Cottage and had curtains at the windows. But it didn't look friendly like Woodcutter's Cottage – it looked like a tiny replica of the house on the hill. A 'Keep Out' kind of house. She wondered who lived in it.

On either side of the drive were fields dotted with oak trees. Phoebe found herself smiling despite her nervousness – she'd always loved the archetypal image of the English countryside. Oak trees and rolling green hills set against a backdrop of white sky. It was so utterly beautiful.

The drive itself was every inch of the quarter of a mile she had guessed, but she was finally almost at the end and now driving past the little woodland where earlier she'd seen the deer. And then suddenly the drive opened out into a wide turning circle, which bordered a fountain on a circular pond, smothered with lilies. There were two white cherubs on either side of it.

Utterly tasteless, Phoebe thought, parking beside a mud-splattered old banger of a Land Rover. That probably belonged to the dodgy henchman.

But it was impossible not to be impressed by the house. The front was even more imposing than the back. It had the same parapet around the top, several chimneys and twelve paned windows overlooking where she stood when she climbed out of the car. Instead of the terrace, there was a jutting-out flat-roofed porch, which also had windows on either side, and a great oak door with a brass knocker. There were steps that led up to it.

Phoebe's heart was beating fast as she skirted the fountain and its tasteless cherubs. In the interests of not upsetting the snooty Rufus further, she should probably look for a staff entrance. On the other hand, she didn't want to risk him catching her snooping around at the front of his house, as well as the back, without announcing her presence.

So, in the end, she decided to go straight to the front door. With a bit of luck, she might end up meeting Old Man Holt instead of his son. Then she could give him her heartfelt apologies without having to grit her teeth, hopefully get Maggie and the New Forest Neddies back in his good books and escape.

She pressed a button on the door, which she assumed was the bell, noticing that the house was protected by CCTV too. There was a jangling inside the house that Phoebe noted was nowhere near as loud as the noise her parents' bell made.

A few moments later, the door swung open. Luck clearly wasn't on her side today. It was Rufus and his expression when he took in his visitor was every bit as hostile as it had been earlier.

It didn't help that, although she was at the top of the steps, he was a step higher, and he was taller than she was anyway, which meant he could look down his nose even more effectively than he had when they'd both been on the terrace.

'Yes,' he said coldly.

Phoebe took a deep breath and held out the box of eggs. 'I'm here to apologise,' she said without preamble. 'For the donkeys.'

There was a gap, but he didn't speak or move or do anything that might have indicated a reaction, so she put the eggs on the doorstep – she was damned if she was going to stand here holding them out – and carried on.

'I should have explained earlier. One of our fences came down in the storm – a fallen tree. That's how the donkeys got out. It won't happen again.'

'Good.'

He obviously wasn't going to make this easy for her and Phoebe wondered in that moment if she should apologise for the mess they'd made on his immaculate lawn too, but he might not know about that. Deciding that discretion was the better part of valour, she kept quiet.

For a long moment, she thought that was it. And she was about to turn away when he spoke again. 'I should apologise too. You caught me off guard. I was...' He touched his stubbled chin with his forefinger and thumb as if struggling for the right word. 'Rude...'

Blimey, she hadn't been expecting that. In fact, it was hard to believe she'd heard him right. But it was an apology she would gracefully accept.

'It must have been a shock.' Impulsively, she held out her hand. 'I'm Phoebe Dashwood by the way. Maggie Crowther's grand-daughter.'

'Good afternoon, Phoebe Dashwood. I'm Rufus.'

They shook hands – Rufus still just inside his doorway and Phoebe still on his doorstep beside the eggs and she was aware of a slant of sunshine on the wooden front door and the smell of something sweet somewhere close by. Just for a moment, the whole day felt brighter and warmer.

Rufus gave her a swift nod and let go of her hand. 'I have things to do,' he said.

'Of course.' She felt herself blush slightly. As if she had suddenly become aware that they weren't equals. Even though for a moment she'd felt that they were. But, no, he was the lord of the manor, and she was just another tenant. In normal circumstances their paths wouldn't have crossed at all. It was ridiculous in this day and age. Nevertheless she stepped back.

'Sorry again.'

This time, she thought she saw the glimmer of a smile in his eyes. But it was gone almost immediately, so perhaps she'd imagined it. All he said, was, 'Thank you for coming.' Then he shut the door in her face.

17

From the privacy of a side window, Rufus Holt watched Phoebe Dashwood cross the yard to her car and get in, and then she was gone.

He'd been surprised she'd come back at all. After the exchange they'd had earlier, that must have taken some guts. And yes, she may have felt obliged to apologise – he wasn't stupid, he knew she might feel that she'd jeopardised her grandmother's tenancy. But she had seemed genuinely contrite. The sparks of fire he'd seen in her earlier as she'd faced his anger had been well under wraps just now.

Besides, she hadn't jeopardised anything. He wasn't that much of a bastard. Mistakes happened. Storms were a pain. According to Harrison, his estate manager, there were several trees down on their land too, but fortunately none had taken a fence with them. It wasn't ideal that the donkeys had escaped into the garden, but it was hardly the end of the world.

The truth was that the shock of seeing Archie so close to those donkeys had swept all sense of reason and rationale from his head.

All he'd seen – all he had felt – in the moments when he'd stepped out onto the terrace was danger.

It was something that happened more often than he cared to admit these days. PTSD. That's what his doctor had finally called it. A condition that Rufus had believed only applied to men who'd come back from war zones until he'd experienced it first-hand.

The first time it happened had been two years ago, just a few months after Rowena's death. It had been triggered by the sight of the hunt in the distance. It was crazy – he'd watched the hunt a thousand times before – although he had never ridden to hounds himself. There weren't many foxes involved these days. Since hunting had become illegal, his father allowed only drag hunts across the estate. A rule that Rufus would make sure continued – he wasn't a fan of the cruelty of fox hunting. And yet there was still something about the sight of the hunt in full gallop that was thrilling and primal. He'd always marvelled at the power and energy of the horses, the age-old tradition of the hounds on a scent, the magnificent red coats of the huntsmen and women, the pure majestic spectacle of the whole thing.

But this time it has been different. As Rufus had watched the hunt streaming across the fields, he'd begun to shake. The nameless fear that had started in his stomach had crept up his spine. It had made the hairs on the back of his neck stand up and his hands sweat and his throat close until he was breathless with terror. It had taken several minutes to subside, but when it had, it was replaced by anger. He had wanted to shout and rage at the world. Scream at the injustice of it all. Rage, rage against the dying of the light. The old Dylan Thomas poem had echoed in his head and for the first time since he'd learned it at school it truly resonated with him.

He had raged against the injustice of Rowena's death.

For that intensely focused moment as the hunt poured across the fields, a dozen splashes of scarlet against a white autumnal sky,

Rufus had truly known what rage felt like. Rage beyond all semblance of reason, rage like a burning red-hot lava gushing from the very heart of a volcano.

Weirdly, he had felt it only briefly when Rowena had first died. In the early days after the accident, he had been more shocked than anything else. Sometimes he felt as though he'd never really moved past the shock. Losing his wife when she was just thirty-three had knocked a hole in the side of his life that had seemed impossible to fill. Some days, it still felt like that.

Archie, who had been just six at the time, was the only reason he had got through it. If it hadn't been for Archie, Rufus thought he might have given in to temptation, locked himself inside a darkened room and never come out.

At the funeral, Rufus and his father had stood at Rowena's grave on what had been one of the most beautiful days of the summer and his father had patted his shoulder and said gruffly, 'The boy needs you. Focus on your son. It will help you to get through.'

Rufus had swallowed hard against the tears and when they'd got home, he had tried to do as his father said.

They had never really talked about it again. Perhaps it would have been different if his own mother had been around, but she had died when he was even younger than Archie was now and Rufus didn't really remember her.

He'd wondered a few times since if that's what his father had done to survive his own grief. Just focus on something else. It certainly hadn't been him his father had focused on. He'd been away at boarding school.

His mother had died after a short illness. Maybe that had made it easier to adjust to what lay ahead. Rowena had died in a riding accident when she'd been jumping a cross-country course at a one-day event. Rowena had loved horses. They had been her passion, her reason for living. Above and beyond even her child and himself, Rufus had occasionally thought.

He had been with her at this particular event. Along with a dozen or so other spectators, he had seen her fall at the ditch and rails – a notoriously difficult fence on this course apparently, which was why spectators gathered there. Just as they clustered around difficult jumps at skiing contests.

Rufus had seen the horse shy at something in the hedge, seen him miss his stride and take off too early and then clip the upright with his foreleg and come crashing down the other side of the fence in a tangle of legs before he rolled onto his trapped rider.

Rufus had been aware of time slowing down to a halt so he had taken in several things simultaneously: the huge gasp from the crowd; the racing of St John Ambulance to the scene; the exact position of the sun in the sky; his own legs carrying him, shaking, across to where Rowena lay so still and unmoving. Every detail of the tragedy was etched sharply in his head. Never to be removed.

Then came the nightmarish ambulance journey to the hospital when Rowena had drifted in and out of consciousness, her face as pale as wax. He'd known it was bad, but he hadn't thought she was going to die. People didn't die in riding accidents. Not in today's world. Even when they'd reached the hospital and she'd been whisked away from him into ICU where she'd been put into an induced coma, he still hadn't thought she would die.

Nothing had prepared him for the solemn-faced doctor coming to the visitor's room, shaking his head, looking at him with eyes that were both sympathetic and exhausted.

Since then, the whole scene had played out in slow motion a thousand times in his head. It would wake him in the small hours. But it happened in the daytime too – over and over again, as if his brain still couldn't quite believe it. Couldn't process it.

Then had come the day when he'd seen the hunt. When briefly

it had been as though every atom of his body had been quivering with fury. The rage had subsided after a few minutes, but only to be replaced by a sobbing helplessness that made him want to curl up, foetal-like, and hide from the world.

The whole intense cycle had been done and dusted in less than twenty minutes, but it had been so severe, so powerful, that it had left Rufus feeling totally washed out and with a throbbing headache.

After that first time, it started happening on a regular basis. And he'd realised it was being triggered by horses – at first, it had been pictures of horses, images of them on television or in one of his father's *Country Life* magazines, but after a while, just the mention of a horse could trigger an attack.

In the end, Rufus had got so sick of it that he'd ignored his natural instinct to push the whole thing to the back of his mind and pretend it wasn't happening and he'd visited the family GP with a complaint about the insomnia that also plagued him.

Doctor Peterson had listened and steepled his hands on his desk and asked him if there was anything else that was bothering him, so a reluctant Rufus had told him the whole story. When he'd finished, his GP had said thoughtfully, 'I'm not entirely surprised. It's only been a matter of months since you lost Rowena, and considering the nature of her accident...' He'd paused. 'Your mind is probably still processing what happened. Do you have any flash-backs at all to the accident?'

'Some,' Rufus had lied.

'And you're not sleeping.'

'No.'

'I'm going to refer you to someone who might be able to help.'

Rufus had nodded, totally defeated. The word psychologist wasn't mentioned at the time and, looking back, he wondered if he'd have gone to see the man if it had been.

But finally he was diagnosed with PTSD. He hadn't wanted to accept it at first, even though it was staring him in the face. But he'd gone along with it, learned ways to manage it: controlling his breathing and focusing on different-coloured objects in his immediate vicinity being two of them. But he'd eventually dispensed with the counselling sessions, convinced he could deal with it himself.

Today had shown him how wrong he was. It was hard to believe, even though he'd just experienced it, that an attack could be triggered by something as innocuous as three donkeys.

The irony was that Archie shouldn't even have been home. He'd usually have been at school, but Emilia, his nanny, had kept him off for a dentist appointment. If the donkeys had turned up ten minutes later, Archie wouldn't have been here at all and Rufus may not have had to encounter the donkeys on his terrace.

Rufus was also sharply aware that if Phoebe Dashwood had come back any sooner to apologise, the whole thing might have escalated into another ugly scene. Round two of 'how dare you trespass on my land?' Because he wouldn't have been able to stay rational.

It had taken Rufus a good half hour to calm down when she'd gone.

But, thankfully, her timing of the second visit – an hour after the first – had been perfect. Even though the thud of a headache still pounded at his temples, the main event, the power of the cycle of PTSD, that was as impossible to stop as it was to describe to anyone who hadn't experienced it, had passed.

Rufus was about to go in search of the paracetamol when the bang of the front door alerted him to the fact that Emilia and Archie had just got back.

Then he heard Emilia's voice from the hall. 'Let's go tell Daddy how brave you were. *Ja?*'

This was followed by his son's slightly higher voice. 'I was, wasn't I?' Tinged with pride.

Rufus smiled despite himself. Archie wasn't one for playing down achievements, especially of the dentist variety. But Rufus could empathise with this. Dentists had always filled him with dread too.

He went to greet them. 'Hello there. How did it go? Did you have to have a filling?'

'Two.' Archie held up two fingers triumphantly. 'And I didn't yell once, did I, Emilia.'

'He did not.' His nanny's face was alight with pleasure as she and Rufus both looked at Archie. 'He was a very brave boy.'

Emilia wasn't the first nanny he'd had since Rowena had passed away. But she was the best. She was Swiss-German but spoke almost perfect English. She was as protective as a mother lion around Archie and she was fiercely loyal to him.

'Two fillings though?' Rufus queried. 'Did the dentist think that was OK? Did he say why?'

'He said sometimes this happens. He gave us leaflets. He also asked about Archie's eating habits, sugar and sweets – this type of thing. I tell him Archie does not eat many sweets and he has good brushing habits. He mention electric toothbrush may help.'

'Can I get one?' Archie asked. 'I think it would help. My other toothbrush is too bristly.' There was a gleam in his dark eyes.

'Too bristly?' Rufus questioned.

'Yes. And it's too big. The dentist thought that might be why I don't use it as much.'

Rufus had a feeling he was being manipulated. 'Did he now?'

He looked at Emilia, who raised her eyebrows and shook her head slightly.

'I suppose if you think it would stop you getting any more fillings, then it would be a good investment.'

'It would,' Archie agreed solemnly.

'Can you organise it?' Rufus asked Emilia.

'*Ja*. Of course.' She hesitated. 'Have there been visitors? We saw a car.'

'It was the tenant who was here earlier. The one with the donkeys.' Rufus tested himself on the word. It was fine. No reaction in his crazy brain to the word. That was a relief.

'Did she forget one?' Emilia joked.

'No, she came to apologise.'

'Good.' Emilia bristled. 'Letting them rampage all over the garden. Frightening Archie out of his head.'

'Out of his wits,' Rufus corrected. That's what he'd told her earlier and she had taken his side immediately. Raging along with him at the outrage of the intrusion. Just as she always did if he told her about any incident that had irritated him. Emilia didn't know about the PTSD. In fact no one, not even his father, knew the full extent of its effect on him.

'I may have overreacted earlier,' he admitted now.

Emilia made a sound somewhere between a huff and a snort. 'I do not think so. You were perfectly within your rights. Did you not see mess they make on lawn?' She wrinkled her nose. 'Disgusting.'

'It'll probably be good for the roses,' Rufus suggested.

'Pfff,' Emilia said, clearly unconvinced.

* * *

Just over a mile and a half away – as the crow flies – Phoebe and Maggie were talking about the visit too.

'Thank you for going, darling. I'm glad he wasn't too obnoxious.'

'He wasn't,' Phoebe said, still feeling surprised. 'He seemed almost human. He actually apologised for being rude.'

'You must have made an impression.'

'Maybe.' Phoebe hesitated, remembering how he'd shut the door firmly in her face, signalling the discussion was over. 'He never thanked me for the eggs though. I was tempted to take them back again. Don't worry, I didn't,' she added quickly, seeing Maggie's face. 'But getting back to the problem in hand. Fixing the fence. I could ask Sam if you like? He did offer to help if we needed anything doing.' She had also told Maggie about Sam's poster idea and her grandmother had agreed reluctantly that she would try it.

'No need for Sam to come. There's a chap in the village who does odd jobs for me. I can ask him.'

'Well, OK, if you're sure.'

'Positive. I phoned him while you were up at the manor.'

Phoebe met her grandmother's eyes. 'I wish you'd let me help more. I could, you know.'

'I'm sure you have better things to do.'

'I don't. Unless you count avoiding Mum's hints about me polishing the silver and Dad's threats to get me answering his office phone while his PA's away.'

'How's the job hunting going?'

Phoebe remembered where she was supposed to have been this morning, but she had no intention of telling Maggie she'd missed the interview because she'd been on a donkey rescue mission. It was difficult enough to get her grandmother to accept help as it was.

'It's going OK,' she said. 'But no takers yet. I promise you'll be the first to hear when I get an offer.' Now she'd cancelled an interview at the last minute she had no idea when that was likely to happen.

18

Fortunately, Phoebe managed to rearrange the interview at Marchwood a week later. The equine vet, Seth Harding, was a surprise when she finally got to meet him. He was older than she'd expected – maybe mid-fifties – and neither was he very tall. Phoebe was five foot ten and she towered over him, even in flats. He looked more like a jockey than a vet, and when they got talking, she discovered that this had in fact been his first choice of career.

'Being a jockey is a young man's game,' he told her ruefully. 'Breaking bones is an occupational hazard and if I'd carried on racing, I think I'd have probably killed myself sooner or later.' He flexed his right wrist, which made a cracking sound that made Phoebe wince. 'As it is, I'm going to end up with arthritis in most of my joints. Being a vet is much safer. Getting a broken toe from being stepped on is the worst injury I've had so far and that was my fault.'

'But you still get to be around horses,' Phoebe said. 'It sounds as though things have worked out well.'

'They have.' He had a gleam in his eyes. 'So, tell me about you. I see from your CV that you've been up in the big smoke.'

She hadn't thought people still called London that, but it did seem appropriate. She still hadn't got used to the fact that even the air was different here. When she'd lived in London, it had sometimes felt as though every inch of earth was slabbed with concrete – the traffic noise was endless. It was never quiet. Even in Hugh's dad's flat, where the double glazing cut them off from the noises of the city, it was never entirely silent. There was far less traffic here and a lot more green and the clear, forest air overlaid everything. She couldn't imagine living anywhere else now and certainly not a big city.

'I don't have a lot of experience with larger animals, as you can see,' she said. 'But I'm pretty au fait with small animal practice.' She told him that she'd got the job at Camberley straight out of vet school and about what she'd been doing at City Vets ever since and he listened thoughtfully.

'I'm really keen to widen my horizons,' she added, 'and practise on a wider breed of animals.'

'Sounds good to me. Why did you leave City Vets?'

She had been dreading this question. She'd contemplated not telling the truth and just saying that she'd felt the call of home, but she didn't want to lie. Besides, it was such a small world and people gossiped, one day he might find out differently. So she gave Seth an edited version.

'I was living with my partner in London. He's also a vet and we worked for the same practice. When we split up – it, er, seemed easier for me to leave than it was for Hugh. We were also living in his dad's flat, you see.'

'I do.' Seth glanced back at her CV, tapping his finger thoughtfully on the paper. 'So when can you start?'

'Seriously?' Phoebe was so surprised, she did a double take. 'You don't want to follow up my references – do any background checks?'

'Should I?' He gave her a quizzical look. 'I think I can trust my instincts. And you have a great champion in Duncan. He speaks very highly of you.'

That could only have come from Maggie, but Phoebe certainly wasn't going to argue with him.

'I also have it on very good authority that you can bring animals back from the dead.'

Phoebe stared at him. He was poker-faced. Then his lips twitched.

'Our veterinary nurse, Shelley, has a child at the same school as Laura Attwell, who works at *New Forest Views*. Apparently you brought her little girl's crayfish back from the dead. You were the talk of the entire school. A vet with superpowers. Just the kind of person my practice needs.' He was smiling broadly now as he held out his hand and she shook it. 'Welcome to the team, Phoebe. I'll get your contract drawn up.'

* * *

'So, when are you going to start?' Tori asked when Phoebe relayed all this back to her later that evening over another late supper.

'The beginning of April. Seth thought that would be simpler.'

'That's only just over a month away. How exciting.'

'It is. I'm thrilled. It's only half an hour's drive too. I never thought I'd get something so close to home. Why are you so late anyway? I didn't think it was a deadline week.'

'It's not. I've been over at Woodcutter's Cottage trying to sort out the latest in the long list of "improvements"–' she mimed the inverted commas around the word '–from Pernickety Pippa. She keeps moving the goalposts. Not only did she want the fencing wood-stained, she now wants the garden doing. I've just employed a gardener to go and take a look and the cheeky beggar was making cracks about needing a flamethrower to clear the brambles.'

It had looked overgrown in December, Phoebe thought, but decided not to mention this. Tori looked tired and irritable enough already.

'Wasn't it a bit dark for him to see anything?'

'I went to Woodcutter's earlier,' Tori explained. 'I've also been on a first date with a guy I met at New Forest Diners just before Christmas.'

Phoebe did a double take. 'You didn't mention him.'

'It was all a bit last minute. Freddie had my number and he's been texting sporadically. We went for a drink at this trendy new bar on the other side of town. He seemed nice on first impressions, but he just banged on about Formula 1 incessantly. It was hard to get a word in edgeways. I didn't stop for a second drink.'

'Shame.'

'Yes.' Her face clouded. 'Never mind. He was one of those guys who's head-turningly hot – all the women in the place were staring at him.' She grinned. 'They're welcome to him and his Formula 1. To be honest, I'm more put out by the price of gardeners. I had no idea they were so expensive.'

'I guess it's a good thing to get on top of it before everything goes mad again though, what with spring just around the corner,' Phoebe said diplomatically.

'Yeah, I suppose so. Although, at the moment, my life feels as though it's all work and no play. I haven't even been to a New Forest Diners event lately, hence going out with Formula 1 Freddie.'

'I thought you hadn't mentioned them recently.' Phoebe had deliberately not mentioned them either. In the interests of not being coerced into going along.

'Anyway, listen to me moaning about my day,' Tori said. 'I'm sorry. I'm absolutely delighted about you getting that job. You must be too. Shall we crack open some Prosecco. I've got one on ice.' She winked. 'Well, I can nip down to the offie and get one from their fridge anyway. Give me two ticks.'

'Prosecco and ham and cheese toasties,' Phoebe said, smiling. 'Sounds perfect to me.'

* * *

Both Phoebe's parents and her grandmother were thrilled about her new job too.

'I guess that means you'll be sticking around,' Maggie said. 'Good. I might get to see a bit more of you.'

'You definitely will. Did you get the fence fixed?' Phoebe asked.

'I did. Yes. Even the most determined of the neddies aren't getting out of that field now. I had someone come and put me up a whole new section of fence.'

Phoebe dreaded to think what that had cost. At least she had finished a poster for Sam to put up. Tori had helped her, so it looked pretty professional.

* * *

The day after she'd told her parents about the job, Sam phoned her up to congratulate her.

'I hear a celebration drink is in order,' he said, sounding pleased. 'My treat.'

'News travels fast. I only just found out myself. How do you know?'

'Your ma told my mine – how do you think?' She heard him chuckle. 'You know what those two are like when they get together. So, are you up for that drink?'

'Yes, please. I can give you a poster to put up in the shop at the same time. Kill two birds with one stone.'

'Great.' There was a pause. 'If you're up for it, I've got some complimentary tickets to go to Exbury Gardens. Ma's always getting stuff like that sent to the shop. We could do that if you like? It's supposed to be nice at the weekend. We could drive out that way on Sunday. Have a stroll around the gardens. The rhododendrons are supposed to be amazing in the spring.'

Exbury Gardens was one of the New Forest's most famous beauty spots. Phoebe had never visited, but the Tourist Board billed it as one of Hampshire's National Trust treasures. It belonged to a branch of the Rothschild family and the two hundred acres of land was made up of woodland, formal gardens and wildflower meadows – there was even a steam train running through it. Set on the banks of the River Beaulieu, it was on the other side of the forest and must be a forty-five-minute drive on a good day.

'OK,' Phoebe said cautiously because it sounded as though a simple celebration drink with an old friend was turning into something more.

'I've always fancied going there,' Sam was saying. He'd clearly sensed her hesitation. 'But if you'd rather not?'

'Exbury's fine,' Phoebe said, thinking it would be churlish to backtrack now she'd agreed to lunch.

'I'll pick you up then,' Sam said. 'About eleven?'

'That would be lovely, Sam. Thanks.'

* * *

When Phoebe told Tori about the trip out to Exbury, her friend raised her eyebrows. 'It doesn't sound as though you need to come to any of my New Forest Diners evenings anyway. Sam's always had a soft spot for you.'

'No, he hasn't. We're just good friends.' Although secretly she was beginning to wonder if that was still true for Sam.

'You might think that, but I reckon he's carrying a torch for you. I think he always has. I was surprised when he started seeing that Judy. Hey – what if you're the reason they split up?'

'I'm not,' Phoebe said. 'He split up with Judy because he didn't think her parents approved and he didn't want to put her in a position where she had to choose. It had nothing to do with me.'

'That's what he told you anyway.' Tori danced around the living room, her eyes gleaming with speculation. 'I bet it was nothing to do with that. I bet he ditched Judy because of his unrequited love for you.'

'He didn't, Tori. Stop it. Besides, I was living with Hugh.'

'Yes, OK, that's fair enough.' Tori's eyes softened. 'Have you never thought that you and Sam might end up together though? It often happens, doesn't it, friendships turning into romances. Girls ending up with the boy next door.'

'It often happens in romantic novels,' Phoebe retorted, glancing at Tori's Kindle on the coffee table. 'I bet you've got dozens of them on there, haven't you?'

'Hundreds,' Tori said proudly. 'Love is what makes the world go round.'

'I thought that was money.'

'Oh, when did you get so cynical? No, don't answer that.' She held up a hand. 'It was that flaming Hugh, wasn't it? Did you ever hear anything else from him?'

'Not a word,' Phoebe replied. 'I thought I might. How can you be with someone all that time and then just stop and never see them again? It doesn't make any sense.' And it also still hurt, but she knew she didn't need to tell Tori that.

Her friend was nodding, her face concerned.

'In some ways I'm not surprised though,' Phoebe went on

thoughtfully. 'Hugh was always very good at compartmentalising things – girlfriends, work, family... mistresses.' She gave a small sigh. 'And he hated confrontations. He wouldn't get in touch with me unless he had a very good reason. That's probably just as well. I wouldn't want him to get in touch with me.' As much as his behaviour had hurt her this was the truth.

'Do you ever look at his social media?'

'He doesn't really do it. He hasn't got a Facebook or Insta account. I think he's got a LinkedIn account and he follows a few people on Twitter. But he doesn't post much. If he did do social media, I'd have tortured myself in the early days seeing if he'd posted any pictures of himself and Cruella.'

Tori grimaced. 'And you haven't heard anything from her either?'

'Not since she called me about my "relocation package", no. I wouldn't expect to. Nor would I want to!'

'I take it you didn't need a reference for the job then?'

'No. Thanks to Laura's little girl.'

Tori frowned and Phoebe realised she hadn't told her about being the talk of the school, so she reiterated what Seth Harding had said.

At the end of it, Tori clapped her hands in delight. 'We really should have done a feature on that. Are you sure you won't let us? It would be really good PR. You might get headhunted.'

'I don't need to get headhunted. I've already got a job.'

'You are such a spoilsport. Do you know that?' Tori gave a mock pout.

* * *

It was only later when she was in bed that Phoebe remembered she had never told Tori about meeting Rufus Holt, although she had told her an edited version about the fallen tree and the donkey escape. She'd just missed out the bit about Archie and Rufus. This was partly a conscious decision. Tori lived and breathed journalism. She was never off duty and the Holts had a reputation for keeping themselves to themselves and being very private. Therefore, any incident involving them, however small, could be built up into hot gossip. Tori might not have been able to resist putting something in the magazine.

The Grass On The Holt side of the Fence is Greener.

Donkeys Visit Shy Lord of the Manor.

They were highly unlikely headlines, Phoebe knew, but from what Phoebe had seen of Rufus Holt, he'd have hated anything that drew attention to him.

Upsetting the Holts could have backfired badly on Maggie. So Phoebe decided to keep quiet. Better safe than sorry.

19

On Sunday, Sam called for Phoebe at eleven prompt, as he'd promised. She was looking out of the lounge window of the flat when she saw his car draw up outside and he got out, locked it, straightened his shoulders and headed for the door. He was wearing his usual Sam outfit – jeans and the brown suede jacket that he'd had for years.

He was freshly shaved too she saw when she went downstairs to meet him. But any guy would do that if they were going out for lunch. It was common courtesy. She didn't think there was any truth in Tori's suggestion that he might be carrying a torch for her.

'Good to see you, Sam.' She leaned in to kiss his cheek. He smelled of citrus aftershave instead of horse. He had made an effort.

'Yeah, same,' he said, smiling at her in the friendly way he always did. There was nothing in that smile except friendship. And there was definitely no chemistry between them. Phew. She'd have hated to lose Sam as a friend.

He'd cleaned his car too, Phoebe noted as she got in. It was a nice drive out to Exbury Gardens. The New Forest had come alive with spring flowers. Patches of daffodils and narcissi grew like blobs of yellow sunshine along the hedgerows and bushes of pink camellias bloomed in country gardens. Now and then, they saw small trees cloaked in pink cherry blossom, one of the most beautiful sights of spring. There would be bluebells in another month, Phoebe thought, pleased. She loved bluebells.

The New Forest ponies were out in force too. There were foals with their mothers – the cutest of soft brown babies, with their long gangly legs and tufty little tails flicking as they romped around in the sunshine.

Sam had been right about the weather. It was a lovely day. It was as if spring had suddenly arrived overnight.

'Penny for them?' Sam asked her as they wound their way along the country roads. Like her, Sam always stuck to the speed limit, too aware of animals wandering without warning into the roads.

'I was just thinking that it's lovely to be back. This beats London hands down. I don't know how I managed to stay away for so long.'

'Me neither. I don't think I'll ever move out of the New Forest. I'm here for the duration.'

'I think I will be now too,' Phoebe agreed. 'Put it this way. I'd need a very good reason to move away again.'

'Good,' Sam said with a world of satisfaction in his voice. 'So what do you fancy doing at Exbury? I think our tickets include a ride on the steam train. Are you up for that?'

'Definitely,' Phoebe said, realising that they'd arrived at the entrance to the car park.

'I've never been here before,' Sam commented as they got out and headed for the main entrance. They passed the train station en route, it was separated from the car park by a fence, and the steam engine was in situ, midnight blue and shiny, puffing out clouds of steam and surrounded by a crowd of admirers.

'Me neither,' Phoebe confessed. 'It's funny how we don't tend to visit attractions that are right on our doorstep. People in general, I mean, not specifically us. Shall we go on the train first?'

'I'm definitely up for that.'

* * *

The steam train ride was a highlight. Although it wasn't quite what Phoebe had expected. It was more Noddy Train than Orient Express with open-air carriages that sat either two or four. As Sam gestured for Phoebe to climb aboard ahead of him into a two-person carriage, she felt her heart lift. It was the first time since she'd split up with Hugh that she'd felt really happy. As if hope had rushed in with the burgeoning spring. As if there really could be a lovely future for her here in the New Forest, surrounded by her friends and family.

'How far does it go?' she asked Sam as the train set off with a whistle, chugging out steam through the warm blue day.

'It's about a mile and a half,' he told her, breathing in steam. 'Don't you just love that smell. It's so nostalgic.'

Phoebe knew what he meant even though she wasn't sure how. Neither of them had been around in steam train days.

'It runs on a narrow-gauge railway – twelve and a quarter inch,' Sam continued. 'Get me on my steam train expertise. It was inspired by Leopold Rothschild apparently. Did you know the gardens were owned by the Rothschilds?'

'I did know that.' She grinned at him. 'They were bankers, weren't they?'

'I dunno. But Leopold died in 1917. He was a racehorse breeder.'

'Trust you to know that.'

'That was the only bit I did know.' And the only bit of interest to him, his face told her. 'I read the rest in the brochure,' he added with a wink.

Phoebe hooked out her phone and tapped buttons. 'The Rothschilds are the most famous of all European banking dynasties – according to Britannica Online. They're also known for their considerable charitable activities.'

'Well, they certainly have some nice places,' Sam said, staring out over the landscape they were passing, which was thick with rhododendron bushes, some of them starting to bud with scarlet blooms. 'It must be amazing to be brought up and have free rein in a place like this.'

Phoebe put her phone away, thinking not for the first time how lucky she and Frazier had been to spend so much of their childhood on their grandparents' farm. Not that they'd had totally free rein, as Sam put it, but it had always felt as though they were surrounded by space. She had never felt hemmed in. She had always felt free.

'It was a great idea suggesting we come here,' she said. 'Thank you.'

For a few moments, they travelled in companionable silence and then Phoebe heard herself saying, 'Talking about lords of the manor type people, I met one of ours the other day. Rufus Holt.'

'Poor you.' Sam screwed up his face. 'I've had the misfortune to bump into him a couple of times lately too.'

'Really. What happened?'

'The first time I saw him, I was riding Ninja. He was in his flash Merc going way too fast along a narrow road, which spooked the horse, whereupon Lord Muck took it upon himself to lean out of his window and hurl abuse at us.'

'Oh my goodness. That's not nice.'

'It wasn't, but the man's an arrogant nob, isn't he? Thinks he owns the forest. He called me an idiot. He said, and I quote, "People like you are a total menace."' Sam had put on a plummy voice that was a passable impression of Rufus Holt. 'That was the bit that got

me,' he added. 'The way he does that whole "me lord of the manner
– you peasant" routine. I thought of half a dozen really good come-
backs, but none of them, unfortunately, until about three hours
later.' He snorted with wry amusement. 'I'm really good at come-
backs, but only if I have a few hours to think them up.'

'Aren't we all,' Phoebe agreed with feeling. 'Did you say you met
him again after that?' She was hoping for a happy ending.

'Yeah – the other time was just in town. He cut me up. I was in
my car, not on Ninja thankfully. I did manage to hurl some insults
that time, but I don't suppose he heard. He was too busy acceler-
ating into the distance.'

'Ah,' said Phoebe, wishing she hadn't brought up Rufus Holt
now. Sam still looked cross at the memory.

'So did you have a better experience?' he asked. They were
sitting beside each other, their knees not quite touching as the train
rattled along on a track that wound through bushes of pink and
scarlet rhododendrons. Every so often, it emitted a whistle, much to
the delight of the children onboard. People exploring the gardens
on foot stopped to wave as the little train passed.

Phoebe told Sam about the great donkey escape and about
meeting Archie. 'He told me he was eight years old and that I was
trespassing.'

'Sounds like a chip off the old block,' Sam commented.

'Yes, but after he'd got that bit off his chest, he was quite sweet.'
She paused to remember. 'He was feeding the donkeys when I got
there. I think he'd been playing chess. But there was no one else
around. That's a bit weird, isn't it – leaving your eight-year-old to
play chess on his own.'

'Maybe his father had just popped inside to pay a visit,' Sam
said, shaking his head. 'Although the whole thing's a bit weird, if
you ask me. It was term-time, wasn't it? I'd have thought he would
have been at school.'

'I didn't see any signs of a mother.'

'I'm not surprised. She probably ditched him. Who'd put up with someone who spends his life hurling abuse at everyone?' Sam's face darkened and he gave her a candid stare. 'Any chance we can change the subject, Phoebe? It's winding me up just thinking about that man.'

'Of course. Sorry.' She had wanted to tell him about the unexpected apology, but she could see he was riled. It took a lot to rile Sam and she didn't want to spoil their outing.

The train had stopped by a small lake, fenced in and fronted by a sign that proclaimed it was Dragonfly Halt. It was clearly a photo opportunity stop. The area thrummed with the birdsong of nesting birds and the air was filled with the fragrance of water lilies.

A short distance from the lake, a woman in a red beret was crouched down, taking pictures of a magnolia bush dripping with pink and white blooms – a candyfloss tree, set against a backdrop of blue satin sky.

Phoebe told Sam about the crayfish being raised from the dead and he chuckled and told her about a little boy he had just started teaching at Brook who was severely autistic. 'He's six and he has virtually no speech, according to his parents, but when he sees a horse, all that changes. He talks to them. Not proper words. He basically talks gobbledygook, but you can tell it means something to him. His voice goes soft and gentle. It's hard to describe, but it reminds me of how a mother speaks to her kid if he's scared. And the thing is that the horses listen. They really respond to it. Their ears flick back and forth and they're so gentle with him.'

'Wow,' Phoebe said. 'That's amazing.'

'It is. You should have seen his face the first time we put him on a horse. They thought he might be scared, but he wasn't. His eyes were so round, I thought they were going to pop out of his head, and then his whole face just lit up.'

'I take it he enjoyed his riding lesson then?' Phoebe asked, pleased.

'Did he ever. His ma said it's the first time she'd seen him connect so strongly with anything outside himself ever. He didn't half squawk when it was time to get off again though. He yelled blue murder.' Sam chuckled.

'I bet.'

'They're coming twice a week at the moment,' he continued. 'On Saturday afternoons and Wednesdays in the indoor school. They say it's made the world of difference to how he is the rest of the time too. I do the Saturday lessons if I can because I'm building a rapport with him too.'

'I'm not a bit surprised,' Phoebe said. Sam was lovely with kids. He'd make a great dad one day.

* * *

Sam was pleased he'd suggested the trip to Exbury, but he was also feeling oddly conflicted and he wasn't sure why.

After the steam train ride, they walked across to the Daffodil Meadow, which turned out to be at the opposite end of the park. It was quite a hike, but worth it when they got there. The Daffodil Meadow was a breathtaking grassland of the bobbing yellow flowers, dotted with silver birch and yews and ancient oaks. This bit of Exbury was bordered by the River Beaulieu. The sun glanced off boats gliding by on the calm water that ran like an aquamarine ribbon past the fields. Above their heads arched a brilliant blue sky with barely a thread of cloud. It was a beautiful day.

In some ways, it reminded Sam of old times. The innocence of long ago when they'd played as kids in the forest. There had always been the four of them. Himself, Frazier, Tori and Phoebe. The fabulous four.

But, in another way, it wasn't like old times at all. Because during the intervening years, they had all changed, and Phoebe had changed the most.

When Phoebe had been at the London Vet School, he'd met up with her quite often. She'd come back frequently then. But the past six years when she'd been living with Hugh had been different. Sam had known that their lives had been separating – going along different tracks, as though they had been passengers on different trains that were running parallel to each other and occasionally crossing close enough for their occupants to wave, but never to really come together.

He hadn't seen so much of her once she'd settled with Hugh. And mostly he hadn't seen her on her own. Hugh had always been with her – so he'd seen them as a couple – and he'd never been overkeen on the slick city boy that he knew Hugh was.

This didn't mean he hadn't been glad Phoebe was happy. Of course he had. She deserved the best. Phoebe was one of those people who everyone liked. She lit up the room with her presence. He'd never heard her say a bad word about anyone. But being back with her today had felt good.

They finally made it back to Mr Eddy's restaurant and were now having a late lunch. Sam had ordered thick cut-gammon, egg and chips and Phoebe had Hampshire sausage and mash with onion gravy.

Over the meal, Phoebe told him about Melissa's 'relocation package'. Even then, when it would have been perfectly justified, she hadn't been bitchy.

'With the benefit of hindsight, I think Melissa did me a favour,' she said.

'How do you work that out?'

'It would have been worse if Hugh and I had got married and I'd found out that he had a roving eye.'

'Yes, that's true. I think the same about Judy actually,' he said. 'Not that either of us had a roving eye, but the fact I found out her parents didn't approve early on, I mean. Relationships are difficult enough without starting off with problems.'

'Thank heaven for lovely friendships,' Phoebe said, her eyes meeting his. 'In fact, I think we should have a toast.' She picked up her glass of Diet Coke and held it up towards him.

'To lovely friendships,' she offered.

He clinked his glass against hers. 'To lovely friendships,' he repeated and he hoped that she wouldn't be able to read in his eyes that actually he was beginning to feel, deep in his heart, that he'd have liked more than friendship.

20

Phoebe's first day at the Marchwood Practice did not go quite as she'd hoped. Seth had said that in the interests of easing her in gently she could start off with the vaccination clinic. 'No nasty surprises, that way,' he'd explained. 'It'll give you a chance to get to know some of our regulars a bit better. How does that sound?'

'It sounds perfect,' Phoebe had said. 'Thank you.'

Not that she was totally unaware of the pitfalls of the vaccination clinic. At City Vets, she'd once had a feline client called Eldon in for his annual booster and general health check. Eldon, a big ginger tom, had yowled at a pitch and volume that would have made Pavarotti proud every time she tried to touch him.

'He's normally as good as gold at the vets,' the apologetic owner had kept saying, giving Phoebe a look that implied it was something she was doing that was sending her 'normally as good as gold' pet into a frenzy.

She'd managed to vaccinate Eldon eventually, but not before the entire practice, including the clients in the waiting room, had been deafened and Cruella had popped her head around the door to enquire if she needed any help.

Ever since then, Phoebe had been wary of big ginger toms. So when her first patient turned out to be a big ginger tom with an uncanny resemblance to Eldon, from what she could see of him through the slatted sides of the cat basket, she was instantly on guard.

This one was called Simon though, Phoebe reminded herself, and he was three years old, and definitely far enough away from London for him not to be related to Eldon in any shape or form.

'So, how has everything been with Simon?' she asked his owner, Pat Sherborne, a petite, fair-haired woman in her early fifties, as she put the cat carrier on the examining table. A pair of wary amber eyes glared out at them.

'Everything's fine,' Pat replied brightly. 'He's such a lovely, gentle boy. A great companion.' She unclipped the front of the cat basket as she spoke, but before she could put her hands in to liberate Simon, he exploded from the carrier, skidded across the examining table and went straight up the opposite wall like a thing possessed.

Pat's mouth made a perfect O shape, as did her eyes, as they both watched Simon reach the top of the wall, cling briefly to the architrave before slithering down, charging across the floor in a blur of fiery gold and hurtling towards the double windows.

The whole thing happened in a matter of seconds. By the time Simon reached the windows – fortunately, these were always kept shut – and had discovered that the slatted blinds gave his claws better purchase than they'd had on the wall, both women were only just recovering from the shock.

Phoebe regained her composure first. She headed swiftly towards the windows, with Pat only a few steps behind her.

'We need to catch him before he does himself an injury,' Phoebe said quietly, looking around for something that might help. A blanket would have been good. Not that there were any convenient blankets to hand. But even as she hesitated, Simon, who was paying absolutely no attention to his owner's entreaties of 'Be a good boy, and come here to Mummy,' seemed to be aware that capture was imminent. He abandoned the blinds, dropped like a stone onto the floor again, landed luckily on his feet and proceeded to tear around the room, hurling himself off every wall and occasionally letting out a banshee howl.

It was impossible to do anything but watch. He was too fast. If he'd been a dog, Phoebe might have risked rugby-tackling him, but she was too scared of hurting him.

'Simon, stop it,' pleaded Pat in vain. 'Stop it now.' She turned frantically to Phoebe. 'It might be your coat; he's scared of the colour green. Maybe if you took it off.'

This seemed unlikely, but Phoebe did as she said, whisked off her vet coat, and on Simon's next breakneck circuit of the room, she threw it over him. Bingo. Her aim was true. She'd somehow covered his eyes and he was disorientated enough to pause from his headlong rush long enough for Phoebe to grab him.

She was as gentle as was possible in the circumstances, holding him tightly, as he struggled frantically in her arms, getting one ginger paw free to scratch her hand. But no way was she letting go again now they'd caught him.

'Hey, it's OK, Everything's fine. Hush now.' She knew she was talking nonsense, but it was working.

The big ginger cat slowly stilled enough for her to hand him back to his anxious owner. Thankfully he was wearing a sturdy-looking collar, and Pat had produced a lead from her pocket, which she was now clipping swiftly onto it.

It would have been handy if she'd done that in the first place, Phoebe thought, but she managed to bite her tongue. Her heart rate must be almost as high as her patient's.

'I think maybe we should let him calm down a bit before we give him his jab,' she murmured.

'Yes, I think you're right.' Pat didn't meet her eyes. 'We did have a bit of an incident once before,' she murmured, going a bit pink. 'But I honestly thought that this time he'd be fine.'

Phoebe sometimes thought that if she had a pound for every owner who said that she'd have been a millionaire!

She dressed the scratch on her hand swiftly, before calling in her next patient.

To her huge relief, the rest of the morning passed without incident. The worst thing that happened was that she was weed on by an overexcited border collie puppy and spat at by a tabby cat called Samantha. But these were occupational hazards when you were a vet.

Phoebe was mightily relieved when, on Simon's second visit to the examining room, he had calmed down enough for her to give him a good check-over and administer his booster jab with his owner hanging on tightly to his collar.

* * *

When she told Tori about it later that night, her friend looked sympathetic. 'It shouldn't happen to a vet,' she said. 'Isn't there a television series called that?'

'There is,' Phoebe replied. 'I can definitely relate. It does feel good to be back working again though, I have to say. How did your day go?'

'I had another run-in with Pernickety Pippa,' Tori said, slightly disconsolately. 'She thinks the kitchen cupboards are dated and that my guests may complain about the temperamental plumbing. The cupboards are a bit dated, I guess. I mean, I doubt it's had a new kitchen for a decade, but they were top of the range at the time. My grandparents never did anything by halves. And there's nothing actually wrong with them. They're solid oak.' She sighed. 'I'm beginning to think that if there are this many issues with Woodcutter's Cottage before I even start, what's it going to be like when I have actual real-life holidaymakers in there?'

'I'd have thought they'd be more interested in enjoying their holiday than complaining about dated kitchen cupboards and temperamental plumbing.'

'Yes I thought that too, but Pernickety Pippa didn't.'

'What's temperamental about the plumbing anyway?' Phoebe asked.

'The downstairs bathroom has one of those really old cisterns and you have to pull the chain in a double flush to get it to work. I was going to write that in the guest information book. I figured that would cover it.'

'What did Pernickety Pippa say about that?'

'The look of horror she gave me, you'd have thought I was suggesting they had to get a bucket of water to flush the loo. Honestly, Phoebe, it's not that bad. You don't even have to do it every time.'

'I know it isn't. Bear with it,' Phoebe said, patting Tori's arm. 'I'm sure it will be worth it in the end. Grit your teeth and think of the money.'

'That's exactly what I've been doing. Grrrrr. I'm not replacing the cupboards. I might paint them – I suppose that would update the look. The plumbing though will have to stay temperamental.' She paused. 'Talking of temperamental, how's your grandmother doing? No more donkey escapes or injured ducks?'

'Not that she's mentioned to me. I'm seeing her on Sunday. Last time we met, I promised that I'd give her a hand. She's just rehomed a couple of Jack Russell terriers with a lady in Southampton, so I'm doing the home check on Friday night after work. Then I'm reporting back to Maggie, and if all is well, the lady is coming to collect on Sunday. But Maggie wants an update first. And that's easier face to face than on the phone. She only uses phones as a last resort.'

'That must be tricky with rehoming animals. Does she rehome very many?'

'Not as many as she takes in,' Phoebe said. 'But you're right. Her phone phobia probably does make it tricky. Not that she's ever admitted any of that to me. But she definitely has more animals than she used to have. She's still got that stray donkey, Diablo. He turned up before Christmas and she said she was searching for his owner. But no one ever came forward.'

'Would it help if we did a feature in the magazine?' Tori asked. 'On New Forest Neddies as a whole, I mean. Not just Diablo. We could do a double page spread – that might prompt a few people who are thinking of buying a dog or cat to get a rescue one instead? But you never know, if we do feature Diablo, someone might recognise him and come forward too.'

'I think that's a great idea. I'll ask her when I see her,' Phoebe said. 'Thank you. Maybe we could mention that she needs volunteers too. Sam put that poster up in the shop, but no one's come forward yet.'

'OK. If she's agreeable, it could go in the June issue, which goes to press the last week of April and comes out at the end of May,' Tori said. 'So you've got a bit of time to talk her round.'

'Perfect.'

* * *

'I think it's a terrible idea,' Maggie said, folding her arms and pursing her lips mutinously when Phoebe raised the subject with her on Sunday morning.

'Why? It would be brilliant publicity – it would help to raise your profile with the locals.'

'I don't need my profile raising. I don't want lots of annoying people tramping around here nosing into things, or worse, dumping even more animals on my doorstep for me to look after.'

'Yes, I guess that might happen, but I was hoping that if we got the tone right, it would have the opposite effect. Tori's idea is that we could put in pictures of the animals needing a home. She could take the photos, so you wouldn't have to do anything. We would also ask for donations – so that anyone wanting to help out financially could do that.'

'We might get the wrong kind of person,' Maggie said suspiciously.

'What do you mean the wrong kind of person?' Phoebe could be as stubborn as her grandmother when the occasion demanded it.

'I mean the kind of person who only wants to rescue a poor little animal – the more maltreated, the better – because it's good for their egos.' Maggie's eyes sparked fire. 'I don't want people like that rescuing my animals.'

'We might also get lovely people who were thinking of getting a dog or cat anyway but hadn't realised there was an animal shelter right here on their doorstep,' Phoebe countered with equal fire.

'I suppose we might.'

Sensing that her grandmother was softening towards the idea, Phoebe took full advantage. 'I was also thinking that if we were taking photographs of animals, I could help you with setting up your sponsor-an-animal scheme again. You said you hadn't kept it up since Eddie moved out.'

In truth, the idea had only just occurred to her, but it was a good idea, and she would have liked to help with raising some more income for the shelter. Especially in view of what Maggie had confessed to her recently about supplementing the day-to-day expenses out of her own savings. That definitely wasn't sustainable, however much she argued that it was.

'All right,' Maggie agreed eventually. 'Tori can do a small feature. And she can take some photographs. But I'll need to approve them all.'

'That sounds perfect,' said Phoebe, adding under her breath, 'hallelujah.'

'Now, if you've finished haranguing me about providing material for the local rag, maybe you'd like to tell me about the woman who wants the Jack Russell terriers. Is she suitable or isn't she?'

'She's very suitable,' said Phoebe, who had done the home check on Friday evening, as she'd promised. 'She has a fully fenced garden, no kids, and she works part-time at a garden centre where she does the occasional weekend, but dogs are welcome, so she can take them in with her if she needs to.' Phoebe consulted the form she'd filled in, as requested, when she'd done the home check and continued, 'Her last dog, CJ, was also a Jack Russell terrier who made it to the age of sixteen before dying peacefully of old age. That was eighteen months ago. She hasn't rushed into getting another one, but she's finally decided that's she's ready.'

'Sounds perfect,' Maggie agreed, before adding under her breath with a triumphant note in her voice, 'hallelujah.'

21

Sam's biggest problem on that Sunday morning was a rattle in his car. It was coming from somewhere on the left-hand side at the front and it was driving him nuts. He wasn't sure when it had started. He didn't remember it being there when he'd taken Phoebe to Exbury, but it had appeared some time since and the more he tried to ignore it, the louder it seemed to get.

Early this morning before he'd left for the stables, he'd done a thorough search. He'd checked the front wheel as well as the back one, in case his directional hearing was off, made sure there were no stones caught anywhere, emptied out the glove compartment. He'd even checked under the bonnet, all to no avail. There was no obvious cause for the rattle.

While he was sorting out Ninja and later teaching a nine-year-old girl called Henrietta whose parents thought was going to be the next Ellen Whitaker, the annoying rattle went out of his mind, but as soon as he got back into his car again to head to his parents for Sunday lunch, it reappeared.

He wasn't often invited to Sunday lunch – as he and his parents frequently joked, he and Ma saw enough of each other at work, but it was Pa's birthday and so, like Christmas, they were having a sit-down meal.

He'd bought his father a new pair of fire tongs for the wood burner, which had seemed like an odd present but was apparently exactly what he'd wanted.

They ate the meal, he volunteered to wash up, Ma made the coffee and now they were all sitting around the wood burner – it was still cold enough to light one some evenings – despite the fact it was April.

'So how did your date go with Phoebe?' his mother asked in her best innocent voice.

'It wasn't a date. It was a lunch,' he protested.

'A lunch date then.' Her eyes sparkled with mischief. 'And if it wasn't one, it should have been. There's absolutely no chance of her getting back with London Hugh. Not from what I've heard anyway. She's just got a new job across the forest.'

'I know she's got a new job and I know she's not planning on getting back with Hugh. But that's got nothing to do with me, Ma. We're just friends.' He shot her a curious look and she tutted.

'I know that, but friends can be a very good basis for a relation-ship. Your father and I were just friends for years. Until he finally wore me down, nagging me for a date.'

His father, who was fiddling with the fire, dropped a bit of hot wood on the hearth, which sent up a shower of sparks, and splut-tered, 'It was her who wore me down, son. Not the other way round.'

'Oh, what does it matter who wore who down, the fact is we got there in the end. And we've been very happy ever since. You should ask her out, Sam. What have you got to lose?'

Sam could think of several things. A very good friendship and his dignity if she said no, being two of them. He shook his head. 'You've been plotting with Louella again, haven't you?' he accused.

'It sounds like they've been planning what hats to buy,' his father said. 'Ignore them, lad. In my book, you choose your own woman, you don't let your parents dictate who you go out with. Although, saying that, I did like that Judy.' He winked. 'What did happen to her?'

Sam didn't want to tell them he'd let Judy's parents put him off seeing her. Oh the irony. 'We drifted apart.'

'Well, I think it's a shame.' His mother was like a dog with a bone. 'It's high time you settled down. A lovely lad like you.'

'I'm thirty-four, Mum, not fifty. I've got plenty of time to settle down.' What on earth had got into her tonight?

'I know, son.' Her voice softened. 'Did Phoebe tell you she's going to be an auntie this year. Frazier and Alexa are having a baby in September. I do envy Louella being a young grannie.'

So that's what this was all about. Being a grannie. She and Louella had obviously been discussing it and his ma was broody. Sam shot her a look and caught the wistful expression in her eyes and knew he was right. Who'd have thought it?

'You're too busy to be a grannie,' he said, giving her arm an affectionate squeeze. 'And I'm way too busy to be a dad. Even if I did have a partner. Besides, you're only fifty-six. You've got years of being young yet.'

His ma wrinkled her nose ruefully.

No more was said about settling down. Serenity was restored. But much later, as Sam got back into his car and drove the short distance home through the quiet Sunday streets, even the annoying rattle couldn't distract him from his thoughts. Although by the time he got home, he'd rescinded that thought and it was loud enough to be annoying again.

Deciding to have one last look, he parked the Subaru and went round and let himself into the passenger side of the car and tried to figure it out logically. Definitely nothing in the glovebox. He checked the side compartment in the door, which looked empty, but as he ran his fingers along it to be sure, they touched cool metal. He pounced on what turned out to be a tiny dark blue tin of mints which had been tucked up at one end and was almost invisible against the black interior. He gave it an experimental shake and the source of the annoying rattle was suddenly clear. It sounded as though there was one mint left. He tucked the offending tin into the pocket of his jeans with a sigh of relief

They must belong to Phoebe. She liked mints. The memory of their day out at Exbury warmed him. And when he let himself into his empty flat and not even Snowball came to greet him, he was struck by the fact that he'd grown tired of the hollow sound of an empty flat.

The rattle that had plagued him for the last week was akin to a niggling thought. Despite all his protestations earlier that he and Phoebe were just friends, he'd already acknowledged to himself that his feelings were changing. The problem was he didn't think hers had changed. In fact, he was sure they hadn't and he'd meant what he'd said to his mother. He'd have hated to lose their friendship.

Sam decided that for now he would keep quiet, maintain the status quo. He was good at that. He'd always been good at it. Sam, the plodder, his school reports had always said. They'd meant academically, but the description summed up how he lived his life too. Quietly plodding on, not creating a stir. Not ruffling any feathers. Not upsetting anyone, not doing anything untoward. But not standing out from the crowd because he'd done something spectacular either.

Sam had realised long ago that he was unlikely to do anything memorable. He wasn't the kind of man who made history. He was similar to his father in that respect. As reliable as the sunrise and as steady as the giant oaks that dotted the forest. The kind of man who wouldn't let you down. A stalwart.

He'd been called a stalwart once by Marjorie Taylor, who owned Brook Stables. Marjorie was old enough to be his grandmother, although she'd never looked any different during the ten years he'd known her. She had grey hair which she kept coiled up in a wispy bun on the back of her head, weather-beaten skin from being outdoors most of her life and kindly button brown eyes.

'You're such a stalwart, Sam,' she'd said to him.

It was obviously a compliment. Not that he'd known what it meant. He'd looked it up when he'd got home and discovered it meant committed and steadfast. While that was all well and good, Sam did wish that just once in a while he could do something that would make him stand out from the crowd. Do something that ruffled some feathers. Do something that would create a major stir.

* * *

Over at Beechbrook House, Rufus had just been creating a major stir. The row between him and his father, which was about Archie wanting riding lessons, had started much earlier in the day. It had just exploded into a major shouting match, from which neither of them would back down.

They were currently in the drawing room, both standing up on either side of one of the three Chesterfields, and Lord Alfred, who rarely got fired up enough to shout these days, was resting his hands against the back of the studded leather and breathing heavily.

'This whole thing about horses has gone on long enough,' he continued. 'It's bloody ludicrous, Rufus, and you need to address it.'

'I have addressed it,' Rufus shot back at him. 'It's been addressed. It doesn't change my decision.'

'Then it hasn't been addressed, has it? Good God, give me strength.' Alfred's face was red as he gripped the back of the Chesterfield. He had high blood pressure at the best of times and Rufus was slightly worried he was going to have a heart attack.

Rufus lowered his voice. 'I don't want my son having riding lessons. I don't want him going anywhere near a horse. It's simple enough. And I'd have thought it would be obvious why, to you, of all people.'

Alfred lowered his voice too. 'You're concerned about his welfare. I understand that perfectly. But this isn't going to go away. The point I'm trying to make is that if you refuse him point blank, all you are going to achieve is to make him want to do it more. You saw how he was earlier. He's determined to learn to ride. And, personally, I think that if you let him try it – without any fuss or emotion – he'll quickly tire of it. Look how he was with the clarinet lessons. And the kung fu classes. He didn't pursue either of them for more than a few weeks.'

'What if he doesn't tire of it?' Rufus said warily. He was starting to calm down from the awful rage part of the violent cycle of PTSD that the mention of his son learning to ride had evoked.

'I think that he will tire of it. But if he doesn't, we both know that fighting him isn't going to help. He's growing up fast, Rufus. You can't protect him for ever and you can't control him either.'

Rufus knew in his heart that his father was right. And he knew that no matter what he thought, how he felt, how much it terrified him, he had to let it go. How he was going to do that was a different matter. His father had no idea – no one did – about the nightmares that still haunted him.

'It was those blasted donkeys that started him off on the riding idea,' he said quietly, meeting his father's eyes. 'He's talked about nothing else since he saw them.'

'Yes. That was an unfortunate incident. But if it hadn't been the marauding donkeys, it would have been something else. We're surrounded by donkeys and ponies, Rufus. Any of the commoners' animals could have strayed onto the estate. I'm surprised it hasn't happened before. Besides, the child only has to look out of the car window when we're driving. In some ways, I'm surprised he hasn't mentioned learning to ride before.'

'He loves all animals,' Rufus said softly. 'He takes after his mum.'

'I should think it's in his genes, son. Rowena came from an equestrian background, didn't she? And she was a very fine horsewoman.'

The atmosphere felt calmer in the room now. It was weird how after the PTSD cycle had run its course, Rufus had a brief window of calm. A brief window in which his thoughts returned to the normal logical pattern that had been there before the PTSD had ripped through them, like a wrong note that had been learned and fixed and couldn't be unlearned. The trigger words briefly quietened and became innocuous, and he could think like a normal human being again. He could be rational.

'She was and it was her passion,' Rufus said, glancing at the sideboard beside the window, where a framed picture of Rowena jumping a cross-country course on her grey mare still had pride of place.

It was the only picture of Rowena on a horse that was still in the house, because it epitomised his wife. The horse was in mid-air, jumping an enormous brush fence against a backdrop of azure sky. Rowena was bent forward, her hands reaching forward along the grey neck, giving her mare the freedom she needed to clear the brush. Strands of her blonde hair had escaped from her hat and although she was in profile, you could see that she was smiling. It was a picture that clearly showed her huge joy of riding cross country. Rufus had taken that picture and Rowena had often referred to it as 'the most perfect moment'.

And although her passion for horses had also killed her, Rufus couldn't bear to take it down. Although it was hard to look at it, these days, too.

'I know you miss her, son. I miss her too. I miss our lunches.'

Alfred's voice cut across his thoughts. His father rarely spoke about emotion and, again, Rufus met his eyes across the room.

'I know you do.'

Sunday lunch was a tradition that had started when Rowena was alive. It had been an excuse for his father to see his grandson and a chance for them all to catch up socially, because although he saw a lot of his father to talk shop, they didn't spend much time together socially.

Back then, Sunday lunches had been a joyous affair. Business talk was banned. His father had loved Rowena as much as Rufus had done and he'd enjoyed taking a back seat and watching the pleasure they took in each other's company, the banter that had flowed around the table.

It was hard not to love Rowena. She had been beautiful, a fair-haired English rose who had a fragility about her that belied how tough she was on the inside. Rowena was a go-getter, brought up by a wealthy family who'd made their fortune in banking. She was academic and funny and sassy – she had a degree in law, which she had never used, but which had been something she'd wanted to do.

'To prove I'm not just a pretty face,' she'd joked to Rufus when they'd first met.

Her mother had been a talented horsewoman who regularly rode to hounds and Rowena herself had ridden from an early age. Rufus, who could ride but had never been passionate about it, had always been pleased she had such a driving force in her life. It meant she didn't mind him working so hard.

It was a common misconception that if you were lucky enough to be a landowner and have a title, you were stinking rich and didn't need to work. This was not true. Or at least it wasn't in his case. Being the only son of a lord came with huge responsibility as well as huge privilege. This was something his father had always drummed into him. And Rufus had always taken it very seriously.

Yes, he had an estate manager who oversaw the estate and a property manager who dealt with the dozens of properties that they owned and rented out to tenants across their land, but, like his father, Rufus had always played an active part in the day-to-day running of the business too. He and Rowena had only moved into Beechbrook House a year before she'd died. The idea being that he would slowly take over more and more duties from Alfred, who had hit sixty-five in the same year and was ready to retire. They would have a slow handover – slow and thorough – the way that Alfred liked to do things.

But Rowena's death had stopped time. Hence, his father still lived in the house. It wasn't as though there wasn't the space – it had seven bedrooms and five bathrooms – but now, while Alfred had what they both called the east wing, Rufus and Archie lived in the middle section. Emilia, who would be a live-in nanny until Archie went away to boarding school at eleven, had her own self-contained accommodation within it.

Rufus had wondered if he should have made Archie a boarder sooner, as his father had suggested. But Rowena hadn't wanted that for their son, and, in truth, neither had he. His own experiences of boarding school had been less than ideal – he'd been bullied and he would have hated that for Archie. When he was eleven, he would be less vulnerable.

Rufus sometimes wondered if he should move out of Beechbrook House and back into one of the estate's properties where he and Rowena had lived before, but inertia and the fact that he had so many happy memories here had so far stopped him. It was also easier to be on hand for the smooth running of the business. He and his father didn't need to schedule meetings; they saw each other at every meal. Besides, Rufus knew deep in his heart that he couldn't leave his father alone and take away his only grandson.

That night as he went up to bed, his father's words still weighed heavy on his mind. They both knew that the real issue wasn't whether or not Archie could have riding lessons – that was something that would have to happen. The real issue was whether Rufus could carry on ignoring the fact that the untreated PTSD was causing such serious disruption to his life.

Rufus had horrified himself when he'd hauled Archie away from those donkeys. He'd acted out of terror, but that had been no excuse to manhandle his son. He'd apologised to him afterwards and Archie had brushed the incident away. He was a surprisingly well-balanced child. But that didn't mean Rufus had forgiven himself.

22

Phoebe quickly settled in at the Marchwood Practice, despite the fact that thanks to the late Easter holiday, she didn't work a full week until week three. It had been nice to catch up for a meal with her parents and Maggie. They weren't big on doing Easter as a family and Frazier and Alexa had gone away, but they still managed a lunch on Bank Holiday Monday.

Phoebe loved being a vet again. Seth was a brilliant boss. Marchwood was a smaller practice than City Vets, which had employed five vets, four part-time veterinary nurses and a couple of receptionists. At Marchwood, there were just three vets, two nurses who job-shared, and one receptionist. Seth looked after the large-animal side of things, and Phoebe and Alison Turner did the small-animal side of things, which had expanded lately, hence the vacancy for another vet. Alison was in her early forties and she was kind and clever and lived with Helena, who was very pretty and one of the veterinary nurses. It took Phoebe a little while to realise that Alison and Helena were also a couple. This was because they were totally professional at work – even when they were off duty, it wasn't obvious – and Phoebe only realised when Helena brought in some leftover biscuits that she said they'd had at the weekend to celebrate their third anniversary. The biscuits, which were cinnamon and ginger, had tiny hearts on them and were utterly gorgeous.

'Oh my God, these are amazing, where did you get them?' Phoebe asked and Helena gave Alison a look of great tenderness and said, 'Baking is one of Alison's many talents. I really do have the perfect woman.'

It was only then that the penny finally dropped and Phoebe realised that she was now truly part of the team.

Marchwood was a lovely place to work. Unlike Cruella, Seth didn't micromanage his staff. He was also very supportive of local charities, like the Bolderwood Deer Sanctuary, The New Forest Wildlife Park, which was near Ashurst, not far from them, and the reptile centre, where he said he always dreaded getting a call just in case it was a snake because they scared him witless.

He was fascinated to hear the inside story on New Forest Neddies, which he knew about via his friend, Duncan Petwell, but he hadn't realised that the shelter had so many other animals.

'I thought it was just a few donkeys,' he remarked when Phoebe told him about the proposed photo shoot that would be going in *New Forest Views* to help raise the shelter's profile.

'It started as a couple of donkeys,' Phoebe explained, 'but my grandmother's a sucker for a sob story. She can't help herself. People turn up at Puddleduck Farm with all sorts of animals and she never says no.'

'Whereas you would be the hard-hearted pragmatist and turn them all away?' Seth quizzed her, raising his bushy eyebrows in disbelief. 'Hmmm, that doesn't quite ring true.'

Phoebe laughed. Seth wasn't silly. He already had the measure of her. 'I think I'd have turned away the geese.'

'No, you wouldn't,' he said confidently. 'Not if you thought something heinous was going to happen to them if you didn't take them.'

That was true.

'Once the feature is in print, you could bring in a laminated copy to put up on the noticeboard in the waiting room if you like?' Seth suggested. 'We tend to get mostly responsible pet owners at the vet's.'

'Thanks, I will,' Phoebe said, knowing he was right. Although even the responsible pet owners could be divided into two groups: the ones who were happy to pay for their animal's care and the ones who begrudged every penny. This did not necessarily depend on how wealthy they were either, she'd discovered. Some of the wealthiest clients that had come into City Vets had quibbled about details and demanded itemised receipts and breakdowns of everything. It didn't seem to make a difference whether they were insured or not either.

She'd also known one elderly lady who had remortgaged her house when her cat had been involved in an accident and had needed extensive work to piece his leg back together.

Pet owners were a very varied mix and the only thing you could be sure of was that you should expect the unexpected.

* * *

The photo shoot was on a Sunday and it turned out to be cloudy, but dry, unlike the rest of the month, which had been living up to its April showers reputation.

'Perfect weather for a photo shoot,' Tori told her as they ate toast for breakfast. 'We don't need the sun to be too glaring.'

'And I presume it won't matter about the mud?' Phoebe said.

'It won't show up in the photos, if that's what you mean. As long as there's a bit of green field somewhere, we'll be OK.' Tori hoisted a bag containing her tripod and cameras over her shoulder and finished her coffee. 'I'm looking forward to this. I have very fond memories of Puddleduck Farm. Do you remember when we were about ten, you, Frazier, Sam and I got into trouble for having a picnic in the cow field?'

'How could I forget?' Phoebe said with a grimace. 'Wasn't that the time Farmer Pete came racing across the field, brandishing a shotgun, saying if we ever did anything so reckless and stupid again, he wouldn't be responsible for his actions?'

'I really thought he was going to shoot us, the way he was shouting so loud,' Tori replied with an amused shudder.

'That was before he knew it was us though.' Phoebe shut her eyes fleetingly, remembering. 'We were surrounded by heifers, weren't we? They were only babies. They weren't going to hurt us. One of them was licking my back.'

'I thought she was going to bite you.'

'I knew she wasn't,' Phoebe said, as an image of the young cow's gentle brown eyes and the rasping sound her tongue had made on the back of her coat flicked into her head.

'All that fuss, but I guess Farmer Pete was just worried,' Tori continued.

'Yes, he'd have had all of our mums to answer to if we'd been trampled to a pulp.' Phoebe grabbed her coat and boots from the back door. 'I haven't thought about that day for years.'

* * *

Less than an hour later, they were at Puddleduck Farm and Maggie was supervising them on a recce of suitable photo locations, accompanied by Buster, who was looking a bit less arthritic today, Phoebe was pleased to see, and Tiny. The ancient black Labrador and the

Irish wolfhound made an odd couple, but they were clearly firm friends.

Not that Tori really needed supervising, Phoebe thought, amused, but Tori was humouring her grandmother and listening carefully to all her instructions about where the sun was, as well as the dozens of directives about which animals were amenable to having their pictures taken and which ones weren't.

'It's really more about which animals are the most photogenic and which ones you'd like to get homes for,' Tori told Phoebe when they were out of hearing range of her grandmother. 'Does Maggie actually want to rehome any of them? And didn't you say there was a donkey whose owner she's trying to track down?'

'I did – and yes, that's Diablo.'

'We'll need a few shots of him then? If he's amenable?' Tori clicked her tongue and grinned. She was in her element when she was working. 'Has this place got an official name? I mean, I know the locals call it New Forest Neddies, but is that how we should bill it? I'm thinking of a headline shot. If it's called New Forest Neddies, we'll need a donkey picture, but if it's called Puddleduck Farm, a duck might be better.'

'I'll see how she feels about the name,' Phoebe said and went to ask her. 'Puddleduck Farm, New Forest Neddies or something else?' she asked, explaining the dilemma.

Maggie shrugged and her eyes clouded a little. 'Does it matter what we call it? Is it that important?'

'We want people to be able to find it. I think that's the main reason. But we can put in an address as well, of course.'

'It had better be something Puddleduck then. Puddleduck Paws and Claws? Puddleduck Animal Rescue. The Puddleduck Shelter. They're all a bit of a mouthful, aren't they? That's why I've never bothered.'

'Puddleduck Pets?' Phoebe suggested. 'Would that work?'

'It's a bit cutesy, but I suppose it will do.' Maggie waved a hand. 'I'll leave it with you girls. You know what the modern world wants. I'm past it.' Again, Phoebe caught a flash of something in her eyes that worried her. A sadness.

'You are definitely not past it,' she said fiercely.

'Nearly past it then,' Maggie amended, and for the first time, Phoebe wondered at the wisdom of organising this shoot. One thing she did know about her grandmother was that she hated change and she was happiest when it was just her and the animals. Maybe she really was worried that she'd have people tramping all over the place if she gave the shelter a higher profile.

Phoebe realised that Tori was beckoning her over. 'I think we'll start with a duck. Are there any particularly photogenic ones or are they all the same?'

'They're similar. But it probably depends on which one we can catch. Jemima's pretty tame. I'll come and catch her for you.'

If anyone had told Phoebe a few months ago that she'd be able to pick one white puddle duck out from a flock of others, she would have disputed it strongly, but she'd just done exactly that, she thought, as she sat on a hay bale with a contented Jemima. Apparently when ducks wagged their tails, it meant they were content.

Not that she'd needed to pick Jemima out – it had been the other way round. She had come waddling across at top speed, quacking.

'She remembers that you saved her life,' Maggie said, in a rare moment of sentimentality. 'Animals don't forget. They're more grateful than humans.'

'She knows you've got treats more like,' Tori remarked and Maggie shot her a look.

'That too,' she said with amusement in her eyes.

At least the sadness had gone now and Maggie seemed happy again with what they were doing.

After they'd got what Tori had said were some cracking shots of Jemima – both posing on a hay bale and splashing about in water with her mates – Tori took some shots of the geese from a distance.

'I'm not a fan of geese,' she said warily. 'I had a run-in with some on a farm where I was doing a story once. Vicious bloody things. I don't fancy having my legs pecked to pieces again.'

Phoebe, who could relate to this, agreed.

Then Tori took some shots of the dogs.

Tiny, the wolfhound, was very happy to sit in the sun, looking directly into the camera with his gentle eyes and pricked ears. Buster had his photo taken too – not because Maggie wanted to rehome him, he was a permanent resident, but to stop him feeling left out.

Laila, an eighteen-month-old golden retriever, was another very photogenic candidate, as was Mutley, a small brown and white terrier of indeterminate breeding.

'They're lovely dogs, all of them,' Tori said. She wasn't animal-mad like Phoebe and Maggie, but she was fond of dogs. 'Why did their owners give them up?'

'People tend to lie,' Maggie said. 'They certainly did in Mutley's case. They said their child was allergic, but I think it was because Mutley never stops barking. That doesn't go down well with the neighbours on your average housing estate.'

'And Laila?' Tori asked.

'She probably just got too big and boisterous. Puppies are cute, but if you don't train them, they grow into dogs that need lots of work. I certainly haven't noticed anything untoward about her. I had her in the house for a while. The worst thing she did was chew up one of my baseball bats.'

'One of your baseball bats!' Tori paused from taking photos. 'How many do you have?'

'Five if you include the chewed-up one. I should probably

replace it now it's not fit for purpose, but... on the other hand, maybe it doesn't matter too much. I have one for every downstairs room. I don't really use them for baseball...'

Phoebe cleared her throat loudly. 'I should stop there, Maggie, if I was you. Don't forget you're talking to a journalist. You don't want to be saying anything that you might later regret...' She giggled at Tori's mystified expression.

'I am perfectly aware of what I'm saying. I may be past it, but I've still got my marbles.' Maggie stuck out her chin and her eyes gleamed with humour. 'As do I still have several larger balls. Bigger ones than marbles, I mean. All around the house. Everywhere.'

Tori gave her a bemused look, shook her head and said in a staged whisper to Phoebe, 'Is it best I don't ask?'

'Definitely best.'

'I'm not deaf either,' Maggie said, and they all laughed.

'Seriously though,' Tori said, in a comment directed at Maggie, 'I won't put anything on record you'd rather I didn't. And you can see the feature before it goes to print.'

Maggie dipped her head in acknowledgement.

One of the least photogenic dogs currently at Puddleduck Farm was a brindle Staffie cross with eczema. 'People take one look at him, see he has a skin condition and decide against it,' Maggie explained. 'It doesn't help that it gets worse when he's stressed. And seeing strangers gets him stressed. I know the feeling,' she added, stroking the dog's head with gentle fingers.

'What's his name?' Tori asked.

'Handsome,' Maggie said without a trace of irony.

'We could focus on that,' Phoebe said, writing it down on her pad. She was taking notes to go with each animal they featured, as she had a little bit of a head start on who was who. 'Also, are you sure Duncan's tried everything? There's a lot of new stuff for eczema on the market?'

'He's tried two or three different potions. And there's a shampoo that's good, but the eczema always comes back. I probably don't bath him as much as I should.' She looked worried again.

Phoebe couldn't imagine it was easy getting the solid-looking Staffie into the bath on a regular basis – the bath was in an upstairs room at the farmhouse – especially if Handsome didn't want to be bathed. And she hadn't met many dogs who were keen on a dip in clean water.

'I'll have a look at what's available and we can try some other things if you like?' She kept her voice non-committal. She didn't want to tread on Duncan Petwell's toes or to ruffle Maggie's pride again.

But, to her relief, the old lady seemed to be in agreement.

Another unexpected bonus, Phoebe was realising, was that she was getting a much more in-depth look at the residents by writing up the details of each one. She had got to know various animals a little bit when she'd come and helped to clean them out and feed them, but it hadn't been in this kind of detail. There had never been a lot of time for chat.

After they'd done the dogs, they went on to the cats. There were four pretty kittens that Phoebe hadn't realised her grandmother had. They were in the haybarn in the enclosure that Jemima had been in while she recovered.

'Someone asked me to rehome their mother a few weeks ago,' Maggie said. 'But failed to mention she was carrying kitties. I didn't realise until it was too late. So they're in here where I can see them. They'll be ready to go soon.' She paused. 'We can put them in the magazine if you like? I've already got a card in the Post Office and Duncan's place. I can usually rehome kittens.'

Tori took some shots of the kittens and their mother, a pretty tabby called Myra.

'Duncan spays all the newcomers,' Maggie told them. 'She'll be done as soon as she's finished with this litter.'

Phoebe spotted a ginger feline prowling along a beam across the barn roof

'You may have trouble catching that one,' Maggie said, following her gaze. 'He's got a touch of the devil in him. He'll bite you as soon as look at you.'

The ginger cat, as if aware that he was the focus of their attention, stopped where he was on the beam, swished his tail from side to side and let out a plaintive meow.

'Don't let that fool you.' Maggie glanced at him – a look that was a mixture of admiration and regret. 'He's half tiger, half cat. I saw him despatch a rat once. It didn't stand a chance against Saddam. I dread him ever getting ill,' she added. 'No sane vet would go near him.'

'I'm sure Phoebe would be happy to sort him out, wouldn't you?' Tori said, flicking Phoebe a challenging look. She knew all about Phoebe's first day at Marchwood.

'Of course,' Phoebe replied, metaphorically crossing everything – fingers, toes and legs – in the hope that she would never be called upon to treat the ferocious Saddam. 'Although I wouldn't want to tread on Duncan's toes, obviously.'

Maggie dashed this hope with her next sentence. 'Duncan won't go near him. He's got more sense.'

23

They came out of the barn, blinking a little as their eyes adjusted to the April sunshine. 'Shall we go up to the neddies?' Maggie asked them, giving the sky a quick glance. 'While the weather's still half decent.'

They trudged up to the big field, accompanied by the ever-faithful Buster and his sidekick, Tiny.

'I don't think you're going to be able to rehome Tiny, are you?' Phoebe said to her grandmother as they walked. 'Buster would be heartbroken.'

'I know. Although if he's staying, he'll have to curb his appetite. He's eating me out of house and home.'

'I bet,' Phoebe said, silently pledging to redouble her efforts on the animal sponsorship front.

Maggie's remarks about subsidising the upkeep of the animals and farm from her savings still worried her. Hopefully, lots of people would see Tori's feature. *New Forest Views* had a big circulation. Phoebe made a note on her pad to include an address or account for donations. Maybe they could set up a special PayPal account.

They had just reached the five-bar gate that led into the donkey field and she could see the new line of fencing opposite them.

The donkeys, led by Roxy, came trotting across the field to greet them. Diablo even broke into a canter for a few strides.

'That'll make a nice shot,' Tori said, in satisfaction, as she clicked away. 'Donkeys are very photogenic. So who have we got here then?'

Maggie made the introductions. 'It would be nice to find out who this fellow belongs to,' she said, rubbing Diablo under his chin while he closed his eyes in blissful contentment.

'He seems to think it's you,' Tori remarked conversationally.

Phoebe agreed. The animals were her grandmother's life. That had become more and more obvious as they'd walked around the shelter. They all loved her, even the ones who didn't like people like Saddam, drew into her orbit when she was nearby.

They had almost finished taking pictures and were so engrossed in the donkeys that none of them realised they had company until they heard the child's voice.

'Hello. What are you doing?'

Phoebe glanced round and saw they'd been joined by the boy she'd seen on the terrace of Beechbrook House. 'Archie?' she said in surprise. 'What on earth are you doing here?'

'I came to see the donkeys.' His face was lit up. Just as it had been when she'd first seen him. His intense dark eyes met hers. He pointed back behind him. 'I came through the woods. I often come to see them.'

'Shouldn't you be at school?' Maggie asked, looking anxiously up towards the belt of woodland that shielded Beechbrook House.

'It's Sunday,' he said, his voice surprised.

'No, I meant the other times. You said you often came. Does your father know you're here?'

'No.' The boy's face clouded a little. He moved closer to stroke

Diablo's neck. 'He's so cute. He's my favourite. I call him Puzzle, like the donkey in Narnia.'

'Puzzle?' Phoebe glanced at Tori.

'He was a donkey in *The Chronicles of Narnia* – you know, of the Lion, the witch and the wardrobe fame. Good to hear it's still being read by kids.'

Tori was a mine of information, particularly when it came to cultural references. She was brilliant at quizzes.

'I didn't read the book,' Archie corrected. 'I saw it on TV when Emilia was phoning her friends.'

Who was Emilia? Phoebe wondered, but before anyone had time to ask, Maggie spoke again.

'We need to tell your father that you're here. He'll be worried.'

'He won't. He's working.' Archie sounded very sure of himself. 'He's always working and Emilia says I'm old enough to make my own entertainment.'

'Is Emilia your sister?' Phoebe asked.

'No, she looks after me. I don't have a sister.'

'Where's your mother?' Phoebe bent down to the child's level. He was so serious and intense. More like a miniature adult than a child.

'My mother is at the Knightwood Cemetery in a mos... mauser... mausey...' He broke off, clearly struggling with the word. 'My mother is dead,' he finished politely and turned back to the donkey.

Phoebe felt her heart contract as she stood up. Bless his little cotton socks. She glanced at Tori, who looked shocked, and Maggie, who was shaking her head. They were both obviously as blown away as she was by this confidence so innocently shared. 'I can take him back,' she told them. 'I think I know which way he came.' She turned back to Archie. 'I think we should probably check that it's OK with your dad for you to be here,' she said. 'In case he is worried.'

'OK.' He sounded reluctant. 'Am I trespassing?'

'No, love,' Phoebe said. She held out her hand and, after a couple of moments' hesitation, Archie took it, then almost immediately he let go again, for just long enough to pat Diablo, before coming back to her and trustingly slipping his fingers into hers.

Phoebe felt warmed. She didn't have much contact with kids, but Archie had opened a door in her heart. For the first time in her life she thought, maybe I do have a maternal instinct after all.

They set off across the field back up towards the woods. Now Archie had started talking, he couldn't seem to stop.

'What's Puzzle's real name?' was his first question.

Phoebe was about to say Diablo, but she stopped herself just in time because she was worried he might ask what Diablo meant. She definitely didn't want to explain that, but neither did she want to lie.

'No one really knows,' she said, 'because he just turned up one day. He was a lost donkey. My grandmother is still trying to find his proper owner.'

'Is your grandmother the very old lady?'

'Yes, that's right.' She tried to imagine what Maggie must look like through a child's eyes.

'My maternal grandmother is a very old lady,' Archie said solemnly, 'and my paternal grandmother died before I was born. She and my mother are together now in heaven.' He looked up at Phoebe and again she felt a jolt of compassion. All of the privileges in the world and yet he sounded so very alone. 'Grandma Claudia is also at Knightwood Cemetery where we go to visit Mother. I don't really know how they can be in two places at once. But my father says I will understand one day. Do you think I will?'

Phoebe was relieved when he didn't wait for an answer. He let go of her hand suddenly and ran to look at a patch of yellow meadow flowers on their left.

'What are these flowers?'

As she caught up with him, he bent over for a closer look and so did she.

'Cowslip, I think. Pretty aren't they.'

'Yes.' He cupped the blooms in his fingers. 'Are these the ones that tell you if you like butter when you hold them up to your chin?'

'I think that's buttercups,' Phoebe said, remembering the old wives' tale. 'I expect we could find some buttercups and try it?'

'No need,' Archie said. 'I already know I like butter.'

They were near the woodland now and he skipped ahead of her, switching suddenly between adult and child. Between the trees, she could see patches of bluebells. As they got closer, she could make out more and more and then they were on the very edges, looking in and it was impossible not to gasp. The entire woodland floor was alight with the blue flowers and their faintly sweet scent filled the air. They shone with that strange blue luminescence that was almost unearthly.

'Wow,' Phoebe said, forgetting for a moment who she was with. 'That has to be one of the most beautiful sights in the world.'

'My father said it's as if the sky has fallen down,' Archie said, grabbing her hand again and looking up at her with those intense dark eyes. 'He also says I'm not allowed to pick them because they are a protected species. Is that the real truth?'

'I think it is,' Phoebe replied. She wasn't used to spending time with children. None of her friends had children of Archie's age. But there was something very appealing about Archie, who seemed to flit from miniature adult to precocious child to total innocent.

He was hunkering down again, and she saw that he had his eyes closed as he breathed in the bluebells' scent.

Phoebe joined him. The woodland felt magical, as if they had stumbled into some enchanted place which was totally devoid of human noise but alive with the sounds of nature – birdsong and the rustling of a faint breeze through the branches of the trees, which were mostly silver birch, but there were some old oaks too. A paradise, not usually accessible to humankind. Phoebe wouldn't have been at all surprised to see fairies or elves dancing through the bluebells.

'Hey?' A woman's voice cut across the air and the spell was broken.

Phoebe glanced up to see that a petite, blonde-haired figure was approaching them. She was on the path that led through the trees and her whole demeanour was of annoyance, which became more apparent as she got closer. She was wearing tight white jeans and a dark jacket and her hair was tied up in a high ponytail, which swung from side to side as she stomped. She couldn't have been more than twenty-five, Phoebe guessed, but she looked very cross.

'Uh-oh,' Archie said under his breath.

Phoebe suddenly felt very vulnerable. It wasn't really surprising that the woman, who she guessed must be Emilia, was angry. She was, to all intents and purposes, trespassing again. She was quite relieved that it wasn't Rufus they'd bumped into.

She waited until the woman was close before taking advantage of the fact that she was clearly out of breath. 'I do apologise,' she said. 'We were just on our way back.'

'Through our woods!' Emilia's eyebrows rose in haughty semi-circles. 'It is private property.' She looked English, but she had a very slight accent – maybe German, Phoebe wasn't quite sure. 'What were you doing here in the beginning?'

'I'm Phoebe Dashwood. I'm your neighbour. I—'

'You thought you would walk to our property and look at pretty *glockenblumen. Ja*?' Her eyes flashed fire.

'No, I did not.' Phoebe felt her hackles rise. 'If you could just let me finish.'

Emilia stopped talking, pursed her lips and folded her arms and

Phoebe realised suddenly that she couldn't very easily explain without getting Archie into serious trouble with this woman, who she was beginning to dislike more and more by the second.

On the other hand, she really should say something about Archie visiting the donkeys. She took a deep breath.

Archie was now focusing intently on a hoverfly buzzing around a bluebell. But as if he had read her mind, he shot her a beseeching look and she knew she couldn't do it. She couldn't drop him in it.

'I'm going back now,' she said. 'I was just worried that Archie seemed to be on his own.'

'Archie is on his own in his own back garden,' the woman mocked. 'Not a major problem, I think. But you are trespassing.' Phoebe was finding her attitude increasingly annoying. 'Maybe if you have urgent need to visit us here again, you use the drive like normal person. *Ja?*'

'I will,' Phoebe replied, gritting her teeth because the urge to react to Emilia's rudeness was so strong. 'Bye, Archie,' she said and the child turned back towards her.

There was the tiniest of smiles on his face now that only she could see. And Phoebe felt as though she'd been played somehow. But she was still glad she hadn't told Emilia his secret.

As she turned around and retraced her steps out of the bluebell wood, Phoebe could still hear Emilia berating Archie. Although he seemed to be giving as good as he got.

A few moments later, she was back in the Holts' meadow. As she walked down the gentle slope towards the donkey field, where she could still see Tori and Maggie with the donkeys, she felt as though some of the sunshine had left the day.

✳ ✳ ✳

'So you didn't see the lord of the manor then?' Tori asked her when she'd explained to them both what had happened. 'That's a shame. I'd like to know what he looks like. Lord Alfred's quite the recluse and his son takes after him from what I gather.' Her eyes gleamed with speculation as she glanced back up the slope towards the woodland.

'No, and I probably should have gone round to see him,' Phoebe replied. 'But that woman was so obnoxious. She made me feel as though I was some lowly peasant. She was about four inches shorter than me, and she still managed to look down her nose. How does that work?'

'The class system is still alive and kicking in England – however much we think it isn't,' Tori said. 'We tend to think that the British peerage is an antiquated term, don't we, but it's just better hidden than it used to be. It's a whole different world behind those locked-away estates – run by posh nannies and groundsmen.'

For a few moments, they all glanced up the slope.

Maggie, who had remained very quiet throughout the conversation, cleared her throat. 'That's as maybe, but I think we probably do need to tell them that Archie was down here looking at the donkeys. It sounded as though it's not the first time and I hate the thought of him getting injured. He must pick his moments; I've never seen him in that field before.'

'No.' Phoebe had a horrible feeling she knew what was coming next.

Maggie was looking at her speculatively. 'I could go, of course, but as you've already met Rufus, perhaps it might be better if you did?'

'You're a dark horse. You never told me you'd met him.' Tori's mouth had dropped open. 'When was this?'

'It was when the donkeys escaped. It was a very brief meeting. Two very brief meetings actually.' Phoebe told her what had happened. She could feel herself going pink. Not that Tori seemed to notice. 'The Holts are Maggie's landlords,' she added. 'You know that they bought the land the dairy farm was on when the herd was sold. So we really do need to keep on the right side of them.'

'I get it.' Tori's voice was serious. 'Wow, you definitely need to go up and see your friend, Rufus. He needs to know his child's been fraternising with donkeys.' She winked and added, 'Not to mention peasants.' She packed up her cameras into the bag. 'We're about done here, aren't we? I'll come with you and give you some moral support.'

Phoebe's heart sank. Facing Rufus again was bad enough, and having Tori, who wasn't known for her tact and diplomacy come along to gawp at him made her feel even more pressured. But she couldn't think of a single way of objecting that wouldn't sound at worst rude or at best unkind. Especially in view of the fact that the only reason Tori was here was to help Puddleduck Pets raise its profile, not to mention extra funds to help her grandmother.

'Well come on then,' Tori prompted. 'What are we waiting for?'

24

Once again, Phoebe drove around the road way, past the high wall to the front entrance of Beechbrook House and Tori chattered as they went. 'I wonder if we'll see the old man. I've never met a lord before. Who opened the door to you last time?'

'Rufus Holt. That was scary enough. How does the lord of the manor thing work anyway? Are they both lords or does the title only get passed down once the last lord is dead?'

'They're two different things,' Tori replied. 'Lord of the manor is an old title that goes back to Anglo-Saxon times and it refers to the landowner of a big estate. I think you can actually buy lord of the manor titles. But you can also be a lord as in a member of the British peerage.'

'How do you know all that stuff?' Phoebe glanced at her, impressed, and Tori tapped her nose.

'It's my job. I'm a journalist.' She laughed. 'Also I interviewed a lord once for the mag and he was very informative. I'm pretty sure that Lord Alfred Holt is a member of the British peerage. He inherited the title from his father, which I think means he has to die to pass it on to his son.'

'Does that mean he can sit in the House of Lords?' Phoebe asked, not because she was terribly interested but to take her mind of the encounter ahead, which she was dreading.

'It used to, but that was changed when Tony Blair was in power. So I'm not sure now. It's complicated.'

'It sounds it,' Phoebe remarked, feeling a strange sense of déjà vu as she drove up the long driveway and parked beside the fountain with the tasteless cherubs.

'It looks like you also get to live in a pretty cool house,' Tori said, glancing up at the mansion. 'What an amazing place.'

'Yes,' Phoebe said as she and Tori got out and walked towards the big wooden front door.

She knew Maggie was right, and that this was the responsible thing to do, but she had a bad feeling about this. She was pretty sure that Rufus was going to be even less pleased that his son had been making regular trips down to see the donkeys than he'd been about the donkeys' impromptu visit to his terrace. After all, if the donkeys hadn't escaped, chances were that Archie wouldn't even have known they existed.

'Don't look so worried,' Tori said, shooting her a glance. 'Lords go to the toilet, same as the rest of us. Imagine Rufus with his trousers down, sitting on the toilet.'

The door opened on the word toilet and they were face to face with Emilia, who looked less than happy to see them.

She flicked her blonde ponytail back and looked, if anything, even haughtier than the last time Phoebe had seen her. 'You! Again. Are you lost? Did you wish to see more of *glockenblumen*?'

'I would like to speak to Rufus Holt please?' Phoebe said politely. 'Is he available?'

'No, he is *not*.'

'Yes he is,' said a voice from behind her. A surprisingly calm voice in the circumstances, Phoebe thought. 'Thank you, Emilia. I can deal with this.'

The nanny made a tutting sound, but she moved reluctantly aside and Phoebe had a brief impression of her flouncing away and through a door deeper into the house before Rufus took her place in the doorway.

He was dressed more casually than when she'd seen him last time, in old jeans and a sweatshirt that had seen better days – if she hadn't known he was a wealthy landowner with a real-life lord for a father, she would have assumed he was an ordinary bloke enjoying a Sunday at home. Shabby was the word that best described him now – although he still had that presence she'd noticed before. The way he moved and spoke was very controlled. Almost as if he was acting out a role that wasn't his normal persona. Maybe it was the 'dealing with the peasants' persona suggested a provocative voice in Phoebe's head.

'How can I help you?'

Was he going to keep them standing on the doorstep? Phoebe had no idea of the etiquette of calling on any type of lord, whether they held a title of peerage or not.

Tori who was less backward in coming forward said, 'It might be easier to talk inside. It's about your son.'

'I see.' His lips tightened and after another moment's hesitation he gestured them into the wide hall and through the first door on the left, which was obviously an office.

The large room, with its high ceilings, was stacked with furniture, but it didn't look cramped. A long dark wood desk took up one wall – there were half a dozen wooden filing cabinets on another. The only thing that shrieked lord of the manor was an ancestral portrait in a brushed gold antique frame. It showed an unsmiling man with sideburns, wearing a dark suit against a dark background. It looked as though it needed a good clean, Phoebe thought. The only bit that was really clear was the man's face and she was just trying to make up her mind if he bore any resemblance to Rufus when Rufus gestured them to sit. Then he took a seat opposite them. Not behind the desk but in front of it.

'You said this was about my son?'

'He came down to see the donkeys today,' Phoebe said, deciding to respond in the same direct manner as he'd addressed her. 'He told me that he's been before – although we haven't been aware of this. I thought I should let you know.'

'But you didn't think his nanny could deal with this?' There was the faintest of questions in his voice and now there was a pulse beating in his forehead. Phoebe had the distinct impression that she'd annoyed him somehow, but she had no idea why.

'Er yes, but I...'

'She wanted to let you know personally,' Tori filled in smoothly.

'And now you have. Which I appreciate, but you really could have said this to Emilia. I will, of course, make sure it doesn't happen again.'

'He would be very welcome to visit the donkeys whenever he likes.' Phoebe found her voice. 'I just think it would be safer if he told you and us that he was coming. So he could be supervised. They are very gentle creatures, but I would hate it if he got kicked. Or injured. Accidents sometimes happen.'

He was standing up. 'I'm aware of this. I will speak to him.'

The meeting was clearly over. Rufus had gone to the door and was holding it open.

Phoebe stood up too. 'Thank you,' she said, because it seemed impolite to leave without saying anything.

He didn't reply. He gestured them ahead of him, back the few steps to the front door, opened it for long enough for them to go through it and then closed it firmly behind them.

Tori stared at Phoebe open-mouthed. 'What the hell was that! Is he the most arrogant, rude man you've ever met or what? No wonder he's a flaming recluse. He couldn't wait to get us out the door, could he?' She paused for breath. 'Or am I overreacting?'

'I don't think you are overreacting. He was certainly keen to get rid of us.' Phoebe glanced back at the heavy oak door.

'What a nob,' Tori said, giving a little shudder.

'Maybe he has some kind of social phobia,' Phoebe said thoughtfully. 'Maybe it runs in the family. Maybe that's why he's a recluse.' He was certainly a moody beggar. He'd seemed quite humble when he'd apologised to her last time, but there had been no sign of that today. He'd been polite enough when he'd invited them in – although even that had been in response to Tori's prompting, she recalled. But as soon as she'd mentioned donkeys, things had deteriorated. 'Maybe he's just really overprotective of his son,' Phoebe continued, as they got back in the car. According to the dashboard clock, it was barely five minutes since they'd arrived.

'Maybe you're just too nice.' Tori was glancing around them. 'This is an amazing place, though, isn't it? Bar those awful cherubs. What I wouldn't give to get a proper look at the rest of the house.'

'I don't think there's much chance of that.' Phoebe pressed the power button to start the car. 'Although I think you're being a bit unfair about my overprotective theory. There's a distinct lack of women in that household. That poor little boy has no mother and no grandmother.' Apart from the imperious Emilia and she didn't seem to be the maternal type.

'Their bodies are probably buried under the terrace,' Tori said. 'That Knightwood Cemetery story they fed Archie is probably just a cover. My theory is they were either murdered by their husbands or they both committed suicide when the utter misery of being married to a nob got too much. I mean, think about it. It can't be much fun living in that great gloomy house with those moody men?'

'You should be a fiction writer not a journalist,' Phoebe said, smiling despite herself.

'Oh, it's not such a great leap as you might think,' Tori retorted. 'There's a bit of fiction in every fact and a bit of fact in every fiction.'

She was silent for a few moments and Phoebe knew she was considering whether or not she should say what was on her mind now. She had a vaguely reflective look on her face.

Then finally she made up her mind. 'Taking the moodiness and the nobbishness out of it though,' she began. 'He is quite hot, isn't he? Our lord of the manor. In a brooding hero cum Heathcliff kind of way.'

'Nobbishness isn't a word,' Phoebe said mildly.

'Journalists are allowed to make up words. It's practically a job requirement. Anyway, never mind about that. Do you agree with me about the hot?'

'No,' Phoebe said. 'I don't. I thought he looked very ordinary today.'

'He had very ordinary clothes on – I'll give you that. But that's a bit of a feature with rich people, isn't it? They often have safety pins holding their jeans together.'

'I didn't notice any safety pins.'

'He didn't have any. I'm just using that as an example. But they weren't cheap jeans. They were Spoke. Did you notice?'

'No.' Phoebe paused for effect and added, 'I wasn't looking below his waist. Unlike you, it would seem!'

'You're definitely not ready to start dating again, are you?' Tori said wistfully.

'Correct,' Phoebe replied. And if she did ever start dating again, it certainly wouldn't be with Rufus Holt!

* * *

Inside Beechbrook House, Rufus closed his eyes and took a few moments. It was all he could do not to sag against the heavy oak door. It had taken every bit of his self-control to hold it together. Had he known what they'd wanted, he would have let Emilia deal with it, but the truth was, he had heard Phoebe's voice at the door and some impulse had made him curious to see her again.

It had been a surprise to see the other woman, the more bolshy one. She was everything Rufus disliked in a female: loud-voiced, pushy and curious – her eyes had been everywhere when she'd walked through his door. And things had deteriorated when the subject of the donkeys came up. But the mention of donkeys hadn't triggered a full-scale PTSD attack, this time. Thank God for small mercies.

He hadn't yet done anything that his father had suggested. He hadn't booked a session with a therapist and he hadn't agreed that Archie could learn to ride, but he knew he couldn't put off either of these things for very much longer.

But first, he would have to sit down with Archie and talk to him. He'd had no idea that his son was sneaking out to see the animals and the thought of it horrified him.

With a small sigh, he went in search of Emilia and told her what had happened.

She listened, although he could see that she wanted to interrupt. As soon as he finished, she said, 'I saw this woman with Archie looking at...' She shrugged. 'I don't remember English word. *Glockenblumen*... blue flowers.'

'Bluebells,' he supplied.

'She did not say Archie had visited her donkeys. Pfff! Why did she not tell me this? I think she just trespass in wood.'

'I've no idea why she didn't tell you. But she said this is what's been happening. And it needs to stop. It's dangerous for Archie to do this. You understand?'

'Of course. I am so sorry. I didn't know he was not on property. I think he is playing in wood all the time.'

'You aren't responsible for his every move,' Rufus said wearily. 'But I will speak to him. I will explain why it's not acceptable to go unaccompanied.'

'You want me to accompany him to do this?' she asked.

He shook his head. He wasn't ready to agree to that just yet. 'Let me speak to him. Where is he?'

'On terrace. He is practising the chess.'

'OK. I'll find him.'

Rufus went to look and saw that she was right. Archie had the board set up and was focusing intently. It looked as though he'd just started a game. Rufus had been worried when he'd first realised that Archie was playing chess alone, but that was before his father had told him that he'd suggested it.

'It's how I did it,' Alfred had told him. 'It's a good way of learning – and it teaches him autonomy. There won't always be people available to play.'

This hadn't entirely assuaged Rufus's feeling of guilt. Archie already did far too many things alone for his liking. It would be better when Archie went away to school. Maybe he should revisit his decision about that too. He'd heard that things were different these days. Better. Maybe it was time to let Archie go. He'd have company of his own age then and not just during lesson time. It was rare that Archie wanted to invite any friends home. He didn't seem to even have many friends. Not close ones anyway. Rufus wished Rowena was still here so they could discuss it together.

He agonised with himself as he stepped out onto the terrace. He stood watching his son, but not interrupting until Archie muttered, 'Bishop C4' under his breath and moved the bishop across the board.

Parenting was a bit like chess, Rufus thought fleetingly.

Although that was probably oversimplifying parenting. But one thing he did know as he looked at his son's small hunched shoulders was that it was getting increasingly hard to be both mother and father to his child.

25

One of the immediate positive effects from the feature – and this was before it even came out – was that Phoebe discovered a possible treatment for Handsome's eczema. They'd just had a new patient join the practice, a Chinese Shar Pei called Billy, and he'd been booked in for an appointment to discuss his dermatitis.

His owner, a well-dressed woman with an American accent, explained that her previous vet had started Billy on a course of immunotherapy which had sorted things out. 'We had thought it was eczema originally,' she drawled. 'But then we had him allergy tested and it turned out to be ectopic dermatitis. The immunotherapy is working wonders. It's been like a miracle cure.'

Phoebe checked Billy's vet records, which had been transferred from his old practice, and agreed they should continue the same treatment. Billy's owner had showed her some photos of Billy before he'd started his treatment and the change was indeed miraculous. Phoebe discussed it with Seth and Alison and they both agreed it was worth a shot for Handsome too.

'We'd have to send away blood tests,' Alison said, 'for the allergy testing side of things, but we can do that. It's definitely worth a try. Is he insured? The tests aren't cheap.'

'No, he's currently homeless – well, he is technically – he's one of the Puddleduck dogs, but I can cover it, don't worry about that.'

'We'll do everything at cost our end,' Seth said. 'That's our policy for registered charities.'

'Thanks.' Phoebe didn't even know if Maggie was a registered charity. She somehow doubted that her grandmother would have given the official registration bit much thought.

* * *

Maggie confirmed this when she was asked. 'It was something I meant to get round to when Eddie was here. He said it was a good idea when we did the animal sponsoring malarkey, but it slipped my mind.'

'I could help you with it,' Phoebe offered. 'And while we're on the "animal sponsoring malarkey", can I run the photos and write-ups past you before I print them out. I thought I could print them on A4 sheets to send out. That's what you did before, wasn't it?'

Her grandmother nodded. It was the Friday after the photo shoot and Phoebe had called in after work, partly to get blood samples from Handsome and partly to show Maggie the pictures Tori had taken.

Maggie was boiling up tripe for the dogs and its stench filled the kitchen.

'Can't you give them anything less smelly?' Phoebe asked.

'I could, but they love it. And it's cheap.' She gestured towards Buster and Tiny, who were both sitting in the middle of the kitchen with expectant looks on their faces.

Then she left the pot simmering on the stove, with the lid on thankfully, which helped contain the foul smell a bit, and now she and Phoebe were both sitting at the kitchen table.

Phoebe lifted out a plastic folder of pictures and began to lay them out. There was a superb one of Jemima slightly in profile to the camera, one beady eye looking their way and her beak partly open. There was also a fabulous one of Laila the retriever. Tori had caught the sun glinting off her gold coat and a look of hope in her eyes. She'd been hoping she'd get one of the treats in Phoebe's hand, but Tori said that to the punters it would look like she was hoping for a home.

She was right, Phoebe thought. It did. Tori's talent for catching exactly the right moment when she was taking photos had always filled her with admiration. It wasn't as if she took loads of shots either – she just had an unerring sense of timing. If she hadn't gone into journalism, she could probably have made a career from photography.

Mutley, the brown and white terrier, had also proved to be very photogenic. He looked cute – one ear up and one ear down. And the kittens in the barn were adorable. Tori had photographed them together and separately. It shouldn't be too much trouble to get them a home.

But the undoubted star of the show was Diablo. His brown shaggy head, with those cheeky brown eyes and white nose, was the epitome of cute. 'That'll make even the most hard-hearted of humans say, Ahh,' had been Tori's comment on that shot.

'He should be on TV,' Maggie said, smiling as she picked up the photo and studied it. 'What he couldn't sell with a face like that.'

Phoebe laughed. 'Hopefully, it will be seen by his real owner, but if it isn't, maybe someone will come forward to offer him a home – or at least sponsor him.'

'I think you could be right,' Maggie agreed.

Phoebe showed her the write-ups she'd done on each animal,

which had their names, photos and a brief description.

Diablo's said simply:

> Diablo was given shelter at Puddleduck Farm after a road accident in the forest. Thankfully, a kindly motorist drew his plight to our attention. Diablo is the friendliest fellow you could ever wish to meet, but also very cheeky. Sometimes we think he prefers the company of humans to his donkey friends. We hope that Diablo's owner might one day come forward to claim him, but if not, his forever home will be at Puddleduck.

'Do you think we should change Diablo's name?' Phoebe asked Maggie.

'Why?'

'I was thinking maybe something cuter like Ee-aw or Pickle. Or even Puzzle,' she added idly, remembering that's what Archie had called him.

'No, I don't. Diablo suits him perfectly.'

'I'm not sure about Saddam either,' Phoebe pressed. 'It's not the kind of name that would inspire people to rehome him, is it?'

Maggie snorted with mirth. 'Nothing about that crazy cat would inspire people to rehome him. His name's the least of his problems. Besides, you know I don't hold with all these PC names. When did it become an offence to call things what they are?' She had that stubborn look in her eyes that Phoebe knew so well. Maggie changed tack. 'Not all of them need to be rehomed, do they? I thought you said that was the point of the sponsorship. To raise money for the animals who can't be rehomed.'

'That's true, I did.' Phoebe knew there was no point in arguing with her grandmother when she had that look on her face. 'And on the subject of money, what do you think about amounts?'

'I think Eddie always did £1 per month or £11 a year if you paid up front.'

'That's ridiculous. It's nowhere near enough. It barely covers the postage and printing costs.'

'I guess it doesn't.' Maggie looked deflated. 'OK, what do you think we should say?'

'£3 a month or £36 a year if people pay up front,' Phoebe said promptly.

'That's three times as much! I don't want people to think I'm being greedy.'

'They won't. And you're not. You'd be lucky to get change from £3 if you buy a drink in the pub.'

'OK, if you really think that's fair.'

'I do. It costs a lot more than £3 a month to keep any of the animals. People aren't daft. They all know that.' Phoebe broke off. 'Is something burning?'

Maggie leapt to her feet. 'Oh dear, the tripe.' She raced back to the cooker to rescue it. 'It's just caught the bottom of the pan,' she yelped.

Phoebe put her hand over her nose as she went to help. Burning tripe was even more pungent than simmering tripe, if that were possible.

When they'd sorted that out, and had opened all the windows, they went back to the table. 'Talking of Diablo... Well, we weren't, but we were earlier,' Phoebe began. 'Have you had any more visits from the youngest Holt?'

'I don't think so. Although I probably wouldn't know, would I?' She hesitated. 'He's been on my mind though, Phoebe, I have to say.'

'Mine too. I keep thinking about him playing chess on his own.' There was something about Archie that had got under her skin and thinking of him in that big house without a female relative had left her reeling.

'I've been thinking about him reading the Narnia books. I used to read them to your mother when she was small? Did she read them to you?'

'They didn't have enough animals in for me,' Phoebe said. 'Most of the books I wanted to read when I was little involved animal heroes – dogs rescuing their families from disaster or cats raising the alarm when the house was on fire.'

Maggie sniffed disparagingly. 'Your average cat would run a mile at the first whiff of smoke. Cats are pragmatists.'

'That's true. But I was lucky enough to have the real thing, wasn't I? Frazier and I were so lucky to have the run of this place when we were growing up.' She hesitated. 'I suppose at least Archie does have the run of the Beechbrook estate. That's even bigger than our playground was.'

'But he doesn't have a brother or a sister, does he? So he comes down on his own to see my neddies. The Narnia books, by the way, are about escaping from the mundanity of your life through the back of a wardrobe to another more exciting world.'

'So you're saying that Archie's woods are like the wardrobe in Narnia.'

Maggie sighed. 'I don't know what I'm saying. Think of it as the ramblings of an old woman. I've been spending far too much time alone.'

Phoebe looked at her, surprised. Her grandmother rarely admitted to feeling lonely. 'You are still OK here though, aren't you?' she queried.

'Of course I'm OK.' Maggie shook herself brusquely as if shaking away her granddaughter's concerns. 'Didn't you say you wanted to take some of Handsome's blood. Shall we go and do that before it gets dark?'

'Yep. Let's do it.'

As they walked down to the kennels in the cooling evening,

Phoebe took a deep breath of the crystal-clear country air. On the horizon, the sun was setting, turning the sky into a sea of pink, blue, orange and gold. A cool breath of air tugged at Phoebe's hair which she hadn't let down from work yet.

The winds of change, she thought, with a little shiver of foreboding. She knew nothing stayed the same for ever, but she hated to think of a time when she wouldn't be able to walk across the land, her boots sinking into the ground underfoot, and look at that fabulous sunset. Maggie and her brusque, perceptive kindness and that amazing view had been there for the whole of her life. It didn't bear thinking about that there might come a day when it wasn't.

* * *

When she got back to Tori's at around nine, Phoebe could see from the street that the flat was in darkness. Tori had said she was going to be late. She had finally got to one of the dinner parties that was being hosted on the other side of the forest.

Part of the reason that Phoebe had gone straight to Puddleduck Farm from work was to avoid bumping into her flatmate, because she knew Tori would have tried to persuade her to go along at the last minute. Despite the fact she'd told her several times she wasn't interested. Tori wasn't very good at taking no for an answer, so it had been easier to just avoid her.

Phoebe felt slightly guilty as she parked and got out of her car. She was just heading past the off-licence towards the front door when a tall figure stepped out of the shadow of Tori's porch. For a heart-stopping moment, Phoebe thought she was about to be mugged. The man had deliberately kept out of sight until the last moment. But then she realised it was worse than that.

This was no mugger. It was Hugh.

26

Phoebe swore under her breath. 'You nearly gave me a heart attack. Why on earth didn't you phone me? What are you doing here anyway?' Adrenaline had flustered her thoughts and now it was making her gabble.

'That wasn't my intention.' He stepped back a pace. He wasn't wearing a coat, just a shirt and jacket as he did when he was working. She wondered how long he'd been standing there. 'But to answer your question,' he continued. 'I didn't think you'd speak to me if I phoned.'

That was true, but she wanted to see him even less.

'And what about my other question. What are you doing here?'

'I wanted to see you,' he said. As though it were obvious and the most natural thing in the world.

'After a four-month silence.'

'It's... just under four months,' he said. 'I believe my last text was sent on Christmas Day.'

'Oh yes, to wish me happy Christmas. That was very thoughtful of you in the circumstances.'

She hadn't realised she was still so angry with him, but she could hear it in her own voice. She was also in a quandary. She didn't want to let him into Tori's flat, particularly when Tori wasn't here, but neither did she want to speak to him out here.

Before she could decide on the best course of action, Hugh cleared his throat and put his hands in his pockets. 'Breaking up with you was a terrible mistake. It is one which I regret very much. In fact, it's the worst mistake I have ever made in my life. I know that now.'

Despite herself, Phoebe stared at him in disbelief. 'It's taken you four months – sorry, just under four months – to work this out, has it? What's happened? Did Cruella tire of you? Did she move on to another toy boy?'

'Phoebe, please give me the chance to explain.' He shifted and his face burned red.

'I don't need you to explain,' she said, shaking her head. 'I've moved on, Hugh. And you should do the same.' This was true, but she was also rattled by his presence.

'I've tried. But I can't get you out of my mind. Today I realised it was time I gave up trying and came to see you.'

'You've wasted your time.'

'Would it help you to know that Melissa and I never became lovers?'

His words stopped her in her tracks. When she'd seen them kissing underneath the mistletoe, her first thought had been that they already were lovers.

'I know that probably sounds like a line. But it's not. It's true.' He let out a sigh that was slightly shaky. 'If you'll just let me explain. I just want to tell you what happened. Please, Phoebe.'

'OK. You have fifteen minutes. But after that, you're gone, whether you're finished or not. Is that agreed?'

'A hundred per cent.' He spread his hands.

Still wondering if she was going to regret this, Phoebe let him in. He followed her upstairs.

'Did Mum tell you I was here?' she asked him, knowing it was unlikely Louella would have said anything without warning her.

'No. I took a guess. This was the first place I tried.'

She hated that she was so predictable.

In Tori's familiar kitchen, as she made the coffee, he waited to be asked to sit down and she was tempted not to ask him, knowing manners would keep him standing. But her own niceness precluded this.

'One coffee,' she said, putting it in front of him. 'Your fifteen minutes has started.'

'Thank you.' There was the tiniest of pauses before he started speaking. 'The thing with Melissa was friendship. I know that I said we'd connected – and we did. But it wasn't on a romantic level.' He rubbed at his forehead, looking suddenly as if his own thoughts bemused him. 'I had – have – a huge amount of admiration and respect for her, but it was for her work, her skill as a practitioner, as well as a businesswoman.'

Melissa had been skilled. Phoebe could accept that.

'I mistook our connection, our friendship and what was really a mutual admiration and respect, if you like, for something else.'

'You kissed her, Hugh. She kissed you back. That was a bit more than mutual admiration and respect.' Even though he was making it out to be oh-so innocent.

'I know. I crossed a line. Because I was drunk. We'd both been drinking.'

'You're saying that it's never happened again?'

'Um, no. I'm not.' He met her eyes. He did at least have the grace to blush. 'We did kiss after that occasion. Not very many times. We talked a lot. Like I told you, we'd connected, but it was not on a romantic level. Which is why we've never taken it further. We have never slept together.' He opened his hands. 'And that's the truth of it.' He dropped his gaze again. 'I know it sounds crazy and unbelievable.'

'You've got that right. It does.' She shook her head as she tried to take in what he was saying. None of it made sense. She couldn't believe that he would cause her all of that pain and anguish, let her uproot her entire life, give up her home, her job and their relationship, for absolutely no good reason.

'I didn't know what I was feeling, Phoebe. You left before I could get my head around any of it.'

'I am so sorry for reacting like a normal human being.'

He blinked. He looked ashamed. 'No, I didn't mean that. I didn't blame you for going. Of course not. I know I behaved really badly. But we never had the chance to talk. I didn't know what I was feeling then. I was so confused.'

'Hugh, two days afterwards, you told me on the phone that you and Melissa had been dating. That you'd been seeing her for some time. That you'd been lying about it.'

'I know, but I hadn't worked it out. You know how I am with feelings. I'm not good with them. I'm too buttoned up. I've been having therapy for the last four months. I'm starting to unravel it all.'

'You needed to have therapy to see how you felt about me? That's not very flattering, Hugh.' Why did she get flippant when she was boiling over with anger? She stood up, wanting him gone.

'Yes. Well, not just about you, obviously. I don't mean that.' He ran his hands through his hair, which had grown since she'd last seen him. He really did look stricken and if he'd have said all this to her four months ago, Phoebe had a feeling they might have been able to save their relationship. But it was too late. It was all far too late. 'There's something else,' he added. 'I've left the practice. I didn't think you'd take me seriously if I didn't. And I want you to know that I am serious. I know I'm in the wrong here, Phoebe, but I want you back. I'll do whatever it takes to prove my love for you.' He blinked rapidly. This was not a Hugh she had ever seen before. So unsure of himself. So insecure. 'The thing is, I now know you're the only woman I ever will love. That's what I wanted to tell you.'

She didn't say anything. Mostly because she couldn't think of a single thing to say. He'd shocked her to the core with this outpouring. In some ways, his admission felt worse than if he'd actually been having a full-on, no-holds-barred love affair. She'd meant that little to him that he could leave her for a work connection with another woman and then spend four months wondering whether it was worth coming to tell her.

The anger that had boiled up in her had already peaked. She felt tearful now and no way was she going to cry in front of him.

'I think you should go,' she said as he looked at her, and for the first time she felt as though she was seeing real emotion on his face.

'But I want to be with you.'

'No you don't.'

'I do.' Hugh leaped to his feet, almost knocking the kitchen chair over in his haste. 'I'll prove it to you. Just give me a few weeks.'

'I can't, Hugh.'

'Why not? Is there someone else?'

'There isn't anyone else.' She would have liked to yell that he'd hurt her so much that the thought of putting herself through it again with someone else was the very last thing in her head, but she felt too raw.

They stood with a few feet between them in Tori's bright kitchen. Hugh's face was pale and she knew he was struggling to hold himself together. But she was shivering inside and she just needed him out of here. She needed to process everything that had just happened.

To her relief, he didn't try to hug her or even take a step closer.

'Thank you for hearing me out,' he said. 'I appreciate that. Whatever happens next.'

They walked in tandem towards the kitchen door and she followed him downstairs to the main door. Neither of them said anything else. She just shut him out and hugged her arms around herself. Her heart was beating very fast and she felt slightly sick. It was ten past nine. It had taken less than quarter of an hour for Hugh to dismantle her for the second time in less than six months.

In some ways, this time had been worse than the first.

* * *

Phoebe was still sitting at the kitchen table when Tori came in just after ten thirty. She had got out her laptop and was working on Maggie's adoption certificates. It had felt like a good idea to focus on something that wasn't Hugh. Something that required her complete concentration. They had decided to make them fairly basic. A nice colour picture, a description, a postcard of the animal, which Phoebe planned to do on Vistaprint (how hard could it be?), and two updates a year, both on the specific adopted animal and on Puddleduck Pets.

Tori bounced in looking very cheerful. She'd clearly had a great evening. 'Hola,' she called from the doorway. 'You still up. I expected you to be tucked up in bed. You should have come, Phoebe. Honestly. I've had such a laugh.' She broke off suddenly. 'Have you been crying? Hey. Are you OK?' Her demeanour changed as she came across to the table. 'No you're not, are you? What is it? Is someone ill?'

'I had a visit from Hugh.' She told Tori what had happened and Tori's expression grew more and more incredulous as she went on.

'That's unbelievable,' she said when Phoebe had finished. 'Did he really think he could just show up, spin you a line and persuade you to go back to him.'

'I don't think it was a line. That's the thing. Hugh has always been "buttoned up", as he put it, emotionally. He had an awful childhood.'

'Lots of people have bad childhoods. It doesn't give them licence to be totally selfish bastards for the rest of their lives.' Tori's eyes flashed fire. 'Don't start feeling sorry for him, Phoebe.'

'I'm not. I don't.' She wasn't entirely sure this was true. His visit had left her reeling.

Tori put her elbows on the kitchen table and her chin in her hands. 'Sorry, I'm not having a go at you. I'm just astounded that he had the audacity. How do you feel?'

'Most of the time he was here, I felt angry. It sounds weird, but I'd almost have preferred it if he had been having a raging affair with her. That would have been some justification for blowing my life to pieces. The fact that he's been calmly sitting up there in London thinking things through and then getting bloody therapy to work out what his feelings were has made me feel worse, I think.'

Phoebe felt a tear run down her cheek.

'Oh, lovely, I bet it has.' Tori reached for Phoebe's hand across the table. 'The stupid, stupid man.'

'He's always been stupid when it comes to feelings. No, stupid isn't the right word. Stunted. Emotionally stunted. It was one of the things that worried me about our relationship. We talked about him getting therapy before so he could learn to open up about his feelings. But he wouldn't have it. He didn't think it would benefit him.'

'But now he's seen the light and come to tell you about it.' Tori's eyes were cynical.

'I know it looks like that. But if there was one thing I could have changed about our relationship, this would have been it.'

'Are you considering taking him back?'

Phoebe hesitated. 'No. No, I'm not. It's weird, but the one thing I did know when he was talking was that it was too late for us. I have moved on. Not in the sense that I want another relationship or anything. I'm definitely not ready for that yet. But I've moved on in here.' She touched her heart. 'As a person. As a woman. I'm happy working with Seth and the team. I'm happy seeing Maggie on a regular basis. And I'm happy living here with you. Even though I know it's not for ever. I mean, you might want a relationship and having me here would cramp your style.'

Something flashed in Tori's eyes when she said that, and just for a second Phoebe thought, *Oh my God, I've hit the nail on the head. She thinks that too.*

But nothing was said. At least nothing was said then.

27

Tori's feature, when it came out in May, looked very impressive. The publication date coincided with a Sunday lunch at Phoebe's parents to celebrate her dad's fifty-sixth birthday, which was on the twentieth, so Phoebe took several magazines along so she could show everyone.

Maggie, Frazier, Alexa and Phoebe had all been invited to the midday feast and Alexa and Frazier had gone early, ostensibly to help with the cooking, but really, Phoebe suspected, so that Louella and Alexa could discuss the forthcoming baby. Louella was almost as excited about it as her daughter-in-law.

Phoebe had picked up Maggie on her way through, who'd been grumbling all the way over about the fact that she couldn't eat big meals in the middle of the day and she hoped there wasn't too much food.

'You don't have to eat it all, do you?' Phoebe told her as they got out of the car at Old Oak Way.

Maggie just scowled and didn't answer. It was unlike her to be so tetchy. Phoebe wondered if she was still thinking about Hugh's visit. Aside from Tori, Maggie was the only person who knew Hugh had turned up again. Phoebe hadn't told anyone else. She was trying to put it out of her head. She hadn't heard any more from him, which had been a relief. With a bit of luck, he'd have gone back to London, although she knew he did have friends in this area. It was one of the links that had joined them when they'd first met and had been doing the 'what else do we have in common?' conversation.

Not that Maggie had given her too much of an opinion on Hugh – although she had agreed with Tori that people shouldn't blame their childhoods for their shortcomings in adulthood.

'It's up to you, of course,' she'd said. 'But it's easier to go through life with a partner who is beside you, on an equal footing. A mature adult.' Which Hugh isn't, her eyes had clearly said.

On the good news front, Handsome's test results had come back and he'd proved to be a good candidate for the immunotherapy, which they'd now started. Phoebe had high hopes for Handsome. Unlike Hugh, his future looked very promising.

She forced her mind back to the present as she and Maggie went into the house and there was a lot of kissing and hugging and Phoebe felt warmed, as she always did when she was surrounded by her family.

Alexa, who was now five months pregnant and displaying her baby bump proudly, looked happy and glowing, the picture of a content mother-to-be.

'Although it wasn't so good last month,' she told Phoebe and Maggie when she opened the door to them. 'But the morning sickness seems to have run its course, thank goodness.'

For a while after they arrived, everyone talked babies. Frazier was full of entertaining facts about old wives' tales that told you the gender of your baby.

'One of the best known is the wedding ring on the string one,' he told them all. 'You tie your wedding ring to a long piece of string and dangle it over Mum's tummy.' He winked at Alexa. 'If it circles, you're having a girl. If it goes back and forth, you're having a boy.'

'What did yours do?' Phoebe asked, knowing he was longing for someone to ask.

'It fell off,' Alexa said, laughing. 'Because someone – who shall remain nameless – didn't tie it on properly. We had to scrabble around under the bed looking for it.'

'Or there's the cravings one,' Frazier continued with an authoritative tone of voice. 'A craving for sweet things means it's a girl and a craving for savoury things means it's a boy.'

'And that's just the father's cravings,' Alexa added, laughing.

'You might mock,' Frazier said, 'but dads can get cravings too.'

'I'll second that,' James put in. 'I had cravings for a peaceful night when you two were on your way. You mother had terrible heartburn through both pregnancies. Are you getting that, Alexa? Or is heartburn worse later in pregnancy?'

'*Heartburn is common during the third trimester,*' Alexa, the virtual assistant, supplied helpfully.

Frazier continued on cheerfully, 'Another way to tell whether you're having a boy or a girl is partner weight gain. If a partner gains weight alongside the mother, then it's a boy, and if they don't, it's a girl.' He patted his tummy. 'We're definitely having a boy.'

'Your expanding waistline is down to ginger nuts, nothing else,' Alexa said. 'That's probably my fault. They were the only thing that helped with the morning sickness.'

'Which I suffered from too,' Frazier announced.

Louella rolled her eyes at her son. 'No you didn't.'

'I did. It's a thing,' Frazier argued. 'It's called Couvade syndrome. Men who are more empathetic and sensitive, such as moi,' he patted his chest, 'will go through some of the same discomforts of pregnancy as their wives, such as weight gain, morning sickness and difficulty sleeping. Ask Alexa if you don't believe me. The

Amazon Alexa, I mean, not the real one. Hey, Alexa?' he shouted across the kitchen. 'What's Couvade syndrome?'

'*I don't know that one*,' Alexa said, which amused everyone greatly.

'She probably didn't hear me properly,' Frazier said, refusing to be deterred.

'Right, you lot, enough of this frivolity,' their mother intervened. 'Sit yourselves down. I'm ready to serve up lunch, and after we've eaten, maybe Frazier and Alexa can tell us whether they actually are having a boy or a girl?'

Alexa blushed prettily and said, 'Absolutely, and of course we're going to tell you. Frazier's just teasing.'

* * *

Dinner was a riotous affair. Everyone was in a really good mood. Even Maggie seemed to have perked up a bit – although Phoebe noticed that she barely touched her food. She'd clearly been serious about not wanting a big meal at lunchtime then.

After dinner, they focused on the present opening. On her mother's advice, Phoebe had bought her father a couple of shirts, which he was thrilled with. Maggie had got him a tie. This was always a good choice as he wore them at work. Frazier and Alexa had got him an electric screwdriver, which he'd apparently asked for as his old one had broken, and Louella, in a rare burst of romanticism, had bought him posh cologne.

'I'll be totally set up,' he had said, thanking them all. He draped one of the shirts around his shoulders, knotted the tie loosely around his neck, sprayed on a squirt of cologne, which did smell amazing, and brandished his electric screwdriver.

It was lovely to see everyone so happy, Phoebe thought, vowing inwardly to come over more often and not just when there was a family celebration. She'd been back nearly five months, and aside from the brief visit at Easter, this was only the second time they'd all been together. It wasn't as though she was living in London any more. She should have more time – although she never seemed to.

'So how much longer are we going to be kept in suspense then?' she asked Alexa and Frazier when there was a gap in the conversation. Her gaze flicked between her sister-in-law and her brother. 'Are you having a boy or a girl?'

They exchanged glances.

'Tell us about this first,' Alexa said, holding up a copy of *New Forest Views*. She opened it up and flicked through it until she found the right page. 'It looks amazing. Are you pleased with it, Maggie?'

'I am. It's a good representation of our animals.'

'They're very photogenic,' Frazier said.

'That donkey is adorable,' Alexa cooed. 'And those kittens. Look at their little faces. We should think about getting a cat, Frazier.'

'I'm not sure cats are a good idea around babies.'

Babies? Was that a slip of the tongue or a general comment? Phoebe wondered. She was about to ask when Maggie, who was sitting opposite her, opened her mouth to speak, then shut it again and looked stricken.

'I... er, I don't feel so well.' Her voice sounded slurred and Phoebe was suddenly on high alert.

'Maggie, what is it?' She jumped up and ran round the table to her grandmother, who also seemed to have slumped to one side in her seat.

Everyone else at the table reacted at various speeds.

Alexa said, 'Oh my goodness. Are you OK, love?'

Louella stood up. 'No, she's not. James, call an ambulance. I think she might be having a stroke.'

Maggie shook her right hand in denial. Her left one was in her lap and now everyone could see that the left side of her face was affected too. The left-hand corner of her mouth was drooping as was her left eyelid. And her eyes were frantic.

Phoebe took her right hand and squeezed it. 'It's going to be OK. Everything's going to be fine.' Oh good grief, no wonder Maggie had been slightly off today. She must have been feeling ill. Why hadn't she picked up on it earlier? Her grandmother never admitted to being ill. But with hindsight that was clearly what must have been going on.

She could hear her father on the phone, answering the operator's questions. 'Yes, it's just happened. Yes, she's in her seventies. No, I don't think so. Yes, she's conscious. Yes, OK, I'll do that. Yes, that's fine. We'll go to Salisbury Hospital.' He finally put the phone down. 'There's up to an hour delay on ambulances,' he said. 'It'll be quicker if we go in the car. They said speed is of the essence. They'll let them know we're on our way.'

Her father drove with Louella in the passenger seat and Phoebe sat in the back with Maggie, holding her hand, reassuring her over and over that it was all going to be OK, and although her grandmother wasn't able to say anything coherent in reply, her eyes were less frantic and she didn't seem quite as tense and frightened.

When Phoebe wasn't talking, she was praying. She hadn't prayed so hard since she was a kid. She'd never been a churchgoer. But now she was praying for all she was worth. Over and over, the same prayer – *Please God, don't let her die. Please God, don't let her be paralysed. It's not fair. She's such a good person. She's helped so many people. She's never hurt anyone in her life. Please don't let her die.*

As if there were any logic when it came to who should die and who shouldn't. It didn't matter. Phoebe prayed anyway. She had never felt so terrified in her life.

* * *

At the hospital, Maggie was whisked away and they all waited anxiously for news, which seemed to take for ever coming, but eventually a doctor with tired eyes and a stethoscope around her neck came to see them.

'Mrs Crowther has had what we call a TIA, which is what is more commonly known as a mini stroke,' she said quietly. 'We've done an MRI scan, which shows that there's been no permanent damage to her brain, but she will need to be monitored for a while. And she will need to take things very easy.'

'What causes them?' Louella asked. 'Is it likely to happen again?'

'To answer your second question first. Yes, there is a very high risk of it happening again, I'm afraid. Especially in the first forty-eight hours, so she will need to be monitored and we'd like to keep her in for observation for a couple of days. As to what causes them, the risk factors are the same as for a stroke. Lifestyle factors, genetic factors, one or two health conditions – for example, diabetes may increase the risk.'

'But it's treatable, right?' This was from James.

'Very treatable. Yes. She's lucky – a TIA is a warning. With lifestyle changes and medication, Mrs Crowther should be fine.'

'Can we see her?' Phoebe and Louella spoke almost in unison.

'Of course you can.'

'Thank you,' Louella said and Phoebe echoed the words in her head as they walked up to the ward. *Thank you, thank you, thank you for answering my prayers.*

Maggie was sitting up in bed. She looked incredibly chirpy for someone who'd just had a stroke, mini or not, but she also looked incredibly vulnerable, out of her natural environment, the starkness of the hospital versus being surrounded by animals and muck with bits of straw in her hair.

Louella and James stood on one side of the bed and Phoebe

stood on the other and Phoebe realised that she was on the good side. Although, even now, on the bad side, the droopiness wasn't that pronounced. Maybe if you hadn't known her, you wouldn't have noticed it straight away.

Phoebe gently took her grandmother's hand. 'The doctor said you're going to be fine.'

Maggie nodded.

'Oh, Mum,' Louella said. 'You had us worried there. How are you feeling?'

'Not bad.' The old lady mouthed the words. 'Bit tired.'

'I bet.'

'You're going to need to take it easy,' Louella said. 'No marathons.'

This raised a lopsided smile, which Maggie swiftly abandoned, and Phoebe wondered what it felt like to have half your face not working properly. At least both her hands seemed to work now, so maybe the mini stroke hadn't affected her as much as they'd first feared.

'My animals?' Maggie asked, and Phoebe squeezed her hand. 'You don't need to worry about them. They'll have a vet on site to take care of their every need. I'll stay at Puddleduck Farm for as long as it takes.'

'Take my keys.'

'What? You mean you've locked the door?'

Phoebe got a nod this time and Louella said softly, 'I won't ask.'

'No, best not.'

Maggie leaned forward towards her daughter and she half mouthed, half spoke, because speaking was obviously an effort. 'Baby's... sex? You... do... know. Don't you?'

'I do.' Louella's face brightened. 'I know they wanted to make a big announcement, but in the circumstances...' She was glowing with pride. 'They're having one of each. They're having twins, Mum.'

Maggie gave that strange half-smile again and lay back on the pillow.

'Oh wow,' Phoebe said, so it hadn't been a slip of the tongue from Frazier earlier. For a moment, it seemed as though the whole room was bathed in a rosy glow. 'Twins! Gosh. That's amazing. How exciting. I didn't know twins ran in the family.'

'I think they might be the first,' Louella said, all lit up with pride. 'It's so exciting.'

Behind her, Phoebe saw her father's shoulders puff up with pride too. Pride and protectiveness.

'Right then,' he said, gathering himself and taking charge of the situation. 'I think it's time we all let Maggie get some rest, don't you?'

For once, there was no arguing from Maggie.

Phoebe looked back over her shoulder when they got to the door, but her grandmother's eyes were already closed.

28

It was seven thirty by the time they got back to Oak Drive. Frazier and Alexa had been given the news that Maggie was OK by phone, but they still waited for them to get back before they left.

'So we could give you all a hug,' Alexa told them and proceeded to do so, followed swiftly by Frazier. 'We're very relieved Maggie is going to be OK.'

'Congratulations on the twins,' Phoebe said to them both. 'Mum told us at the hospital.'

'We're so excited,' Frazier said, beaming from ear to ear. 'We've always wanted a big family and now we get two for the price of one.'

'It's OK for you, you don't have to carry them,' Alexa scolded. 'Not to mention give birth to them!' But she looked just as ecstatic as he did.

It was the joyful times that brought families together, Phoebe thought, as she drove back to Tori's to collect an overnight bag to go to Puddleduck. The joyful times were just as important as the difficult, painful times, such as the shock they'd had today. And very briefly Hugh flicked into her head.

She would have put money on the fact that he wouldn't have

run to his parents when they'd split up. He'd stayed at the flat for Christmas, so his parents probably didn't even know she had moved out. Poor Hugh had needed to go to a therapist to work out what he was feeling because his own parents had done such a hatchet job on his emotions when he was a child. Child abuse had been a hot topic for a few years now, but the emotional abuse of children wasn't mentioned as much as the physical side. Yet it could be just as devastating.

Phoebe sighed and put the image of Hugh firmly out of her head. He wasn't her responsibility.

Back at Tori's, once more, Phoebe gave her a friend an update of the day's events and what she was doing now, at the same time as packing an overnight bag, while Tori stood in the bedroom doorway, her face concerned.

'I texted Seth from the hospital and asked for a couple of days off, which will make things a bit easier. I could do the animals as well as work for a couple of days, but I'll be totally frazzled if I do. He said to take as long as I need.'

'That's nice of him. And thank God it was just a mini stroke. I'm guessing that's a warning though, isn't it?'

'Yes it is. Maggie needs to slow down a bit. Well, a lot, probably. I'm not too sure where that leaves Puddleduck Farm.' She glanced at the magazine on the carpet that she'd brought back from her parents' house. 'Maggie loved your feature by the way. Everyone loved it. Alexa wanted to adopt a kitten. Oh my God, I haven't told you that bit. They're having twins. A boy and a girl.'

'Blimey. That's exciting. Frazier being a daddy – it seems hard to believe.' Tori's eyes were shining suddenly. 'I still think of him as your little brother. How come he beat us to the proper grown-up stuff?'

'Is that having babies or settling down?'

'Both.'

'I'm not sure.' They looked at each other and a tingle of intuition ran down Phoebe's spine. Tori's eyes were shining a little bit too much. 'You've been up to something. What's going on?'

Tori could no longer contain herself. 'Actually, I've had quite an exciting day too, as it happens. I've been on a date with a guy I met at dinner club.'

'Who? Where? How did it go?' Phoebe glanced at her watch, aware of the time. 'I really should go – all the animals' dinner times are long overdue. But I need to know details. Can I phone you when I get to Puddleduck?'

'Yes, of course you can. Or I can text you – there's a chance he'll phone me.' On cue, her mobile trilled. 'Oooh, that might be him now. Yes it is. I'll definitely text you. Now go. Shoo.' Tori made shooing motions with her hands. 'Full update later.'

* * *

It felt strange going into Puddleduck Farm and knowing Maggie wasn't there. Phoebe was relieved to find that she needed the key to get in the front door. At least Maggie locked it when she left the house then. That was something.

Buster and Tiny came enthusiastically to greet her. Buster bright-eyed but hobbling a bit – so she wondered if his medication needed upping – and Tiny giving her a slow wag of his grey tail. Nothing about wolfhounds was small, but his tail was definitely spindly in relation to the rest of him.

She hadn't seen Duncan Petwell since she'd got the job at Marchwood, although she had phoned him to say thank you for his recommendation.

'You didn't really need it,' he'd told her with amusement in his voice. 'I heard that your reputation for bringing animals back from the dead had gone ahead of you!'

She had laughed, trying not to feel self-conscious. 'I also wanted to say that I didn't want to tread on your toes with regard to my grandmother,' she had added cautiously. 'I know you've always treated the Puddleduck animals.'

'You won't tread on my toes, don't worry. To be honest, I'll be retiring soon anyway so it would be good to have a few less clients.'

Tiny nudged Phoebe's arm and Buster gave a small whine and she came back to the present with a start. 'Sorry, guys. I'm getting your dinner, right now.'

Dogs could definitely smile, she thought, feeding Tiny and Buster who, once they were served, politely kept to their own bowls and didn't try to steal each other's food.

Then they both accompanied her out to the kennels to feed the kennel dogs. There was a chart on the wall in the utility room which showed what each of them ate – Phoebe guessed that was there for when Natasha came in to cover – and fortunately she knew where most of the food was already.

The cats were easy. Their bowls were in the barn and so was their food, she seemed to remember, but the steel bins where it was kept had locks on, which gave Phoebe a bit of a jolt. She checked the keys she'd been given and eventually found one that fitted. The bin contained a 15kg sack of Fishy Feline – a gourmet cat biscuit – Maggie didn't mess around.

The cats had the run of the farm, not just the barn, they came in and out via the stable door, the top half of which was never closed, even when the bottom half was. Phoebe wondered if the locks were to keep foxes out. She'd heard of some clever foxes, but really – a fox who could raid a bin when the lid was closed? She made a mental note to ask Maggie.

Phoebe fed the cats and made sure they had fresh water and then she played with the kittens for a while. Kittens were so endlessly entertaining. She also gave Myra, their mother, a quick check-over. One of her teats looked a bit sore, but it didn't look like mastitis. She would just keep an eye on it for now. The kittens would be weaned very soon. Being a vet was second nature, Phoebe thought. She couldn't imagine doing anything different.

She was just about to collect the cat bowls, most of which were now empty from the selection of felines in the barn, when she heard a clang. Spinning round, she saw that Saddam was balanced on the steel food bin, which was now open. The lid was on the floor – good grief – she'd never have thought a cat would be strong enough to do that.

Sighing, she went to shoo him away, but before she'd got within a foot of the bin, Saddam set up a low growling noise and glared at her with malevolent orange eyes.

Oh great, that was all she needed to finish off her day. A run-in with a crazy cat. What was it with her and ginger toms?

'Get out of there,' she said in her sternest voice, taking a step forward. 'Go on – SCOOT. NOW!'

Saddam bared his teeth and swished his tail. Phoebe wasn't sure whether that tail was swishing in annoyance or whether he was actually preparing to launch himself at her. Deciding not to take the chance and remembering that even Duncan Petwell didn't go near him, according to Maggie, she backed off.

Could a cat look triumphant? Saddam was certainly doing a great job. Taking full advantage of her retreat, he dipped a ginger paw into the bin and hooked out a Fishy Feline cat biscuit, which fell onto the barn floor.

Good Lord, she'd never seen a cat do that either. Phoebe got out her phone, wishing she'd had a chance to video the whole thing. It would amuse Maggie no end. Mind you, Maggie would already know, of course.

She abandoned her phone. She couldn't just leave the bin open.

There wouldn't be any biscuits left. And it would encourage rats. Although it would have taken a brave rat to challenge Saddam.

She would have to try the coat trick. It wasn't as if she had to catch him – just unbalance him long enough from his position on the bin to close it.

The first time she threw her coat, it missed and Saddam looked outraged. The second time she threw a coat – an old one of Maggie's this time as she didn't fancy going close enough to retrieve hers – she struck her target and he landed in a flailing paws heap on the floor. He freed himself in seconds and was away, a streak of furious amber, across to the other side of the barn.

Phoebe darted in, retrieved the bin lid, locked it securely and stood back with a sigh of relief. Her heart was thudding with adrenaline. She wouldn't make that mistake again.

From the other side of the barn, Saddam watched her with malevolent eyes. Why did she have the feeling he was plotting revenge?

* * *

Phoebe collected Tiny and Buster – both of whom were waiting patiently outside the barn, they were obviously old hands at this and were wary enough of Saddam not to come in – and the three of them walked down to the donkey field. The grass was lush and green. The donkeys didn't need extra feeding at this time of year. If anything, they'd need to be reined in a bit to prevent them overeating and getting laminitis.

They came to greet her, Roxy whickering softly and Diablo blowing on her hands. Phoebe hoped her grandmother wasn't missing her animals too much. She hoped that Tori's feature would bring in some more money and maybe even some extra volunteers. They'd also added a box at the bottom: Ways you can help. Rehome an animal if you can. Sponsor one if you can't. Be a volunteer dog walker. Be a volunteer fundraiser.

There were enough animal lovers in the surrounding villages who might want to volunteer. With a bit of luck, they'd get some kids doing the Duke of Edinburgh award.

And, of course, there was the PayPal account for donations. Phoebe decided to check that when she got back to the farmhouse. It was early days – the magazine had only just been delivered – but you never knew.

However, she got sidetracked before she could look. Firstly, by her mother, who rang to say she'd just been speaking to the hospital and Maggie was absolutely fine and settled for the night.

'This is one occasion when I really wish she would use a phone,' she added. 'If they are keeping her in for any length of time, I'm going to take her one in.'

'Good idea.'

As soon as she disconnected, her mobile rang again. It was Tori. 'Everything OK your end?' she asked.

Phoebe said it was and told her the update on Maggie and then, in an afterthought, about Saddam.

'I don't know whether to be impressed or afraid,' Tori quipped. 'Although it's probably a good job you're not putting him up for adoption. Just as well I didn't take his photo! But anyway.... Would you like to hear about my man?'

She sounded like the cat who'd got the cream herself, Phoebe thought, smiling.

'Of course I want to hear. Tell me everything.'

'OK. Here goes. In a nutshell. His name's Daniel. He's a forty-four-year-old stockbroker from Essex. He's tall, dark and *hot*. He's been married once – that was a red flag, but he told me she ran off with his brother, so I forgave him. He's only just moved into the area and we have exactly the same sense of humour.'

'Wow. A match made in heaven.'

'I know. I'm really happy, Phoebe. It's high time I had some proper fun. We took some selfies earlier. Hang on, I'll send you a pic.'

Phoebe's phone pinged several times and she paused to look at the pictures of Daniel and Tori making silly faces and grinning. Daniel wasn't bad-looking. He had kind eyes and great teeth and a decent haircut. And they did look happy together.

'I'm thrilled for you. I really am.'

By the time they'd finished chatting, it was gone ten. Phoebe made up the bed in the spare room, got in it and lay listening to the unfamiliar night-time sounds of the old farmhouse. She'd meant what she said about being thrilled for Tori. But she was also slightly worried. There was a part of her that knew she had already outstayed her welcome in Tori's flat. Tori would need her privacy if she had a new man. She should look for somewhere more permanent to live.

It needed to be close to Puddleduck too. She was all too aware that Maggie was going to need more help with Puddleduck Pets. A lot more help. And it really needed to be on a more permanent basis.

29

Phoebe was woken the next day by the sounds of faint barking. Not Buster and Tiny, who she'd left sleeping by the Aga in the kitchen, but the kennel dogs, presumably wanting the day to start. A quick glance at her watch showed it was only six fifteen, which wasn't too much different from her usual alarm.

She got up, put on thickish jeans – a precautionary measure for Bruce Goose and for Saddam – and ten minutes later, she was out in the yard, beginning the breakfast round.

The geese were probably less of a hazard than Saddam, despite the fact that there were a lot more of them, she thought, as she filled up their feed containers, removed poop from their coops and checked for eggs. Then she did the same with the ducks. She knew that geese and ducks didn't lay the same quantities of eggs as hens, but there were still a few. As she collected them, she wondered what Maggie did with them. She'd never said and there didn't seem to be any lying around in the farmhouse.

The kennel dogs were thrilled to see her. They had big outside runs, but she knew that Maggie also let them into the field for a run about daily and – just as importantly in Maggie's book – she gave them all a hug and some individual attention. Leads were hung up outside each run. Cleaning up the kennels and removing the poop wasn't the most pleasant of jobs, but it was satisfying getting the animals' living areas all clean and comfy. It did bring back Phoebe's concerns about Maggie though. This wasn't a job for an old lady. It was hard, physical work. This whole place was hard physical work.

An animal sanctuary in the New Forest might sound amazing and idyllic, but the reality of looking after animals day after day, with no time off, would be gruelling. Not to mention a major commitment. There was no way Maggie could carry on doing this on her own.

To Phoebe's relief, Saddam was nowhere to be seen in the barn. He didn't materialise when she unlocked the feed bin and then carefully relocked it as soon as she'd finished. Phoebe checked on Myra and the kittens. Definitely not mastitis. Then she escaped from the barn and headed back to the house for her own breakfast, which turned out to be coffee and some toast she made from a loaf of bread found in the freezer, which was so dried out that it was more like crispbread. What on earth did Maggie eat? A diet of duck and goose eggs possibly? She would have to get some shopping today.

While she was eating her breakfast, she checked the Puddle-duck Pets PayPal account that she had set up and she got the shock of her life. Someone had donated £1,500.

Phoebe blinked. Had she seen that right? Surely the decimal point was in the wrong place. It wasn't the only money in the account. The total figure was £1,587.87 – the rest was made up from smaller donations that varied between £2 and £10. One person had paid £1.87. This was much more the kind of thing she'd expected.

Phebe's head spun. Well, it was brilliant news, that was for certain and something lovely to tell Maggie when they spoke on her next visit to the hospital, which she planned to do later.

At lunchtime, she phoned her mother to see if there was an update.

'She's fine, but they're keeping her in for observation,' Louella told her. 'To be honest, I think that's just as well. You know what she's like. She wouldn't rest if they discharged her and she's highly unlikely to do anything else they tell her to, either. Frankly, love, I'm a bit worried. She seems very down and I know the stroke – mini or not – must have been a huge shock. But I don't think it's just that.'

'Did you speak to her?' Phoebe asked. 'You haven't been to the hospital again, have you?'

'I haven't been to the hospital, but Alexa and Frazier went in first thing. Frazier took her a mobile phone, all charged up and ready to use, with all our numbers programmed in, so all she has to do is press a button. Isn't your brother a superstar! I don't know when he got so grown up.'

'Tori and I were saying exactly the same thing yesterday. Things change so quickly, Frazier and Alexa being parents to twins, you being a granny to twins. I'm sorry we didn't get the chance to celebrate that properly.'

'We will. We've got years ahead to celebrate our twins, I'm sure. Anyway, Maggie actually rang me just now. I think she's going to phone you too. She's fretting about her animals, naturally.'

'I'll try calling her. Have you got the number?'

'I'll text it to you, love. I've got to go. I'm teaching in about five minutes.'

They said their goodbyes and, as promised, her mother texted her the number, but Phoebe got no answer when she called it. She would try again later.

She headed back outside to walk the kennel dogs.

* * *

It was a busy day. As well as sorting out the animals, Phoebe took phone calls from two people who'd seen the feature in *New Forest Views*. One of them wanted to rehome Handsome, and the other one was a woman wondering if Puddleduck could rehome her mother's seventeen-year-old cat, as her mother had just died and she was allergic to him.

Phoebe gulped and said that yes they could if the woman would drop him off. Remembering that this was one of the things Maggie had worried might happen, she hoped it wasn't the start of an influx.

She eventually spoke to Maggie on her mobile around five and Maggie launched into a barrage of questions before Phoebe could get a word in edgeways.

'All the animals are fine,' she reassured her. 'As am I? How are you?'

'I feel like a prisoner in here. They might as well chain me to the bed. And the food hasn't improved since the last time I was in hospital – that was when I had your mother – in fact, I think it's worse. Even Tiny would turn up his nose.'

'Oh dear,' Phoebe said, but at least her grandmother didn't sound sad now. I'm planning to come over at visiting time.'

'Don't bother. I'd rather you were there looking after the animals.'

Phoebe told her about Saddam and heard her sharp intake of breath.

'Are you OK? I did warn you that cat was dangerous. How's Bruce Goose?'

'Bruce Goose is fine. As am I. But talking of geese. What do you do with the eggs? I couldn't see any in the house. The ducks and the geese are laying, I noticed.'

'I eat some of them and I donate the rest to the Vale Pantry. It's a local food bank in Brook. They take as many as I can give. I go at least once a week so they're nice and fresh.'

'Wow, I didn't even know they existed.' Her grandmother went up another few notches in her estimation. 'I'll do the same.'

'There are some egg boxes in the utility-room cupboard and if you run out, there's a sack under the stairs. I buy them in bulk from the wholesaler.'

'Thanks.' She told Maggie about the donations and got another gasp.

'Really. How extraordinarily generous. You will say thank you on my behalf.'

'Of course I will. You just focus on getting better.' Phoebe paused. 'Also, there's a woman who is interested in rehoming Handsome. I said she would need a home check first, but I can do that. She seems happy about his skin condition too. She said she had a boxer who had that problem once, which is handy because she knows what she's doing. Also someone wants us to rehome a cat because her mother died. I said that was OK.'

'Of course it's OK. I try not to turn anyone away.'

The doorbell rang and Phoebe jumped. She hadn't known her grandmother even had a doorbell. 'That's probably her now. Let's speak tomorrow. I'm happy to stay here as long as you need me to. You're going to need to recuperate when you get back. I don't want any arguments.'

She disconnected before Maggie could start on one and went to answer the door, which was when she got the second shock of the day. It was Hugh.

She looked at him in amazement. 'What are you doing here? Why didn't you ring?' She had a feeling of déjà vu. Hadn't she asked those exact same questions last time she'd seen him?

'I think we've had this conversation before,' he said. 'Same answers as last time. I wanted to see you and I thought you'd say no if I rang first.'

'But how did you know I was here?'

'I was passing and I saw your car outside.' He sounded as though this was a perfectly rational statement as he gestured behind him.

'So you thought you would stop by.'

'Yes.' He put his hands in his pockets and shuffled from foot to foot. 'But that wasn't the only reason I was passing. I saw the feature in the local magazine. And I wanted to offer my services.'

'You want to adopt an animal?' she asked, raising her eyebrows. She wouldn't have been much more surprised if he'd said he wanted to fly to Mars and adopt a Martian. Hugh had never wanted a pet. His attitude being that he saw enough animals at work.

'No, I don't want to adopt one. I want to offer my services.'

'As a vet.'

'Gratis, of course. Puddleduck must need one. All the animals coming in and out.'

'We have a vet already,' she said, taken aback. 'I'm a vet. Or had you forgotten that?'

'No, of course not. But another vet wouldn't hurt, would it? And to prove I'm serious, I've made a donation to Puddleduck Pets. It's quite a sizeable one.'

So it had been Hugh who'd given them the £1,500. Phoebe blinked, wondering what he wanted in return. There was no such thing as a free lunch.

'It's my way of making amends,' he said, as if he'd tuned into her thoughts. 'I know this place is really important to you. I want to prove that I'm sorry for my behaviour, Phoebe, and that I still love you.'

'Your donation is to my grandmother, not me,' she said quietly, hoping fervently he wouldn't retract it if he thought it wouldn't make any difference to her feelings. Not now she'd told Maggie about it.

'I know that.' He looked taken aback. 'But this place is important to you too. My donation stands. Whatever you think about me. I mean that.'

He held her gaze steadily and something close to respect rose up in her.

'Thank you,' she said. 'That's very decent of you, Hugh, but I still don't think—'

'Please don't finish that sentence,' he interrupted. 'Please tell me you'll just consider what I've said. And let me make amends.'

'OK. And thank you again.'

A car was indicating to draw through the five-bar gate – they were still standing on the doorstep – and they both turned.

'I think this might be a lady about rehoming a cat,' Phoebe said.

'I'll disappear then.'

She didn't contradict him, even though she could see now it wasn't the lady about the cat. Or even a lady. It was Sam. What was he doing here?

Hugh didn't recognise him, or if he did, he didn't acknowledge him. He got back into his car, lifted a hand to wave at her and pulled out, just as Sam parked the Subaru and turned off his ignition.

Phoebe stayed where she was on the doorstep, feeling a slight sense of surrealness, as Sam strode across the gravel towards the front door.

'Hi, Phoebe, sorry to turn up on spec, but I just heard about Maggie. And I heard you were holding the fort. I came by to see if there's anything I can do to help?'

She felt warmed by the concern in his eyes.

'The grapevine is working well then. Our mothers?'

'Yep.'

'But thanks. I appreciate it. Come in. I'll make you a coffee.'

'Was that Hugh I just saw leaving, by the way?' Sam asked as they reached the kitchen.

'Yes it was. Well spotted.' Avoiding his eyes, she made them both coffee and brought it to the kitchen table, where Sam was getting acquainted with Tiny.

'I've always wanted one of these. Is he a deerhound or wolfhound?'

'Wolfhound. They're slightly bigger. Very similar though. He's up for adoption, I think. Shall I ask Maggie?'

'I can't have a big dog in my flat. More's the pity. He's gorgeous, isn't he?' He cleared his throat. 'Feel free to tell me to mind my own, but what was Hugh doing here? Are you two getting back together?'

'Hugh would like us to get back together...' She hesitated. 'But the feeling isn't mutual.'

'I see.' Sam stirred his coffee. 'Is that because you haven't forgiven him for having an affair?'

'It turns out that he didn't actually have an affair. At least not in the strictest sense of the word.'

She told him what had happened and he listened without interrupting. Sam had always been a good listener.

'Oh boy,' he said when she'd finally told him everything, including the fact that Hugh had just made a big donation to Puddleduck Pets.

'Which we are badly in need of,' she added.

'Do you feel beholden to him?' Sam's lovely blue eyes were solemn.

'Yes. No... A bit. Gosh, I don't know.' She rubbed her forehead, which had begun to throb. A stress headache. 'It did give me a shock, I know that.'

'Yeah, I'm not surprised. Flash bugger.' There was a hint of annoyance in his voice. That wasn't like Sam.

Phoebe gave him a curious glance.

He caught her gaze and blinked. 'Sorry. That was uncalled for. I'm just jealous, I guess. That he can afford to do something like that. And all I can do is come round and offer to muck out a few animals.'

'Sam, that's actually better. And more helpful. It takes effort and kindness... and it's one of the things that I love about you.' She broke off. Oh God, had she just said one of the things she loved about him. Not that it wasn't, but she didn't want to give him the wrong idea.

Now he was smiling. 'And on that note,' he said, 'why don't we wander down now and you can show me how to do something useful. I'm guessing it must be nearly teatime for the Puddleduck strays.'

* * *

As they walked out into the early-evening sunshine, Sam clenched his hands in his pockets. He could have kicked himself. He'd just had the perfect opportunity to tell Phoebe that his feelings of friendship had grown into something else and he'd blown it. She'd actually just said, one of the things she loved about him. *One* of the things. And he'd gone and changed the subject. What the hell was the matter with him? Any other bloke in the world – possibly the entire universe – would have taken the bull by the horns and said something, even if it was fairly innocuous like, 'One of the things, huh?' with a wink.

There were probably a thousand retorts he could have made and all he'd managed was an offer to muck out the animals. Very romantic, Sam!

Phoebe seemed oblivious to his churning thoughts. She was walking just ahead of him, straight-backed. She looked so at home strolling across the land that had been in her family for generations. That was one of the things he loved about her – her total ease in the countryside, as if she completely belonged there. She was as much a part of this landscape as Sam was himself. So many of their friends who'd grown up in the New Forest had left, moved away in search of cheaper housing or sometimes a more exciting place to live. But he had never wanted exciting. He was pretty sure now that Phoebe was here to stay too and the prospect of spending more time in her company overjoyed him. And yet he still couldn't bring himself to tell her this.

He glanced at her again. A strand of her long brown hair had come loose from its ponytail and was lying along the back of her Barbour and Sam longed to take a step closer and tuck it in.

One step, but it might as well be a thousand miles.

30

'Well, I have to say that – shocks aside – it does sound as though you had a better Monday than I did,' was Tori's comment when Phoebe told her about Hugh's donation and then Hugh and Sam turning up one after the other the previous evening.

It was now Tuesday evening and Phoebe had just popped round to see her flatmate on the way back from a supermarket run. Being surrounded by animals was wonderful, but she hadn't realised how much she missed being around people too. Now they were in the kitchen sipping coffee and nibbling Tunnock's Tea Cakes that Tori had decided were low calorie because they were full of marshmallow.

'Why? What's happened? It's not your new man, is it?'

'Mmm, partly.' Tori frowned. 'I took it upon myself to do a bit of online research and now I wish I hadn't.'

'Why?' Phoebe looked at her in concern. 'He's not a secret serial killer, is he?'

'Like that would be online!' Tori rolled her eyes. 'No. Worse. He's a serial online dater. I should have checked before.'

'Does that matter? Maybe he was just looking for the right woman?'

'Yes, well, that only works if he's stopped looking. But just as an experiment I had a chat with Laura, who happens to be on the same online dating site as he is, and she sent him a message asking him if he'd connected with anyone or if he was still available, and he answered and said he hadn't connected with anyone he liked. He'd actually only met losers. He was still TOTALLY AVAILABLE, that bit was in capital letters, and VERY open to offers. Bloody cheek. He sent the message this morning,' she added disconsolately. 'After that lovely day we had on Sunday and the lovely messages he's been sending ever since. I couldn't believe it! I thought we'd connected.'

'Maybe he's just keeping his options open,' Phoebe ventured. 'I mean, as you've only had one date.'

'Huh!' Tori said, devouring half a tea cake in one mouthful and swallowing it. 'That does NOT excuse him for calling me a loser. I had such high hopes too. I should have checked online before. I usually do. But I liked him so much at the dinner club that I didn't. Lessons learned.'

'I am sorry. He did sound nice.'

'I sent him a copy of the "losers" comment he'd made to Laura and asked him to explain himself. And he didn't even have the balls to reply. Still, there are plenty more fish in the sea.' Tori brightened. 'As it happens, there's another dinner club date on Saturday. Which I wasn't going to go to, but now I might. Do you fancy it?' She pushed the box of tea cakes across the table.

'I don't really think it's the right time for me,' Phoebe said, taking another tea cake. 'I will come, one day, I promise.'

Tori's eyes narrowed. 'You're not contemplating getting back with Hugh, are you?'

'No, I'm not. And I really hope that doesn't make him change his mind about the donation. But I don't think it will. He does seem to be genuinely trying to make amends. As well as trying a spot of bribery. He's always been single-minded when he wants something.'

'Yes, I can imagine.' Tori grimaced. 'Well, good luck.'

'Thanks, and I'm sorry about your man. Did you say he was only part of the reason you've had a bad day?' she asked, remembering as she unwrapped her second tea cake.

'I had a run-in with Pernickety Pippa. Remember her?'

'How could I forget? How come she's been in touch? I thought you were all signed up now.' She had a vague memory of Tori saying that.

'I am. But apparently a guest complained because there was a screw loose on the toilet roll holder. A screw loose! It's not exactly hanging off the wall or anything. You'd think they'd have better things to think about, wouldn't you, while they were on their wonderful spring break in the forest.' She huffed. 'Honestly, Phoebe, I'm beginning to regret that I ever let it out as a holiday cottage. It was so much work to get it up to Pernickety Pippa's standards and so far they've got me two measly bookings and the second one has complained.'

'That is annoying.'

'I'm seriously contemplating letting it out long term again. It would be far less hassle.'

'I'd rent it?' Phoebe said and although she hadn't contemplated it until that moment, it suddenly seemed like a very good idea. 'I can't stay here for ever,' she added, looking into Tori's startled eyes. 'You need your own space.'

'You're very welcome to stay as long as you like,' Tori said firmly.

'I know, but it's true, isn't it? We'll both need our own space sooner or later, especially if either of us get into a relationship. That's much more likely to happen to you than me – what with all these dinner parties.' She smirked. 'Or do you just go for the yummy food?' She leaned across the table, turning serious. 'I love Woodcutter's Cottage. It's close to Puddleduck Farm too and Maggie's going to need a lot more help when she gets out of hospital. I've offered to stay with her for a while, but I can't stay there permanently. Much as I love her, we'd drive each other bonkers.'

Tori looked thoughtful. 'You're serious, aren't you?'

'I am. And I promise I won't complain about you having a screw loose.' She raised her eyebrows.

Tori laughed. 'That's true! You already know about my mental foibles. OK, I'll look into it. I'm tied into a contract for a minimum period. I forget what that is, but I'll check. You're not in a rush to move out, are you?'

'No, not at all. I'm thinking long term. But talking of rushing, I'd better get back. Tiny and Buster are used to having someone around twenty-four seven.'

'Give them a hug from me,' Tori said. 'And let me know how Maggie is and if there are any more developments with Hugh. Or with Sam,' she added with a wicked little sideways glance at Phoebe.

'Sam?'

'Well, he didn't waste any time, did he? Heading round with offers of help the second he found out you were all on your lonesome.'

'He was just being nice. That's Sam all over.'

'Hmm,' Tori said with a world of meaning in her voice. 'Well, time will tell, won't it?'

* * *

Maggie was finally proclaimed fit enough to come out of hospital on Thursday, once she'd seen the doctor, and Phoebe arranged to pick her up as soon as she'd been discharged.

She spoke to her mother before she went in and Louella said, 'I've tried to talk her into coming here for a while – so she could recuperate properly and I could make sure she takes her medication, but she won't hear of it. She wants to be in her home.'

'You can't blame her for that. Don't worry, Mum. I'll take care of her. I won't let her do too much. And I'll keep an eye on the meds.'

'Good luck with that,' Louella muttered. 'Let me know when you've picked her up and I'll pop over later with your father. I think we should have a family confab.' She hesitated. 'You can't stay there for ever, love. What about work? You've only just started that job.'

'Seth's fine with it. I'm on leave.'

'Yes, OK. But we still need to make plans. Set up some kind of rota to help.'

'That's a good idea, but I think what we really need is some more money. Maggie runs this place on a shoestring. She has volunteer helpers. But no one helps out full-time. She's been subsidising the animal care with her savings, so I can see why she doesn't want to hire someone permanently, but it's not sustainable, Mum.'

Louella sighed. 'Yes, I had a feeling she might be doing that. OK, we'll see you later.'

'Thanks,' Phoebe agreed, feeling worried. Ever since she'd discovered first-hand the extent of the work that was required purely to keep Puddleduck ticking over, she'd been racking her brain for solutions. But, as far as she could see, more hands-on help was really the only one. Running an animal sanctuary was a young person's game. Maggie couldn't do it on her own. Especially not now. Her doctors had said that another stroke was a very real possibility if she didn't slow down considerably. She couldn't do that at

Puddleduck without full-time help. And full-time help was not going to be cheap.

* * *

Maggie was finally discharged at just after two and Phoebe was relieved to see that her face was fine now, albeit pale, and she was speaking normally again.

Phoebe drove her back to Puddleduck Farm in the Lexus.

'This is a nice car,' Maggie said, twiddling with the heated seat button as they drove through the forest past gorse bushes dotted with yellow flowers and the ubiquitous New Forest ponies, who you had to keep an eye out for as they wandered without warning across the road.

'Yes, well, you'd go in it more often if you weren't so stubborn and independent.' Phoebe gave her a sideways glance.

Maggie pursed her lips and didn't reply and Phoebe felt guilty.

'I'm sorry, I'm not having a go at you. I'm just concerned about you. We all are.'

'Well, you've no need to be. I'm perfectly capable of looking after myself.'

'That's the thing. You don't have to. I love being at the farm. I have amazing memories from when I was small, and anyway, I love your company.'

Maggie clasped her hands in her lap and didn't say any more. Phoebe decided not to push it because she didn't want Maggie to decide she couldn't stay on at Puddleduck Pets and help out. Which Phoebe knew she was very likely to do if she was backed into a corner. That blasted pride.

Neither had she told her grandmother about the family confab that was happening later because she was very likely to put a stop to that too.

Back at Puddleduck Farm, Maggie walked ahead of Phoebe into the house, where she got an ecstatic welcome from Buster and Tiny that nearly knocked her off her feet.

'Steady on,' Phoebe said, making a grab for the wolfhound's collar.

'They're OK. Leave them be.' Maggie bent down to fondle Buster's soft black ears – she didn't need to bend to stroke Tiny – and Phoebe saw a tear roll down her grandmother's cheek and fall onto the wolfhound's shaggy head.

She swallowed, feeling incredibly moved. The love that Maggie felt for these two shone out brighter than the sun and it was a love that Phoebe knew she felt for all of her animals. From Bruce Goose to the stroppy Saddam. It wasn't dependent on them loving her back or even being grateful for her care. It was all-encompassing and totally unconditional. Maggie Crowther might run Puddleduck Pets on a shoestring where money was concerned, but she also ran it on an abundance of love and hope.

* * *

Phoebe's parents arrived at just before five. To Phoebe's surprise, Frazier was with them, although not Alexa, who he explained was at home putting her feet up.

'We come bearing gifts,' Louella said, putting a pot of purple hyacinths on the worktop and coming to the table where Phoebe and Maggie were sitting to kiss them both.

'Oh great. Something else for me to look after,' Maggie grumbled, but she did shoot her daughter a look of affection.

'Don't get up,' Frazier ordered. 'We're here to help.' He put a carrier bag on the worktop. 'Waitrose essentials,' he said, glancing at Phoebe. 'In case you didn't have a chance to go shopping. It'll all freeze if you did.'

'That's sweet of you.' She got up and kissed her brother. When she peeked in the bag, she saw milk and bread and some cheese, and some chocolate biscuits. There were even a few dog treats.

'I'm not an invalid,' Maggie said.

'Ah, but you will be if you carry on overdoing it,' said Phoebe's father, which was very diplomatic for him, Phoebe thought. He must have been primed.

'Which is why I have no intention of carrying on overdoing it,' Maggie said firmly. 'I have a plan.'

That got everyone's attention.

She waved a hand. 'Now, if you would all like to sit down, I will tell you my plan.'

Phoebe and her mother exchanged glances. Neither of them had expected this, but everyone did as Maggie suggested and after some shuffling and scraping of chairs and some gentle shifting of the dogs who were already around the table, albeit on the floor, everyone sat down.

'I know you're all worried about my health,' Maggie began, 'and, despite what you all think, I'm not entirely oblivious to the fact that I'm getting towards being old.'

'Getting towards...' Frazier blurted and Louella hushed him with a look.

'Yes, young man, getting towards.' Maggie shot him a defiant glare. 'There are dozens of men and women my age who still work full-time. Lots of them run marathons. Several of them have been presidents of America, I believe. It's immaterial.' She paused and cleared her throat. 'I've always said that I'd slow down if and when my body said so. Which, I'm sad to say, may have just happened. So, I've just put plan B into action.' She took a deep breath. 'I'm selling up. Puddleduck Farm is on the market. And as soon as it's sold, I intend to retire. I've always fancied retiring to the sea, so I'm buying a McCarthy and Stone retirement flat in Milford on Sea.'

There was a stunned silence around the table. This was a bombshell that Phoebe had not been expecting and it was clear the others felt the same. Milford on Sea was twenty-five miles away on the coast. A neat little suburban town full of retirement homes and pavements with street lights. It was a world away from the ancient forest and farmland where Maggie had spent her whole life. Not to mention an hour from Louella.

Then there was a babble of voices. They were all talking over each other, so it was hard to hear any one individual voice, but the overall consensus seemed to be the same.

It was a crazy idea.

Maggie couldn't get rid of what was left of her heritage. The farmhouse that had housed four generations of her family.

It was Phoebe's father who banged the table to quieten them all and then said in a voice of great authority, 'You'll hate living in a McCarthy and Stone flat. I'll give you six months before you die of boredom.'

There were murmurings of agreement from everyone except Maggie, who sat there looking rather flushed, with her chin jutting out stubbornly.

Before anyone could say anything else, the doorbell jangled and Phoebe jumped to her feet. 'I'll get it. Are you expecting anyone?'

Maggie shook her head and Phoebe, accompanied by Tiny, went to answer the door.

Standing on the doorstep was a woman holding a cat box. Through the bars, Phoebe caught a glimpse of marmalade fur.

'We spoke on the phone a few days ago about my mother's cat,' the woman began. 'I'm Ingrid Bellamy and this is Garfield.' She held out the box. 'I do hope it's still OK for you to take him.'

31

Rufus had made Archie a promise that he had regretted the moment he'd done it because he'd known it would be an impossible promise to keep, and today it had come back to haunt him.

He had promised that if Archie agreed not to visit the Puddle-duck donkeys again, he would book him a course of riding lessons.

'Will you come with me?' Archie had asked.

'I'd like to but...'

'Please, Dad.' Archie had looked up at him pleadingly with an expression so like his mother's when she had wanted something that Rufus had capitulated.

'Of course I'll come with you.'

'You promise?'

'I promise, son.'

He'd got Emelia to book the lessons. Brook Riding School was their local stables and it had, according to Emelia, got excellent reviews on TripAdvisor, but she'd hit a snag.

'They are booked up for weeks on the future,' Emilia had said with a sigh in her voice. 'Shall I book another school? It is shame, because it is best school in area.'

Hating himself for it, Rufus had breathed a sigh of relief. 'No. We'll wait. I want Archie to have the best. And it's weeks *in* the future not *on*.'

'Weeks *in* the future. OK. I will ask they put him on waiting list. Hopefully it will not be too long.'

Rufus had prayed that it would be months and that in the meantime Archie would lose interest and decide he was no longer interested in learning to ride. Rufus hadn't bargained on there being a cancellation. But that was exactly what had happened.

Emelia had told him this with great excitement. 'Great news for Archie. One of the regular learners had block booking. This is right word, this block – *ja*?'

'Yes. It's the right word.'

'Thanks. They have cancelled. They have now offered to us this block booking so Archie may start riding at Brook Riding School. We have first lesson booked for ten on Saturday morning. I check your diary. This is OK for you to go. Yes?'

Emilia had told him this on Wednesday morning and he had said, yes, it was fine. A promise was a promise.

'I will make sure he has riding clothes before Saturday,' Emilia had added. 'I will pull out all the plugs.'

Rufus had been too distracted even to correct the phrase.

Archie had been ecstatic ever since. Rufus had hardly slept. The PTSD raged within him. It was as though it was a living entity and it had upped its game, the slightest of triggers could set off a cycle of fear, rage and utter demoralisation. The triggers were everywhere.

Emilia had taken Archie to get kitted out at a nearby country equestrian store and the boy had paraded in his new kit – riding hat, boots, jodhpurs and crop – past his traumatised father. That had set off an attack.

Emilia had shown Rufus Brook Riding School's brochure with

pictures of their ponies, one of which Archie would no doubt ride. That had set off another one.

Emilia had even sent him a link via TripAdvisor to the glowing reviews about Brook Stables. Even that had sent Rufus spinning into a PTSD cycle and after each gruelling round, he'd felt more and more debilitated.

It was like walking across a minefield, pitted with PTSD trip-wires. Whereas once he had managed to avoid most of his illness's tripwires, or at least contain the consequences, now it seemed impossible. He kept stumbling into them and the symptoms would explode in his face before he had time to draw breath.

* * *

It was now nine fifteen on Saturday morning. Archie's lesson was at ten and Rufus felt as though he was hanging on to his sanity by a thread.

If the merest mention of anything connected to horses threw him into such turmoil, how the hell was he going to sit through an hour of seeing his child ride one?

In the past, if the PTSD cycles were triggered in public, he'd mainly managed to keep his behaviour in check by the sheer force of his willpower. But he wasn't sure if that was going to be enough today. He felt as though he was going to the gallows.

'Are you excited, Dad?' Archie asked him as they got ready to go out of the door.

'Yes,' Rufus managed to croak. The one thing he was clinging on to was that once a cycle had begun and run its course, he was usually immune to having another one for a while. But he was unsure whether this was because he was usually able to remove himself from whatever had triggered the initial attack.

There would be no chance of doing that today.

They got in the car and Rufus set up the satnav with fingers that were so sweaty the touchscreen wasn't responding to them.

'Shall I do it, Dad?' Archie offered and Rufus nodded gratefully, thankful for once that his son was streets ahead of him when it came to all things technological.

As they drove towards Brook Riding School, Rufus practised the deep-breathing exercises that he'd learned from his sessions with the psychologist he'd seen in the past, and he did his best to focus on the steering wheel he was gripping so tightly and on the excited chatter of his son. None of this stopped the thunderous pounding of his heart or the sensation that he was driving towards his own destruction, but it did help a bit.

At nine forty-five, which was the time they'd been told to arrive so someone could go through the 'new rider' paperwork with them, Rufus parked the car on the road that bordered Brook School and he and Archie walked along to the double gates that opened out onto a yard, surrounded on three sides by stables. There were no actual horses in the yard they had to cross, although a couple of equine heads peered out over the tops of their loose boxes.

Rufus longed for blinkers, like the ones worn by racehorses or trap-pulling horses in the old days. Oh, the irony, he thought, as Archie gripped his hand.

'Are you OK, Dad?'

God, it must be bad if Archie had noticed something amiss.

'Yep.'

'I won't fall off like Mum did, will I?' Archie said, sounding suddenly vulnerable. And it was that vulnerability that pierced through Rufus's terror enough to divert him from the first crippling plunge into full-blown PTSD.

He gripped his son's hand tighter. 'Of course not. You'll be going very slowly, and someone will be holding the reins. And I'll be there. Ready to catch you. Just in case.'

'Thanks, Dad.' Reassured, Archie let go of his hand and skipped ahead of him into a large wooden building that was signposted 'office'. Rufus followed him out of the morning sunshine into the relative dimness of a room that smelled strongly of horse and leather – possibly because it also appeared to be the tack room and the place where riding hats were hung up on rows of hooks for riders who didn't have their own.

Rufus was sent tumbling back in time to when he'd gone to the stables with Rowena and the memories rushed in on him so forcibly that his legs turned to jelly and he had to put out a hand to steady himself. His fingers touched the rough surface of a notice-board on the wall beside him.

'Focus, focus,' he said under his breath, staring hard at the only thing in the room that didn't scream horse, which was a woman, who could have been any age between forty and sixty, with wispy grey hair and weather-beaten ruddy skin. She was dressed in shabby trousers and an ancient tweed jacket with leather patches on the elbows. She looked as though she didn't have two pennies to rub together, but Rufus knew instinctively that here was the owner of the establishment.

She was looking at him with concern. 'Are you OK, sir? Can I help you at all?'

'We're here for my first riding lesson,' Archie answered for them both. 'I'm Archie Holt and this is my dad.'

'And I'm Marjorie Taylor,' said the woman. 'Nice to meet you, Archie. And Dad.' She looked at Rufus consideringly. 'Can I reassure you that Archie will be in very good hands. So please don't worry. He's with our top instructor, Sam Hendrie. I'll take you round and introduce you in a moment. And...' She glanced at an open book on the desk in front of her, '...It looks as though he'll be riding Cranberry, who's our gentlest pony. Very safe.'

Rufus couldn't manage any more than a nod. He could feel

sweat dripping down the back of his neck. He was here. That was the main thing. He didn't care if the entire staff of Brook Riding School thought he was stark raving bonkers. It didn't matter. He was keeping his promise to his son.

* * *

When Sam had seen the name Archie Holt on his list of scheduled lessons, it had given him a jolt. But he'd quickly dismissed the idea that Archie Holt would have anything to do with the Holts at Beechbrook House. There must be plenty of others in the vicinity.

He'd just turned a sweaty Ninja out into his field, having been on an early hack through the forest. It was a gorgeous day, the sky was a pastel blue, flecked with wispy clouds that looked as though they'd be gone by lunchtime. There was a warmth in the air that held the promise of summer just around the corner.

Sam was in a very good mood. He'd been thinking about Phoebe a lot since he'd been over to Puddleduck and he had a plan. He'd asked her out for a drink tonight – pie and chips at the Brace of Pheasants to be precise – saying there were a couple of things he wanted to talk to her about – and she'd agreed straight away.

He was picking her up from Puddleduck, where she was still staying with her grandmother, at seven thirty. That gave him time to get home for a wash and a brush up first, and he'd decided to grab the bull by the horns. Tonight, once they'd eaten, he would tell her how he felt. He would keep it very gentle. He would tell her that he was in no hurry – he knew she didn't want to go diving back into a full-blown relationship – but that he was willing to wait for her to be ready, however long it took.

He knew that if he didn't do that and she ended up back with Hugh – or with someone else – just because he hadn't had the balls to ask her out – then he would never forgive himself.

Back at Brook Riding School, he strolled round to the office, whistling. He saw his new client as soon as he went into the dimness of the big barn – a child with an unruly dark mop of hair. The boy's father was talking to Marjorie, but he had his back to Sam. Then, as Marjorie looked his way, the man turned too, and Sam felt himself bristle.

Shit. It was Rufus Holt. That was all he needed. That arrogant nob watching his every move while he taught his son to ride. No doubt he'd be interfering at every available opportunity, presuming he knew better. What on earth was he doing here anyway? Surely he could have afforded to hire a private riding instructor to go up to the manor and teach his boy. They must have horses there.

He knew at once that Rufus didn't recognise him. Mind you, why would he? He was a nobody, a peasant. The phrase 'people like you' echoed in his brain.

Oh for God's sake, Sam, get that chip off your shoulder, he scolded himself inwardly. This was his turf. His home ground. His rules.

Forcing himself to be professional, he stepped forward.

'Ah, Sam, this is Archie Holt and his dad. We've just been doing the paperwork.' Marjorie introduced them and then glanced back at Rufus. 'I shall leave you in Sam's very capable hands. Enjoy your lesson.'

'Good morning, Mr Holt,' Sam said. 'It's good to meet you.'

The man looked very stressed. Sam could see sweat dripping down his face. How odd. He glanced at Marjorie and she gave an almost imperceptible shrug of her shoulders. So she'd noticed something amiss too.

Sam turned his attention to Archie, who, to his relief, looked like any other excited child about to do their first riding lesson. 'Good morning, Archie. Shall we go and meet your pony?'

'Yes please.'

Sam led them back out into the yard, deciding it was best to focus on Archie. But, on the other hand, maybe his father was ill. It would be awful if he had a heart attack while he was at Brook Riding School. What if he collapsed and died in their yard? That would be terrible publicity. Sam struggled with himself. Maybe he should say something.

He turned again. 'Are you all right, sir? I hope you don't mind me saying, but you don't look well.'

Rufus met his eyes for the first time and Sam saw something he hadn't expected. The man's pupils were so dark that his eyes were almost black. Sam recognised that look. It was something he saw often in his job. Fear. He stopped in his tracks, empathy lending him a compassion he hadn't expected to feel.

'Has your son had a bad experience with a horse?' he asked quietly. Not that it looked like it. Archie was ahead of them in the yard. Every loose box had a nameplate over its door and he'd gone straight to Cranberry's. The bay pony was in situ, already tacked up ready for the lesson, and Archie was now stroking her nose. Cranberry was as daft as they came and she was enjoying the attention. Sam knew Archie was unlikely to come to any harm with the gentle schoolmistress pony.

Rufus hadn't answered Sam's question. He was clearly struggling to speak. His Adam's apple bobbed and he finally managed to shake his head.

'OK, well...' Sam felt at a bit of a loss. If the man wasn't having a heart attack and the boy wasn't afraid of horses, he guessed he should just get on with his job. He called across to Archie, 'Right then, let's get that pony out and we can all go round to the outdoor school. Now, there are a couple of things I need to tell you about ponies – number one, they can kick if they're startled. So don't be going around the back of them, especially if they don't know you're there. And number two, they're pretty heavy. If they stand on your toe, you'll know about it. So treat them with respect. Is that clear?'

Archie nodded. His eyes were huge with wonderment.

Sam felt himself warming to the boy, despite the ambiguous feelings he had about his father.

In his experience, there were two types of kids who wanted to learn to ride. There were the ones who wanted to get on and gallop off into the distance as soon as humanly possible. And there were the ones who loved horses and were in it for the long haul. The first type usually fell off quite quickly, hopefully without hurting themselves too much, and subsequently gave up riding, which was as much a relief to Sam as it was to them. The second lot listened to everything you said and were a joy to teach.

Sam was pretty sure Archie fell into the second category.

He unbolted the stable door and Archie stood back as he'd been instructed while Sam led Cranberry out into the morning sun.

The sunshine glinted off her reddish bay coat and her shoes clip-clopped across the concrete and the smell of horse hit Sam's nostrils.

'This is how you hold a pony's reins when you want them to go with you,' Sam said, taking the reins over Cranberry's head and showing Archie how to use both hands to hold them. 'Right, are you ready?'

'I'm ready,' Archie said, and they set off out of the yard, along the track at the back that led towards the outdoor school.

Rufus muttered something about a phone call and stepped back several paces.

When Sam glanced over his shoulder to check that Rufus was following them too, he realised he wasn't behind them.

Archie hadn't seemed to notice, so Sam decided to carry on alone with Archie's lesson and hope that his father caught them up.

32

To Sam's relief, the lesson had gone really well, despite the fact Rufus had watched it from a distance. He'd spent most of the time on the far side of the outdoor school, the side that bordered the road, communicating with his son via the occasional hand signal.

Archie hadn't seemed to mind, so Sam had focused on the child, relieved that at least his fears about Rufus interfering had been unfounded. Rufus hadn't said another word all morning and after Archie's lesson he'd practically run out of the stables.

As soon as he'd finished his afternoon lessons, Sam had gone home for a spruce-up and headed for Puddleduck, via the supermarket to get a box of posh chocolates and some flowers for Maggie, who he was relieved to see looked surprisingly well for someone recovering from a stroke, mini or otherwise.

He'd taken Phoebe chocolates and flowers too. 'Just so you don't feel left out,' he'd said, as he'd pecked her cheek, inhaling the lovely light floral scent she wore and fighting off the urge he had to take her in his arms and declare he was in love with her right that second.

'That's so sweet of you, Sam. Thank you.' She'd blushed prettily and then turned towards her grandmother. 'Maggie, are you sure you don't want to come with us? We're going to pie and chip night at the Brace of Pheasants. You'd be very welcome to join us. Wouldn't she, Sam?'

'Er yeah. Of course.' Sam hoped fervently she wouldn't. That definitely didn't fit in with his plans.

'I'm fine here,' Maggie had said. 'I don't fancy a pie at this time of night. You two youngsters go and enjoy yourselves.' She'd winked at Sam, unseen by her granddaughter, and he'd wondered fleetingly if she'd guessed at his intentions. Hopefully not. Although it was true that not much got past Maggie Crowther.

Phoebe was quiet in the car. She seemed thoughtful and reflective. 'Penny for them,' Sam said, as he drew into the pub car park.

'I'll tell you after we've eaten,' she replied. 'We must have loads to catch up on. So much has happened lately.'

'Yes,' Sam said, feeling his heart beat a little faster. 'In my life too.'

* * *

A few minutes later, they were installed at the table he'd booked with their drinks – wine for Phoebe and a J2O and lemonade for him – in front of them. It was bank holiday weekend, so it had seemed prudent to book. Sam had asked for the table in the alcove, which had the inglenook fireplace on one side and a window with a view out over the pub garden on the other. There was no fire this evening, but there was a row of tea light candles in pots around the hearth and the pub smelled sweetly of rosemary and pastry every time the door to the kitchen opened on the other side of the room.

They'd already ordered their pies. Phoebe had ordered chicken and mushroom. He was having steak and kidney. Bar staff hurried about with trays of food, but they were in an intimate little corner where they were unlikely to be interrupted or overheard. Sam hadn't wanted to leave anything to chance.

They talked trivia until their pies arrived and as they ate them, Phoebe asked him about his Saturday. 'Do you have any promising new pupils? How's Ninja?'

'Ninja's great.' He told her about Archie Holt and the strange behaviour of his father. 'The man was obviously very anxious about something, but we didn't get to the bottom of it. To be truthful, I was shocked he brought the lad himself. I'd have thought he'd have come with his mother...'

'There isn't one,' Phoebe said, surprising him. 'His mother died when he was younger, apparently. I think there's a nanny.' She told him about Archie visiting the donkeys. 'He hasn't been since, as far as we know,' she added. 'His father must have put a stop to it. I'm glad he's having riding lessons. He was a sweet kid.'

Sam grunted. 'He was... is... He obviously loves horses. I don't think his father will bring him again. Not personally anyway. He only watched bits of the lesson.'

'That is odd. Hopefully his nanny will bring him next time.' Phoebe had finished her pie and she put down her knife and fork. 'That was delicious. Thank you for suggesting it.'

'My pleasure.' Sam rested his elbows on the table and his chin on his hands and looked at Phoebe. 'Tell me how you are. It was good to see Maggie looking so well.'

'I'm fine.' There was a small frown on her forehead and her beautiful hazel eyes were troubled. 'That's not true. I'm not fine. Oh, Sam, it's Maggie. She's selling Puddleduck Farm.' Pain edged her voice. 'I don't think I can bear it. She's looking for a buyer to take over the animal sanctuary, but if she can't find one, she says she's going to try and rehome all the existing animals and sell the land and farmhouse as it is. There's hardly any land anyway – she rents most of it from the Holts. I know things have to change, but I can't imagine her not being there. I can't imagine not going there any more. It just feels so terrible.' She rummaged in her handbag for tissues and pulled out a pack. 'I'm sorry. I knew I'd cry if I started talking about it.' She wiped her face with a tissue and blew her nose. 'I'm being selfish. I've always known Maggie couldn't carry on with that place for ever.'

'Bloody hell.' Sam shook his head in disbelief. He hadn't been expecting that. 'What is she going to do?'

'She's decided to buy a McCarthy and Stone retirement flat in Milford on Sea and nothing that I, nor any of the family, can say will change her mind. She's already put down a non-refundable deposit. She's hell-bent on selling up.'

'Is this because of the stroke?'

'Yes.' Blinking rapidly, Phoebe sipped her drink. 'I mean, I get that she's worried about her health We're all worried about her health and we all want her to make changes, but none of us thought she would be so radical.'

'No,' Sam said. 'I wouldn't have thought it either. She loves that place.'

'She does. But I think she's terrified of not being able to manage. The bottom line is that it's a huge money pit and she's been subsidising it. It's not self-supporting at all. I think that's another reason she wants to sell it. She's probably scared that if she doesn't do something soon, she won't have any money left to buy a retirement flat. Puddleduck Farm needs shedloads of money spent on it. It's not going to be an easy place to sell.'

'No,' Sam agreed. A dozen thoughts were whirling through his mind. 'I don't suppose you can raise the money to buy it?'

She was already shaking her head. 'Not unless I marry a rich man whose only aim in life is to spend all his money on lost causes.' She gave him a rueful smile, even though her eyes were bright with tears. 'I don't know any rich men, unless you count Hugh. He's pretty well off. His parents owned the flat we lived in at Greenwich Park. If they sold that they could probably buy Puddleduck Farm three times over.'

'You can't marry Hugh.' Sam blurted the words before he'd had a chance to edit them. 'What I mean is that it wouldn't be good for you – obviously, it's not my place to say.'

'Oh, Sam.' She reached across the table and put her hand over his. 'I would never marry someone for their money. You know me better than that.'

'I know.' He squeezed her hand. 'Shit. Ignore me. Do you still love Hugh? I mean, is there a chance you'll get back together?'

'No, I don't think so.' But her eyes were doubtful. 'I know he wants us to give it another go, but I wouldn't have considered it at all if he hadn't come to see me. It's weird, Sam. Our whole life in London feels as though it happened to someone else. I've only just started to feel really OK again.' She broke off. 'But one of the things I've also realised is that I don't need a relationship to be complete. I'm already complete. I feel as though I've just started to find things out about myself. One of those things is that I've discovered where I want to be. Here. I love it here. My roots are here. All the people I love are here.' She looked at him and added softly, 'You're here.'

He realised they were still holding hands and his heart soared.

'I love our friendship,' she added.

The word friendship brought his heart jolting back down to earth again.

He swallowed. It was now or never. 'Phoebe, I love our friendship too, but lately I've felt that I... I...' God, why was this so hard? He started again. 'I've felt that – well, that I've wanted it to be more.'

She was looking at him. She had gone very still.

Sam knew his face was probably flaming. But he'd gone too far to backtrack now. He had to get this out. 'The truth is that I'm in love with you, Phoebe. I think I always have been. In one way or another. But I also value our friendship so much that I've been scared to tell you. In case I wreck things. That's not what I want. I don't want to wreck things.'

'You haven't,' she said quietly. 'You couldn't wreck things. You're too lovely.'

'But you don't feel the same,' he asked, already knowing the answer. It was in her eyes. He realised that her hand was still over his and he withdrew his fingers gently, although he still held her gaze. There was a part of his heart that felt as though it was breaking.

'At the moment, I don't want a romantic relationship. But that's not just with you, Sam. I don't want a romantic relationship with anyone.'

'But there's a possibility that you might, one day.' He kept his voice as neutral as he could.

'Anything is possible.' She touched her face. 'But I'm not going to sit here making promises about the future. Because I don't know what will happen.'

'Of course. I totally get that. Thank you for hearing me out.'

'Thank you for being so honest. I'm really glad you've told me how you feel.'

'No problem.' He swallowed.

Behind Phoebe's head, he saw that all but one of the tea lights had gone out. The last one flickered bravely. There was still a flicker of hope, Sam thought. Phoebe may have been letting him down lightly or maybe she really meant it. He had a feeling it was the latter. Nothing was impossible. Neither of them knew what the future held.

* * *

They didn't stay much longer after that conversation. Phoebe had known Sam felt awkward, after what she knew must feel to him like a rejection. Just as she also knew there was nothing she could do or say to change that.

But it was still gone ten when Sam dropped Phoebe back to Puddleduck Farm. As they drew into the parking area at the front, she glanced up at the house and saw that her grandmother's light was off. She must have gone to bed.

'I won't invite you in for coffee,' she told Sam. 'But thank you for a lovely evening. And thank you again for being honest.' She leaned across from the passenger seat to kiss him and he moved his head so that her kiss landed on his ear.

Awkward, but better in the circumstances, she thought with a pang, than it landing on his lips.

'Goodnight, Sam. We'll always be friends.'

'Goodnight, sweetheart.' His voice was neutral. 'Let me know if there's anything you need. Any time.'

'I will.'

She was aware that he was waiting until she'd let herself in the front door. At least Maggie had got into the habit of locking it now. Then his tail lights drew off into the darkening night.

Phoebe cuddled the dogs, let them out for a last wee stop, then closed the kitchen door on them and sneaked up to bed. She could hear Maggie snoring quietly.

But she felt way too hyped up to sleep.

In some ways, she hadn't been surprised at Sam's declarations. She had felt something lately, a change in him.

She pinged Tori a text.

Are you still up? I could really use a quick chat.

Absolutely. Give me ten minutes.

Phoebe brushed her teeth, unplaited her hair, took off the tiny amount of make-up she'd put on for the evening, got into bed and phoned her friend.

'Is it Maggie? Has she had a change of heart?' was Tori's first question.

'I'm afraid not. No, it's Sam. Turned out you were right about him wanting us to be more than friends.'

She told Tori what had happened and she heard her friend's sharp intake of breath.

'Oh my goodness. That's the most romantic thing I've ever heard.'

'It is? How?'

'It's swords at dawn, isn't it? Or at least it would have been in the olden days. You'd have had two men fighting to the death for your affections. On the one hand, the ex, returning to the woman he loves, begging for her forgiveness. And on the other hand, the best friend, who's been carrying a torch for years, finally plucking up the courage to declare his true feelings.'

'Tori, this is serious. It's not a romantic epic. It's my life. And they're hardly fighting at dawn.'

'No, but they would be if that was the kind of thing we did these days. Hugh would have definitely thrown down a gauntlet at Sam's feet. Or maybe it would be the other way round. Yes, I think it might. I think Sam would have been the challenger.' She paused. 'Sorry. I've just been watching *Downton Abbey*. Ignore me. Are you OK? You haven't fallen out with Sam, have you?'

'I'm fine,' Phoebe said, smiling now, despite herself. 'And thank you for cheering me up. No, I haven't fallen out with Sam. I love Sam. I've always loved him.'

'But not as a prospective beau?'

Tori was clearly still in period-drama land.

'I don't think so.'

'But you don't know for sure?'

'I'm too worried about Maggie and Puddleduck to know anything for sure at the moment. I'm definitely not up for a relationship. I do know that.'

They talked for a bit longer, but when they finally said their goodnights, Phoebe still couldn't sleep.

It was true what she'd told both Tori and Sam. She wasn't up for a romantic relationship with anyone right now. There were too many other things up in the air. She didn't feel attracted to anyone.

Except that the last bit wasn't true. There was someone she'd felt attracted to – very attracted to – but she hadn't dared to acknowledge it until now. Not even to herself. Because it was madness. Perhaps it had been prompted by Tori's mention of *Downton Abbey*, she thought as his face popped into her mind.

There was nothing about him she liked. He was arrogant, rude and, as Sam had said often, a total nob. But none of that stopped her tummy crunching when she thought about him, or her skin prickling with attraction. The only man she'd been attracted to lately, however much it pained her to admit it, was their very own lord of the manor. Rufus Holt.

33

Rufus had finally accepted defeat. Saturday had been horrendous. He'd managed to stay in the vicinity of the stables by the sheer force of his will. Logistics had helped. The outdoor school where Archie's lesson had taken place had, by some stroke of fate, backed onto the road where he'd parked his car. So he'd made an excuse about an urgent phone call and gone to the far side of the school, where he'd been able to lean on the fence, gripping tightly to his phone, and watching from a distance.

He'd been far enough away for neither Archie nor the instructor to see just how much he'd lost it. Too far for them to have seen the panting, the shaking, the sweating, the sheer bloody nightmare of a full-blown PTSD attack unravelling him. Every so often Archie had glanced across the school, looking for approval, and Rufus had lifted his hand in a wave. Or, once, given him the thumbs up sign. *I'm watching, son. I'm here.*

The horrendous cycle of terror, anger and finally the numbness had left him spent and exhausted. When the lesson had finished, Rufus had dragged himself together for long enough to go and fetch his son. On the drive home, he had been glad of Archie's bright chatter washing over him like a soothing balm.

'Did you see me, Dad? Did you see when I was riding on my own?'

'I did, son.'

'I mean, when the man let go of the reins?'

'I saw it.'

'And I was riding Cranberry all by myself.'

'I know. You were brilliant.'

Rufus had felt calmer as they'd got farther away. His shirt, soaked with sweat, was glued to his back, but his heart no longer felt as though it would explode. The one thing he did know though, as he drove beneath the stone archway into the drive of Beechbrook House, was that there was no way he could do this again. The experience had taken everything he had. He had to get help. For Archie's sake and for his own.

He thought about Rowena as he parked his car, and Archie, too impatient to wait for his father, ran helter-skelter into the house to find Emelia to tell her about the lesson.

Rufus followed more slowly. He knew he owed it to Archie not to waste any more of his life, being haunted by the tragedy that had stolen Rowena. If he carried on like this, the PTSD would destroy him too. Archie wouldn't have a mother or a father.

He was about to escape upstairs to change his clothes when his own father called out to him from the downstairs study. Rufus hesitated, one foot on the bottom stair, and then his father appeared. He was wearing his golf attire. Rufus had assumed he'd have already left for the game. He realised he must have been waiting for them to get back.

'How are you, Rufus?'

'I must admit, I've been better.' He met his father's eyes 'It was much tougher than I thought.'

His father nodded. For a few seconds, neither of them spoke and then Rufus managed to get out the words he'd never wanted to say.

'I think I need some more help to get over this, Dad, don't I?'

'You do, son. I've taken the liberty of speaking to a friend of mine. I don't want to argue with you. But I think it would be greatly beneficial for you to listen to what he has to say.'

'OK. Who is it?'

'His name's Bartholomew Timms. He's a doctor.'

'A psychiatrist?'

'Yes.'

'Give me his number.'

'Actually, he's here. I asked him to come over this morning. He's waiting in the study.'

Rufus blinked. 'I see.'

'I thought if you spoke to him informally, you could make an appointment to see him professionally.' His father leant back against the banister of the stairs. 'It's up to you.' He gestured towards the study. 'He's in there. He's a member of the golf club.' He glanced at his watch. 'We've got a few minutes before we leave for the game. I thought you might like a quick word before we go. No pressure. Only if you're ready.'

Rufus gathered himself and glanced at the study door. 'I'm ready,' he said. And somehow making the decision to get help, to step into that room and admit he was totally beaten, completely done with fighting this thing on his own, brought with it an unexpected relief.

He reached for the handle of the door, and for the first time in a very long while, Rufus felt a sense of peace.

* * *

Phoebe had just finished packing up the few bits and pieces she'd brought with her to Puddleduck Farm in preparation to move back to Tori's. It was bank holiday Monday. She was going back to work on Tuesday.

She had wanted to stay longer, but Maggie had insisted, and there was no arguing with her grandmother when she had made up her mind about something.

Not that this stopped Phoebe trying. She went into the kitchen, where her grandmother was stirring a pan of tripe on the stove. 'Are you sure I can't stay for another couple of days?' she asked. 'I can go to work from here just as easily as I can go from Tori's.'

'I don't need a babysitter,' Maggie said stubbornly as Phoebe went across the kitchen, holding her nose.

'If you're trying to stink me out, then you're succeeding,' Phoebe muttered.

'Good.' Maggie smirked. 'It's not that I don't appreciate your help. I do. Very much. But you've got your own life to lead. You have a job to go to. You can't be messing about here, cleaning up after a load of old strays.'

'I love it,' Phoebe said. 'I love being here. I love helping you. I love the animals.'

'Even Saddam and Bruce Goose?' Maggie taunted.

'Yep. Them too.' Phoebe was using her best flippant voice and she knew that her grandmother was doing the same. They were covering how they really felt – or at least she knew she was. Because, inside, her heart felt as though it was breaking. Why did this feel like an ending? Why did she feel as though once she had left, a whole era would be over, that she would never come here again? She grabbed the wooden spoon from Maggie's hand and reached forward to move the pan from the Aga hotplate. 'Will you just stop stirring that a minute and say goodbye to me properly?'

'All right. All right. Don't crowd me.' Maggie turned finally towards her and Phoebe saw that her grandmother was crying. Tears were wet on her cheeks and there were more brimming in her eyes. 'Are you happy now?' she asked, swiping at the tears crossly with the back of her hand. 'Now I'm a blubbering mess, worse than a woman giving up a dog.'

'Oh, I'm sorry, Gran. I'm so sorry. I just don't want to leave you. I don't want to leave this place. I can't bear it.'

They were both crying now and in each other's arms, standing by the Aga warmth in the steamy smelly kitchen.

'Isn't there a way to save it? There must be a way. Do we know anyone who'd like to invest?'

'Invest in a money pit of a farmhouse that needs a new roof, a new central heating system and is rammed full of hungry animals that no one wants. It's hardly an investment.'

'A crazy billionaire animal lover then. Or maybe one who's dying but doesn't have any heirs and wants to make a difference. Isn't there anyone like that? There must be loads of people like that in the New Forest.'

'Why don't we advertise in your friend's rag? Billionaire Animal Lover Wanted. Don't apply unless you're dying. I'm sure we'd be swamped.' Maggie's voice was heavy with sarcasm. 'Pipe dreams and pie in the sky.'

'We probably wouldn't even need a billionaire. We could crowd-fund it. Maybe get lots of people to donate a little. Or even a lot if they were wealthy. I hadn't thought of crowdfunding, but that could work. How much would we need for a new roof? We could set up a petting park and charge people to come here. I know you don't like people wandering about, but if they were actually paying money, we could put up with them, couldn't we, and I could help you with that. I'm free most weekends. And Handsome got rehomed, didn't he? We never thought that would happen. She was really happy to pay for his treatment too. There must be other lovely people like her around.'

Phoebe didn't care any more that she was gabbling, she needed so much for there to be hope.

At least now they weren't crying.

'How much would a new roof cost anyway?' she added.

Maggie was looking thoughtful. 'We probably don't need a new roof right away. This one could maybe last a few more years. If it was patched up. There's a lot of missing tiles, but it doesn't actually leak. They've got sell-by dates, roofs, did you know that? Or at least the tiles have. Farmer Pete used to say that the roof tiles on Puddleduck passed their sell-by date in the nineties, but the roof still does the job.'

'Every day's a school day,' Phoebe quipped. 'What else did he say?'

'He said that if anything happened to him, I shouldn't hang about here because the outgoings were horrendous. I should cut my losses and buy a little bungalow by the sea. He was right about the outgoings,' she mused. 'And that was before I filled the place up with hungry animals.' She sighed. 'I would have gone for the bungalow, but a flat's cheaper. I can buy a flat outright and your mother will still have her full inheritance.'

'What do you mean her full inheritance?'

'The compo money.' Maggie's eyes clouded. 'It's been ring-fenced ever since I got it. It's for your mother and you and Frazier. So you never have to worry about money. It's a guaranteed pot for the future.'

Phoebe stared at her, mystified. 'Hang on a minute. Are you saying that you have some money somewhere – some kind of compensation money? What for?'

Now Maggie met her eyes. 'It was compensation, paid by the insurance company after your grandfather's accident. And his death. I've never touched it. It wasn't compensation, you see – not in any sense of the word. Nothing could ever have compensated for us losing our last years together. Our happy retirement.' Her eyes clouded at the painful memories. 'I just wanted to forget about it. So I took advice from the financial advisor and she invested it for me. It's for you and Frazier and your mother. Because I know that's what my Pete would have wanted.'

'Does Mum know about this?'

Maggie shook her head. 'No. I've never told her. I've never told anyone about it.'

'How much was it? Do you remember?'

'Of course I remember. It was £365,000 ten years ago. I think it's probably more now.'

'Oh my God.' Phoebe's head was spinning and her heart was pounding so loudly, she could hardly breathe. 'Are you saying that you have all this money sitting doing nothing?'

'It's not doing nothing. It's waiting to be your inheritance.'

Phoebe led her bewildered grandmother back to the kitchen table. 'But it's the answer to saving Puddleduck, don't you see? I don't need an inheritance and I know Frazier will say the same. Neither does Mum. We need to tell them.'

Maggie shook her head. 'I can't spend everyone's inheritance.'

Phoebe took her hand. 'You wouldn't be. You might even be increasing it. Imagine it, a revamped farmhouse with a new roof. When it needs it, of course. That would be worth so much more than a dilapidated one. We could refurbish the barns – they definitely need some attention. Maybe one day we could turn one of them into a veterinary practice – that could be my part of the inheritance. Imagine that. Puddleduck Vets – an integral part of Puddleduck Pets.' Phoebe was on a roll. 'It would be awesome.' She couldn't believe she'd just used the word, awesome. 'I've always dreamed that one day I'd have my own practice. And what better place to have it than here?'

'But what about your job at Marchwood?'

'I'm not planning on giving in my notice next month. I'm talking about the future. Oh wow. This is the answer to everything. We need another urgent family confab. We need to phone Mum. You need to phone Mum.'

'Could you phone her?' Maggie looked slightly less bewildered. She put out a hand to stroke Buster, who'd been waiting patiently for her attention. Tiny was less bothered – he was stretched out full length on the flagstone floor, his nose turned in the direction of the stove. He was asleep, but every so often, his nose twitched and his ears flickered and Phoebe guessed he was dreaming of tripe dinners.

'It would mean I could keep these two.' Maggie gestured towards the dogs. 'And the neddies.'

'And Saddam and Bruce Goose,' Phoebe added. 'Ah well... Into every sunny day a little rain must fall.'

They both giggled.

Phoebe stretched out her hand and took her grandmother's fingers in hers. 'And I won't need to marry Hugh.'

'Maybe you could marry Sam.'

Her grandmother hadn't been oblivious to Sam's change of feelings then.

'I don't want to marry anyone,' Phoebe said firmly.

Her phone pinged with a message in her bag and when she looked, she saw there were two messages. One was from Hugh and one was from Sam. What strange synchronicity was this?

Phoebe could read the one from Hugh without even opening it. It was short and to the point.

Have you had any thoughts about us getting back together? x

The one from Sam was longer. It began:

I've had some ideas on ways to raise money for keeping Puddleduck…

Phoebe opened it and as she read it, warmth stole through her. Sam truly was lovely.

She typed out a message in response.

I've just found out something that may be the answer to Maggie's prayers. I will tell you more as soon as I'm sure.

34

The family confab took place at 5 Old Oak Way the following Saturday evening. They'd had a chippie tea, picked up by her father and a posh sticky toffee pudding supplied by Alexa and Frazier, to save anyone cooking.

Then they had all sat around the table discussing the future.

Phoebe was right in her assumption that her family would want Maggie to use the compensation money that had been paid out by the insurance company to invest in Puddleduck Farm. It was a unanimous decision.

'I can understand you would want me to spend your money on putting the house in proper order,' Maggie said. 'But it seems wrong to spend money on employing a full-time person to run the place.'

'The wrong thing would have been letting you go into sheltered housing,' Frazier said. 'We'd have all hated that and you'd have loathed it too. Will you be able to get back your deposit?'

'I'm not sure. But that's my problem.' Maggie frowned. 'And for your information, I wouldn't have hated it.' Two bright pink spots of colour appeared on her cheeks. 'I'd have sat in an armchair in the communal lounge and bored the pants off anyone who'd listen about being a dairy farmer.'

'Nonsense,' James said. 'You'd have bored the pants off them about animal sanctuaries. That's a subject far closer to your heart.'

No one disputed this. Not even Maggie.

They moved on to talk about the repairs and improvements that would now happen. Even though there was now a pot of money to dip into – a pot that was rather bigger than even Maggie had dared to hope, thanks to the canny investments her financial advisor had made – no one wanted to waste any money.

Maggie had finally accepted she needed someone full time and planned to offer Natasha the full-time job. She'd been a volunteer since she was fifteen, she was now twenty and had never taken any form of payment. She had always worked for love, but Maggie knew that she wasn't overkeen on her office job and would love the chance for a paid full-time position.

'That means you can take a back seat,' Louella said. 'Never mind sitting in a communal armchair – you can sit in your very own armchair at Puddleduck and issue commands.'

'And when you get bored of that you can come and supervise my vet practice being built,' Phoebe said, seeing that the matriarch was about to argue.

Maggie closed her mouth again and gave a sweet smile. Her eyes were full of hope. Her whole demeanour had gone from sad and defeated to sparkly and alive. And she looked totally at peace with the world.

Phoebe felt happier than she could ever remember feeling too. Five months ago, when she and Hugh had split up and she'd lost her job, and her home to boot, she hadn't thought she would ever feel happy again. She certainly hadn't expected to feel it so soon. And yet here she was looking forward to a future that seemed bright.

* * *

She also replied to Hugh's message by asking him to meet her the following week for a lunchtime coffee in Bridgeford. She didn't want to tell him they were definitely over by text or by phone call. It didn't seem fair or very nice in the circumstances. And this way, their time was restricted because she was working.

They sat in the coffee-scented warmth of Nell's Café, one of Bridgeford's independent coffee shops. Then she told him, face to face, that she didn't want them to get back together. 'I just don't feel the same way any more, Hugh,' she said. 'I'm so sorry.'

He was very gracious about it. 'Thank you for being straight with me, I do appreciate it. Even though your answer isn't the one I'd hoped for.'

'What will you do? Will you go back to London?'

'I'm not sure. Maybe.' He caught hold of her hand across the clutter of the table. 'I must admit, I've grown to like this part of the world. I can see why you love it. I might try to find work in the area.'

'Good luck,' she said.

'You too, Phoebe. Take care, lovely girl.'

* * *

Phoebe reported this conversation back to Tori at the end of the following Friday evening when they were both together in Tori's flat, sharing a bottle of wine and a takeout pizza. They'd been passing like ships in the night lately: Tori had been on a deadline and was working all hours and Phoebe was also working all hours in an effort to pay Seth back for his generosity at all the leave he'd given her.

'Hugh actually said "lovely girl"?' Tori asked, looking amazed, as she helped herself to another slice of ham and pepperoni.

'He did. Those were his exact words.'

'He must have had a major personality change.'

'I know. I thought that too.' Phoebe frowned. 'Maybe I was mad to turn him down.'

'You're not having second thoughts, are you?'

'No, I'm not. That ship's sailed. And I know it sounds weird, but I've realised lately that I don't need a man to be happy.'

'Actually, it doesn't sound weird. Not even to a hopeless romantic like myself.' Tori clicked her tongue. 'Although, while we're on the subject of romance, did I tell you I've got another date on Saturday? Not tomorrow, sadly, as I think I'll be working late again, but next Saturday.'

'Really? Who with?'

'A guy who was at the same dinner party as Mr Serial Dater, funnily enough. He hooked up with one of the girls there at the same time I hooked up with my no-hoper, his didn't work out either. We've been chatting on the phone.'

'Well, fingers crossed,' Phoebe said. 'Maybe he'll be the one.'

'I doubt it,' Tori said idly. 'But I don't really mind. I like first dates. Even when they don't go anywhere. All that hope and expectation. All those unsullied dreams of the future. Mind you, I have been on quite a few. I worked it out the other day. I've been on eleven first dates in the last eight months.'

'Blimey, have you? I didn't know that. When did you go on all those? You didn't tell me.'

'I don't tell you everything I do,' Tori said archly. 'And talking of not sharing everything we do on the romantic front, how's Sam? Now his rival is off the scene, is there going to be any action there?'

'I don't want any action,' Phoebe said, transferring another slice of pizza to her plate. 'Not that kind anyway. Sam and I will always be friends. In fact, I'm seeing him next Saturday too. It's not a date,' she added swiftly, seeing Tori's eyes start to sparkle. 'We're going round to Puddleduck Farm in the evening after work because Sam wants to chat about some fundraising ideas he's had and I thought Maggie might want some input. She said she's always up for listening to fundraising ideas if we are to keep Puddleduck sustainable.'

'That's nice of him. He is lovely, isn't he? Do you not think he's lovely?' Tori pressed.

'I've always thought he was lovely,' Phoebe said, refusing to be drawn. 'We're also going to chat about my idea of converting the barn into a fully fitted-out vet practice and see what he thinks about the feasibility. That's another reason we're meeting at Maggie's.'

'I thought Sam worked in the Post Office and taught riding lessons. What does he know about converting budlings?'

'A surprising amount. His dad's a kitchen fitter, remember, and they did up Sam's flat together. Sam and I have talked about it before.'

'O-kaaay...' Tori drew out the second part of the word. She didn't look very convinced, but she didn't pursue it. 'So what does Seth think about you handing in your notice barely three months after you've started working for him and setting up on your own? Won't you be in competition with him?'

'I haven't handed in my notice. I'm not going to be leaving Marchwood any time soon. For a start, the building would have to be done and we haven't even done a feasibility study yet. There are a lot of other things that need doing at Puddleduck. We have to apply for charitable status. Do everything by the book.' She finished her pizza and said, 'My whole family have been talking about it. We think that Puddleduck Pets could be sustainable with a bit of hard work and investment – even Dad thinks it could be self-funding and he's a hard-headed solicitor. Well, he's a solicitor,' she amended with a giggle.

'It's great to see you looking so happy,' Tori commented. 'Are you still thinking about renting Woodcutter's Cottage too, or do you have other plans now?'

'I am thinking about it, yes. But maybe not this month. Unless you're anxious to kick me out?'

'Never. Like I said, you're welcome to stay here as long as you like.'

'Thanks,' Phoebe said. 'I am happy, you're right. I was so sad Maggie was selling Puddleduck, but I also knew she couldn't manage to keep running it either, so it felt like we were out of options.'

'And then you discovered you weren't.' Tori looked thoughtful. 'It's amazing isn't it, how things work out. I'm happy too. I'm really looking forward to this date. He's got a lot going for him. He's a journalist like me. Only he's on one of the nationals.'

'Sounds promising. I'll keep my fingers crossed it works out.'

'Thank you.'

'Thank you too,' Phoebe said.

'What for?'

'For being there when I was at my lowest ebb. For taking me in and letting me live here and get under your feet. I know it's been a bit cramped at times.'

'It's been fine,' Tori said. 'I've loved it.'

'You're the best friend I've ever had,' Phoebe added.

'Are you drunk?' Tori's voice was suspicious.

'Probably a bit.'

'You're the best friend I've ever had too,' Tori said, reaching for the bottle and finding it empty. 'I'd better open another one. We need to make a toast.'

'A toast to what?' Phoebe asked.

'Best friends and future possibilities.'

'I'll certainly drink to that,' Phoebe said, as Tori hotfooted it to the fridge to get another bottle.

She came back to the table, popped the cork and said thoughtfully. 'Talking of future possibilities, did you know that next Saturday is the solstice? It's a great day for a date.'

'Is that so?' Phoebe said, wondering what was coming. Tori had a reflective look on her face.

'Yep. Midsummer Night's Eve is steeped in myth and magic, especially around love and fertility. It's traditionally the time for baby-making, because back in pagan times, babies born in spring had a better chance of survival than ones born in winter. So the solstice was a great time to mate.'

'Very romantic.'

Tori carried on unabashed. 'It's big in Sweden apparently. There's even a Swedish proverb that roughly translates as, "Midsummer's night isn't long, but it sets many cradles a rocking."'

'You're a mine of information.'

'I know. I've done loads of research. I just put a feature in the mag "Love on the Longest Day". Don't look so cynical. There's romance too. Look at Shakespeare's *A Midsummer Night's Dream*.' She refilled their glasses. 'So all I'm saying,' Tori added, narrowing her eyes speculatively and giving Phoebe a direct look, 'is that next Saturday is the perfect day for romance.'

35

The following Saturday evening, Tori got ready and put on her make-up to the sound of Ed Sheeran's 'Shape of You'. When she came out into the open-plan lounge, she was still singing it.

'How do I look?' she asked Phoebe when she paused for breath. She was wearing a black belted shirt dress with a wine-coloured jacket, which set off her red hair perfectly.

'Like a hot girl going on a hot date,' Phoebe said. 'You look stunning.'

'You don't think it's too short?' Tori tugged at the hem.

'No. You've got amazing legs.'

Tori blushed. 'What are you wearing for your date?'

'What I've got on.' This was skinny jeans and one of her favourite floral tops, which was pretty but definitely not a date outfit. 'And before you say anything, A – it's not a date, and B – we're just going to be chatting to Maggie and walking around Puddleduck Farm. There's absolutely no point in me dressing up.'

'Hmmm,' Tori said pointedly.

* * *

Phoebe and Sam arrived at Puddleduck Farm at the same time, just before seven thirty. He was dressed casually too, Phoebe noticed, jeans and a black T-shirt and a jacket draped over his arm. Sam never seemed to feel the cold. He was carrying a rucksack and she saw a clipboard peeking out the top.

They went in to see Maggie, who it seemed had finally decided to open her Christmas cards and was standing them up on the kitchen table amidst a dusting of glitter and envelopes.

'I thought it was better late than never,' she said, when Phoebe reminded her it was June. 'I thought there might be some messages I needed to read. Like this one.' She pounced on a card with a reindeer on the front and read aloud. 'Season's greetings from Arthur and Doris – we've just had our seventh grandchild. We hope you are well.'

'Who are Arthur and Doris?' Phoebe asked.

'No idea. But it's nice, isn't it, that they've had another grandchild.'

Phoebe and Sam exchanged glances and Phoebe shook her head. 'She doesn't get any better.'

'Don't talk about me as though I wasn't here.' But there was a glint in Maggie's eyes. 'So come on then, pull up a chair. Let's hear about these fundraising ideas. Are you sure I can't get you anything to eat?'

'I've eaten, thanks,' Sam said, glancing at Phoebe.

'Me too, but thanks.'

He was tanned, Phoebe noticed. Sam was always tanned – he spent so much of his time outdoors – and it suited him. She studied him surreptitiously as he sat at the table. Thinking about it, he may have had a haircut. It was hard to look at Sam objectively – he had always been just Sam.

For the next hour or so, they talked fundraising. Open days, fetes and a petting zoo. Sam had brought brochures he'd down-loaded from other animal shelters up and down the country.

'The sponsorship is starting to take off,' Phoebe told him. 'Rufus Holt made a donation the other day. A sizeable one. He said it was in loving memory of Rowena and her passion. I think that's the name of his late wife. And he sponsored a donkey for Archie, which was nice. I keep meaning to ask you if Archie's still having riding lessons.'

'Yes he is.' Sam looked non-committal. 'His nanny brings him. He's doing really well.'

'That's great news.' Phoebe dropped her eyes. She hadn't told anyone about her feelings for Rufus Holt. Not even Tori. She was doing her best to suppress them. It worried her a bit that the only man she was actively attracted to was way out of reach. She had a niggling suspicion that this was behind the way she felt. If there was no chance of them ever dating, there was no chance of her ever being hurt either.

'A lot of them do gifts. Christmas cards and the like,' Sam was saying and Phoebe was jolted from her thoughts by his voice. He was gesturing towards Maggie's collection and looking at the old lady questioningly.

'I'm trying to cut down on my workload, not give myself even more to do, young man,' Maggie said, but her voice was full of affection. She had always liked Sam, Phoebe thought, and he had always liked her.

Eventually, Phoebe had to tap Sam's arm. 'We should probably go outside while it's still daylight,' she murmured.

'Yeah. We should. Sorry. I'm getting carried away.'

'Not at all. I really appreciate you coming over.'

'Take the dogs with you, will you,' Maggie added, as they stood up, gathering belongings, before heading out on their mission to recce the barn.

It had been a beautiful day, which had turned into a beautiful evening. The sky was a pale blue and the evening sun had turned the light to amber gold so that everything looked soft and rose-tinted.

'Thank you for coming over, Sam,' Phoebe said, as they walked across towards the barn, accompanied by Buster and Tiny.

'My pleasure.'

'I want to ask your dad to do the barn – if he can fit us in some time,' Phoebe said, 'but I thought you could tell me if it looks feasible or whether you think it would be best to just build a completely new building.'

'No problem at all. Very happy to help. As I said on the phone.'

He had the clipboard under his arm.

'I'll take a few pictures and a few measurements,' Sam said, 'and I'll show Pa. Just so he's got an idea what to expect.'

'Thank you.' Her heart lifted as they went inside the barn, breathing in the sweet scent of hay.

Tiny peered cautiously round the door and then backtracked when he saw a cat.

'Sensible hound,' Phoebe remarked. She glanced around warily. 'Watch out for a big ginger tom. He's definitely not up for rehoming. He's not a fan of people. Or, at least, he's not a fan of me!'

All except one of the kittens had been rehomed and this one, who Maggie had nicknamed Tabitha, skittered across to greet them.

'He's a cutie,' Sam said, scooping up the black and white kitten. 'He or she?'

'She. She's up for rehoming. Do you fancy a playmate for Snowball?'

'Sadly not. I think being a one-cat family is probably enough when I work full-time.'

'Very sensible. I'd love a dog or cat too, but you're right. It's hard when you work full-time. And it's not like I don't have enough animals to play with here.'

There was no sign of Saddam, but a few minutes later as Sam was taking photos on his phone, the big ginger cat appeared. To Phoebe's amazement, he walked straight up to Sam, purring.

Sam hunkered down and held out his hand for the cat to inspect.

'Wow, what are you? A cat whisperer?' Phoebe said in admiration. 'I've never seen him that friendly before.'

Sam clicked his tongue. 'I just like cats. They can tell.'

'I like cats,' she protested.

'Yes, but you probably smell of vets and medicine too. Cats have a better sense of smell than dogs. That's something we've only recently discovered apparently. It was always thought to be the other way round.'

'Is that so?' Phoebe looked at him, intrigued.

'Yep. But I don't think I'll risk stroking him too soon,' Sam said, straightening and snapping shut his clipboard. 'I'll show the pictures to Dad, but by the look of it, this barn is in pretty good shape, structurally. Let's go outside. I need to take some more of the roof. That didn't look so good.'

His verdict was delivered a few minutes later.

'It'll probably need a new one, but still cheaper than starting from scratch.'

'That sounds like very good news.' Phoebe paused, wanting suddenly to prolong the evening. 'Shall we go down and say hello to the donkeys while we're here?'

'Yep. I'm up for that.'

As they strolled side by side down to the donkey field, Phoebe told him about Hugh. 'At least he knows we have no future now. I'm not going back to him, Sam. Whatever was between us has gone. Or at least it has for me.'

'How did he take it?'

'Surprisingly graciously. He said he might stay in the area, but I think that's because he likes it here. I don't mind what he does. I'd prefer us to be on good terms than bad.'

They reached the donkey field and Roxy and Diablo came ambling across to greet them, with Neddie a little way behind.

'What are their names?' Sam asked and Phoebe told him and how to tell which one was which. Neddie with his dark ears, Diablo, brown with his white nose and Roxy who was a very light grey, your classic donkey colour.

'Diablo was a stray,' she added. 'Maggie hoped someone might come forward to claim him, but no one has yet.'

For a while, they stood petting the trio and Phoebe thought how quiet her friend was.

'Are you OK, Sam? Are you still thinking about what we spoke about the other week?'

'You know me so well.' He turned towards her, and his face was bathed in golden evening light and, for a moment, Phoebe wanted more than anything to take his hand and reassure him that she loved him as a friend and that maybe one day that love would turn into something more. But she couldn't make him promises she couldn't keep. That would be far crueller than saying nothing at all.

'I meant what I said about us always being friends,' she began. 'But I can't say anything beyond that. It wouldn't be fair.'

'I'm fine with that. Truly I am.' Sam shielded his eyes and looked up towards the woods that bordered the fields. 'Hey, isn't that a goshawk. I'd heard they were getting more common in the forest again, but you don't see very many.'

He pointed and she followed his gaze to the bird's silhouette, soaring against the blue of the sky.

'Wow, I think you're right.'

For a few seconds, they both focused on the bird as it circled.

And Sam thought, yes, he was fine with being friends with her. He would wait. He would wait for ever, if that's what it took. After all, he had waited this long.

And Phoebe thought, *Maybe it is just a matter of time. Maybe one day I'll look at him and I'll want to be in his arms. Or I'll feel fire when we touch. A crackling of chemistry. The kind that Tori loves about first dates. Or maybe I'm longing for something that doesn't exist. Maybe love and chemistry don't survive for very long in each other's company. Maybe it really is one or the other.*

Another goshawk had joined the first, Phoebe saw and she nudged Sam's arm. 'They must have a nest somewhere. How amazing. They must know they're safe here. Do you think?'

'Do I think they know they've rocked up at Puddleduck Pets?' Sam glanced at her. 'Maybe they do. Maybe they heard on the grapevine that the place has a secure future.' He lifted his eyebrows and she laughed.

'Oh, Sam, I'm so glad this place has a future.'

'You and me both.' But he wasn't looking at her any more. He was looking at the birds again and Phoebe followed his gaze.

They were calling to each other, a kikikikiki sound on the air as they circled.

Up on the slope at the top of Five Acre Field, the stretch of woodland was becoming a darker silhouette against the backdrop of a lilac sky. And just above the trees, the sun had begun to streak the air with gold.

Gold was the colour of hope, Phoebe thought. And Puddleduck Farm was a place full of hope and love and sanctuary. A place where her grandmother could spend her sunset years. But it was also a place full of new beginnings. A place that would live on to rescue many more animals in all the days that lay ahead.

It was the longest day, Phoebe remembered – and so different from the shortest day, just before Christmas, when she'd been filled with despair and everything had felt grey and hopeless. Right now, it seemed to Phoebe that the very air around them was beginning to turn golden too – as though Midas had strolled across the fields, scattering handfuls of liquid gold air as he went – along with a sprinkling of optimism and hope.

Sam felt it too. The approaching sunset didn't feel like an ending any more, but rather a beginning. The ache of poignancy he'd felt just moments before was dissipating into the golden air and he knew deep in his heart, that just as the beautiful sun would set across the fields and forest tonight, then so it would rise again tomorrow.

And as they stood there bathed in the amber light of the setting sun, with the donkeys in front of them and the endless lilac sky above their heads, Phoebe smiled at Sam. And Sam smiled softly back...

ACKNOWLEDGMENTS

Thank you so much to Team Boldwood – you are amazing. Thank you to every single one of you who works so hard to bring my books to my readers in paperback, audio and digital.

As always, my special thanks go to Caroline Ridding, Judith Murdoch, Jade Craddock, Shirley Khan and to Alice Moore for the gorgeous cover.

Thank you to Beth Yeatman for her veterinary knowledge. Thank you to Ben's dad, he knows who he is.

Thank you to Tony for his fabulous geographical knowledge and the recce trips and the Christmas bauble. Much appreciated. Thanks to Adam for the London background. Also to Alison Jacinth Landymore for her insight on all things 'duck'.

Thank you to the Dunford Novelists for your perceptive comments.

Thank you to Gordon Rawsthorne for his enduring support. He endures a lot!

Thank you, perhaps most of all, for the huge support of my readers – without whom it would be pretty pointless writing novels. I love reading your emails, tweets and Facebook comments. Please keep them coming.

MORE FROM DELLA GALTON

We hope you enjoyed reading *Coming Home To Puddleduck Farm*. If you did, please leave a review.

If you'd like to gift a copy, this book is also available as an ebook, digital audio download and audiobook CD.

Sign up to Della Galton's mailing list for news, competitions and updates on future books:

http://bit.ly/DellaGaltonNewsletter

Sunshine Over Bluebell Cliff, another glorious escapist read from Della Galton, is available to order now.

ABOUT THE AUTHOR

Della Galton is the author of 15 books, including *Ice and a Slice*. She writes short stories, teaches writing groups and is Agony Aunt for Writers Forum Magazine. She lives in Dorset.

Visit Della's website: www.dellagalton.co.uk

Follow Della on social media:

f facebook.com/DailyDella

twitter.com/DellaGalton

instagram.com/Dellagalton

BB bookbub.com/authors/della-galton

Boldwᴑᴑd

Boldwood Books is an award-winning fiction publishing company seeking out the best stories from around the world.

Find out more at www.boldwoodbooks.com

Join our reader community for brilliant books, competitions and offers!

Follow us
@BoldwoodBooks
@BookandTonic

Sign up to our weekly deals newsletter

https://bit.ly/BoldwoodBNewsletter

Printed in Great Britain
by Amazon